# THE TWO-PENNY BAR &
# THE SHADOW PUPPET

While visiting a criminal in his cell, Inspector Maigret is told of a man who'd been spotted dumping a body in a Parisian canal some years ago. Later, at a popular inn, Maigret finds himself in the very place the suspected killer was last seen, and is pulled deep into a web of blackmail and deceit . . . A scientist is shot dead in his laboratory, his body within easy view of the surrounding apartments. Did anyone see anything? Why was he killed? Summoned to investigate, Maigret uncovers a tragic story of desperate lives, unhappy families, addiction, and a terrible, fatal greed.

GEORGES SIMENON

◆

# THE
# TWO-PENNY BAR
# &
# THE SHADOW
# PUPPET

*Complete and Unabridged*

# ULVERSCROFT
*Leicester*

*The Two-Penny Bar* first published in French as
*La Guinguette à deux sous* by Fayard in 1932

This translation first published in Great Britain as
*The Bar on the Seine* by Penguin Books in 2003,
and revised in 2014

*The Shadow Puppet* first published in French
as *L'ombre chinoise* by Fayard in 1932

This translation first published in Great Britain in 2014

This Ulverscroft Edition
published 2020
by arrangement with
Penguin Random House UK
London

A catalogue record for this book is available
from the British Library.

ISBN 978–1–4448–4366–8

Published by
F. A. Thorpe (Publishing)
Anstey, Leicestershire

Set by Words & Graphics Ltd.
Anstey, Leicestershire
Printed and bound in Great Britain by
T. J. International Ltd., Padstow, Cornwall

This book is printed on acid-free paper

# Contents

# The Two-Penny Bar

Translated by
DAVID WATSON

# 1

## Saturday with Monsieur Basso

A radiant late afternoon. The sunshine almost as thick as syrup in the quiet streets of the Left Bank. And everything — the people's faces, the countless familiar sounds of the street — exuded a joy to be alive.

There are days like this, when ordinary life seems heightened, when the people walking down the street, the trams and cars all seem to exist in a fairy tale.

It was 27 June. When Maigret arrived at the gate of the Santé prison he found the guard gazing soppily at a little white cat that was playing with the dog from the dairy.

Some days the pavement must be more resonant underfoot: Maigret's footsteps echoed in the vast courtyard. He walked to the end of a corridor, where he asked a warder:

'Does he know? . . . '

'Not yet.'

A key turned in the lock. The bolt was pulled back. A high-ceilinged cell, very clean. A man stood up, looking unsure as to which expression to adopt.

'All right, Lenoir?' the inspector asked.

The man nearly smiled. But a thought came into his mind and his face hardened. He frowned suspiciously, and his mouth twisted into a sneer for a moment or two. Then he shrugged his shoulders and held out his hand.

'I see,' he said.

'What do you see?'

A resigned smile.

'Give it a rest, eh? You must be here because . . . '

'I'm here because I'm off on holiday tomorrow and . . . '

The prisoner gave a hollow laugh. He was a tall young man. His dark hair was brushed back. He had regular features, fine brown eyes. His thin dark moustache set off the whiteness of his teeth, which were as sharp as a rodent's.

'That's very kind of you, inspector . . . '

He stretched, yawned, put down the lid of the toilet in the corner of the cell which had been left up.

'Excuse the mess . . . '

Then suddenly, looking Maigret in the eye, he said:

'They've turned down the appeal, haven't they?'

There was no point in lying. He knew already. He started pacing up and down.

'I knew they would . . . so when is it? . . . Tomorrow?'

Even so, his voice faltered and his eyes drank in the glimmer of light from the narrow window high up the cell wall.

At that moment, the evening papers being sold on the café terraces announced:

The President of the Republic has rejected

4

the appeal of Jean Lenoir, the young leader of the Belleville gang. The execution will take place tomorrow at dawn.

It was Maigret himself who had arrested Lenoir three months previously, in a hotel in Rue Saint-Antoine. A split second later and the bullet the gangster fired at him would have caught him full in the chest rather than ending up lodged in the ceiling.

In spite of this, the inspector bore him no grudge; indeed, he had taken something of a shine to him. Firstly, perhaps, because Lenoir was so young — a twenty-two-year-old who had been in and out of prison since the age of fifteen. But also because he had a self-confidence about him.

He had had accomplices. Two of them were arrested at the same time as him. They were both guilty and on this occasion — an armed robbery — they probably played a bigger part than the boss himself. However, Lenoir got them off the hook. He took the whole blame on himself and refused to 'spill the beans'.

He never put on an act, wasn't too full of himself. He didn't blame society for his actions.

'Looks like I've lost,' was all he said.

It was all over. More precisely it would be all over when the sun, which was casting a golden strip of light on the cell wall, next rose.

Almost unconsciously, Lenoir felt the back of his neck. He shivered, turned pale, gave a derisive laugh:

'It feels weird . . . '

Then suddenly, in an outburst of bitterness:

'There are others who deserve this, and I wish they were going down with me!'

He looked at Maigret, hesitated, walked round the narrow cell once more, muttering:

'Don't get excited, I'm not going to put anyone in the frame now . . . but all the same . . .'

The inspector avoided looking at him. He could feel a confession coming. And he knew the man was so prickly that the slightest reaction or sign of interest on his part would make him clam up.

'There's a little place known as the 'Two-Penny Bar' . . . I don't suppose you're familiar with it, but if you happen to find yourself in the neighbourhood you might be interested to know that one of the regulars there has more reason than me to be putting his head on the block tomorrow . . .'

He was still pacing up and down. He couldn't stay still. It was hypnotic. It was the only sign of his inner turmoil.

'But you won't get him . . . Look, without giving anything away, I can tell you this much . . . I don't know why this is coming back to me now. Maybe because I was just a kid. I couldn't have been more than sixteen . . . Me and my friend used to do a bit of filching around the dance halls. He must be in a sanatorium by now — he already had a cough back then . . .'

Was all this talk just to give himself the illusion of being alive, to prove to himself that he was still a man?

'One night — it must have been around three in the morning — we were walking down the street. It doesn't matter which street. Just a street. We saw a door opening ahead of us. There was a car parked by the roadside. This guy came out, pushing another guy in front of him. No, not pushing. Imagine you're carrying a shop dummy and trying to make it look like it's your friend walking next to you. He put him in the car and got into the driver's seat. My friend shot me a look and we both jumped up on to the rear bumper. In those days they called me the Cat . . . that tells you all you need to know! The guy drove all over the place. He seemed to be looking for something, but seemed to keep losing his way. In the end we realized what he'd been looking for, because we arrived at the Canal Saint-Martin. You've worked it out, haven't you? It was over in the time it takes to open and shut a car door. One body at the bottom of the canal . . .

'Smooth as you like! The guy in the car must have put lead weights in the stiff's pockets, because he sank like a stone.

'We kept our cool. Another wink and we're back on the bumper. Then it was just a case of checking the client's address. He stopped in the Place de la République to have a glass of rum at the only café that was open. Then he drove his car to the garage and went home. We could see his silhouette through the curtains as he got undressed . . .

'We blackmailed him for two years, Victor and me. We were novices. We were afraid of asking for too much . . . a few hundred at a time . . .

7

'Then one day he moved house, and we lost him . . . Then three months ago I ran into him again at the Two-Penny Bar. He didn't even recognize me . . . '

Lenoir spat on the ground, automatically searched his pockets for his cigarettes.

'You'd think they'd let me smoke, in my situation,' he muttered.

The shaft of sunlight above their heads had disappeared. Footsteps could be heard out in the corridor.

'It's not that I'm making out that I'm better than I am, but this guy I'm telling you about should be up there with me, tomorrow, on the . . . '

Suddenly the beads of sweat stood out on his forehead, and his legs buckled. He sat down on the edge of his bunk.

'Leave me . . . ' he sighed. 'No, don't . . . don't leave me alone today . . . It's better to talk to someone . . . Hey, do you want me to tell you about Marcelle, the woman who . . . '

The door opened. The prisoner's lawyer hesitated when he saw Maigret. He had pasted on his professional smile, so that his client wouldn't be able to guess that his appeal had been turned down.

'I have good news . . . ' he began.

'I know!'

Then, to Maigret:

'Guess I won't be seeing you, inspector . . . Well, we've all got a job to do. By the way, I wouldn't bother checking out the Two-Penny Bar. This guy is just as cunning as you . . . '

Maigret offered his hand. He saw his nostrils

8

twitch, his dark moustache moisten with sweat, the two front teeth biting the lower lip.

'Better this than typhoid!' Lenoir joked, with a forced laugh.

★   ★   ★

Maigret didn't go away on holiday; there was a case involving forged bonds that took up nearly all of his time. He had never heard of the Two-Penny Bar. He asked around among his colleagues.

'Don't know it. Whereabouts? On the Marne? The lower Seine?'

Lenoir was sixteen at the time of the events he had described. So the case was six years old, and one evening Maigret read the reports for that year.

There was nothing sensational. Missing persons, as always. A woman chopped up into pieces, whose head was never found. As for the Canal Saint-Martin, it had thrown up no less than seven corpses.

The forged bonds turned out to be a complicated case, involving many lines of inquiry. Then he had to drive Madame Maigret to her sister's in Alsace, where she stayed for a month every year.

Paris was emptying. The asphalt grew sticky underfoot. Pedestrians sought the shady side of the street, and the café terraces were full.

Expecting you Sunday without fail. Love from everyone.

Madame Maigret's summons arrived when her husband had failed to turn up for a fortnight. It was Saturday, 23 July. He tidied up his desk and warned Jean, the office boy at the Quai des Orfèvres, that he probably wouldn't be back before Monday evening.

As he was about to leave, he noticed the brim of his bowler, which had been torn for weeks. His wife had told him a dozen times to buy a new one.

'You'll have people throwing you coins in the street . . .'

He spotted a hatshop in Boulevard Saint-Michel. He tried on a few, but they were all too small for his head.

'I'm sure this one will be just right . . . ' the spotty young shop assistant kept insisting.

Maigret was never more miserable than when he was trying things on in shops. In the mirror he was looking in, he spotted a man's back and head, and on the head a top hat. As the man was dressed in hunting tweeds, he cut a rather droll figure.

'No! I wanted something a bit older-looking,' he was saying. 'It's not meant to be smart.'

Maigret was waiting for the assistant to return from the back of the shop with some new hats for him to try on.

'It's just for a little play-acting . . . a mock marriage which we're putting on with a few friends at the Two-Penny Bar . . . there'll be a bride, mother of the bride, page-boys, the lot! . . . Just like a village wedding! . . . Now do you see what I'm after? . . . I'm playing the part of the village mayor . . . '

The customer gave a hearty laugh. He was about thirty-five, thickset, with rosy cheeks; he had the air of a prosperous businessman.

'Maybe one with a flat brim . . . '

'Hold on! I think we've got just the thing you're after in the workshop. It was a cancelled order . . . '

Maigret was brought another pile of bowlers. The first one he tried on fitted. But he dallied and made sure he left the shop just before the man with the opera hat. He hailed a taxi, just in case he needed it.

He did. The man came out of the shop, got into a car parked next to the pavement and drove off in the direction of Rue Vieille-du-Temple.

There he spent half an hour in a second-hand shop and emerged with a flat cardboard box, which obviously contained a suit to go with his top hat.

Then on to the Champs-Élysées, Avenue de Wagram. A small bar on a street corner. He stayed there only five minutes and left accompanied by a buxom, jovial-looking woman who must have been in her thirties.

Twice Maigret looked at his watch. His first train had already gone. The second would be leaving in a quarter of an hour. He shrugged his shoulders and told the taxi driver:

'Keep following him.'

Much as he had expected, the car drew up in front of an apartment block on Avenue Niel. The couple hurried in through the entrance. Maigret waited a quarter of an hour, then went in, taking

11

note of the brass plate:

Bachelor apartments by the month or by the day.

In a smart office which had a whiff of adultery he found a perfumed manageress.

'Police! . . . The couple who just came in here . . . '

'Which couple?'

But she didn't put up much of a struggle.

'Very respectable people, both married. They come twice a week . . . '

On his way out, the inspector glanced through the car windscreen at the identity plate.

Marcel Basso,
32, Quai d'Austerlitz, Paris.

Not a breath of wind. The air was warm and heavy. All the trams and buses heading for the railway stations were packed. Taxis full of deckchairs, fishing-rods, shrimp nets and suitcases. The asphalt glistened blue, and the café terraces resounded with the clatter of saucers and glasses.

'After all, three weeks ago Lenoir was . . . '

There hadn't been much talk about it. It was an everyday case — he was what you might call a professional criminal. Maigret remembered the quivering moustache and sighed as he looked at his watch.

Too late now. Madame Maigret would be waiting with her sister at the barrier of the little station that evening and would not fail to mutter:

'Always the same!'

The taxi driver was reading a newspaper. The man with the top hat left first, scanned the street both ways before signalling to his companion, who was lurking in the entrance.

They stopped in Place des Ternes. He saw them kiss through the rear windscreen. They were still holding hands after the woman had hailed a taxi and the man was ready to drive off.

'Do you want me to follow?' the driver asked Maigret.

'Might as well.'

At least he'd found someone who knew the Two-Penny Bar!

Quai d'Austerlitz. A huge sign:

Marcel Basso
Coal importer — various sources
Wholesale and retail
Domestic deliveries by the sack
Special summer prices

A yard surrounded by a black fence. On the opposite side of the street a quayside bearing the firm's name, with moored barges and a newly unloaded pile of coal.

In the middle of the yard a large house, in the style of a villa. Monsieur Basso parked his car, automatically brushed his shoulders to remove any female hairs and went into his house.

Maigret saw him reappear at the wide-open window of a room on the first floor. He was with a tall, attractive blonde woman. They were both laughing and talking in an excited fashion. Monsieur Basso was trying on his top hat and looking at himself in the mirror.

They were packing suitcases. There was a maid in a white apron in the room.

A quarter of an hour later — it was now five o'clock — the family came downstairs. A boy of about ten led the way, brandishing an air rifle. Then came the servant, Madame Basso, her husband, a gardener carrying the cases . . .

The group was brimming with good humour. Cars drove past, heading for the country. At Gare de Lyon the specially extended holiday trains whistled shrilly.

Madame Basso got in next to her husband. The boy climbed into the back seat among the cases and lowered the windows. The car was nothing fancy, just a standard family car, dark blue, nearly new.

A few minutes later they were driving towards Villeneuve-Saint-Georges. Then they took the road towards Corbeil. They drove through the town and ended up on a potholed road along the bank of the Seine.

Mon Loisir

That was the name of the villa, on the river between Morsang and Seine-Port. It looked newly built, bricks still shiny, the paintwork fresh, flowers in the garden that looked as if they had been washed that morning. A diving-board over the river, rowing-boats by the bank.

14

'Do you know the area?' Maigret asked his driver.

'A bit . . . '

'Is there somewhere to stay around here?'

'In Morsang, the Vieux-Garçon . . . Or further on, at Seine-Port, Chez Marius . . . '

'And the Two-Penny Bar?'

The driver shrugged.

The taxi was too conspicuous to stay there much longer by the roadside. The Bassos had unloaded their car. No more than ten minutes had elapsed before Madame Basso appeared in the garden dressed in a sailor's outfit, with an American naval cap on her head.

Her husband must have been more eager to try out his fancy dress, for he appeared at a window buttoned up in an improbable-looking frock coat, with the top hat perched on his head.

'What do you reckon?'

'Shouldn't you be wearing the sash?'

'What sash?'

'Mayors all wear a tricolour sash . . . '

Canoes glided slowly by on the river. In the distance, a tug blew its siren. The sun was sinking behind the trees on the hillside further downstream.

'Let's try the Vieux-Garçon!' said Maigret.

The inn had a large terrace next to the Seine. Boats of all sorts were moored to the bank, while a dozen or so cars were parked behind the building.

'Do you want me to wait for you?'

'I don't know yet.'

The first person he met was a woman dressed

all in white, who almost ran into him. She was wearing orange blossom in her hair. She was being chased by a young man in a swimming-costume. They were both laughing. Some other people were observing the scene from the front steps of the inn.

'Hey, keep your dirty paws off the bride!' someone shouted.

'At least until after the wedding!'

The bride stopped, out of breath, and Maigret recognized the lady from Avenue Niel, the one who visited the apartment with Monsieur Basso twice a week.

A man in a green rowing-boat was putting away his fishing tackle, his brow furrowed, as if he were performing some delicate and difficult operation.

'Five Pernods, five!'

A young man came out of the inn, his face plastered with greasepaint and rouge. He was made up to look like a freckly, ruddy-cheeked peasant.

'What do you think?'

'You should have red hair!'

A car arrived. Some people got out, already dressed up for the village wedding. There was a woman in a puce silk dress which trailed along the ground. Her husband had stuffed a cushion under his waistcoat to simulate a paunch and was wearing a boat chain that was meant to look like a watch chain.

The sun's rays turned red. The leaves on the trees barely stirred. A canoe drifted downstream; its passenger, stripped to the waist, sat at the back, doing no more than lazily steer it with a paddle.

'What time are the carriages due to arrive?'

Maigret hung around, feeling out of place.

'Have the Bassos arrived?'

'They passed us on the way!'

Suddenly, someone came and stood in front of Maigret, a man of about thirty, already nearly bald, his face made up like a clown's. He had a mischievous glint in his eyes. He spoke with a pronounced English accent:

'Here's someone to play the notary!'

He wasn't completely drunk. He wasn't completely sober, either. The rays of the setting sun turned his face purple; his eyes were bluer than the river.

'You'll be the notary, won't you?' he asked with the familiarity of a drunkard. 'Of course you will, old chap. We'll have a great time.'

He took Maigret's arm and added:

'Let's have a Pernod.'

Everyone laughed. A woman muttered:

'He's got a nerve, that James.'

But James wasn't bothered. He dragged Maigret back to the Vieux-Garçon.

'Two large Pernods!'

He was laughing at his own little joke as they were served two glasses full to the brim.

# 2

## The Lady's Husband

By the time they got to the Two-Penny Bar, things hadn't yet clicked for Maigret, as he liked to say. He hadn't had any high hopes in following Monsieur Basso. At the Vieux-Garçon he had looked on gloomily as the people milled about. But he hadn't felt that nibble, that little shift, the 'click' that told him he was on to something.

While James was forcing him to have a drink with him, he had seen customers come and go, helping each other to try on their ridiculous costumes, laughing, shouting. The Bassos had turned up, and their son, whom they had made up as a carrot-headed village idiot, had gone down a storm.

'Don't mind them,' said James each time Maigret turned round to look at the group. 'They're having a good time and they're not even drunk . . . '

Two carriages had drawn up. More shouting. More laughing and jostling. Maigret sat next to James, while the landlord, his wife and the staff of the Vieux-Garçon lined up on the terrace to see them off.

The sun had given way to a blue-tinted twilight. The lights from the windows of the quiet villas on the far bank of the Seine

18

glimmered in the dusk.

The carriages trundled onwards. The inspector took in the scene around him: the coachman, whom everyone teased and who responded with a laugh through gritted teeth; a young girl who had made herself up as the simple country lass, and who was trying to put on a peasant accent; a grey-haired man dressed like a granny . . .

It was all very confusing. Such an unexpected mix of people that Maigret could scarcely work out who went with whom. He needed to get things in focus.

'See her over there? That's my wife . . . ' James told him, pointing out the plumpest of the women, who was wearing leg-of-mutton sleeves. He said this in a cheerless tone, with a glint in his eyes.

They sang. They passed through Seine-Port, and people came out on to their doorsteps to watch the procession go by. Little boys ran after the carriages for some distance, whooping with delight.

The horses slowed to walking pace. They crossed a bridge. A sign could just about be made out in the half-light:

Eugène Rougier — Licensee

A tiny little whitewashed house squeezed in between the towpath and the hillside. The lettering on the sign was crude. As they approached, they could hear snatches of music, interspersed with a grinding noise.

What was it that finally clicked? Maigret

couldn't put his finger on it. Perhaps the mildness of the evening, the little white house with its two lighted windows and the contrast with this invading circus troupe?

Perhaps the couple who came forward to see the 'wedding party' — the man a young factory worker, the woman in a pink silk dress, standing with her hands on her hips . . . ?

The house had only two rooms. In the one on the right, an old woman was busy at her stove. In the one on the left could be seen a bed, some family portraits.

The bistro was at the back. It was a large lean-to with one wall completely open to the garden. Tables and benches, a bar, a mechanical piano and some Chinese lanterns. Some bargees were drinking at the bar. A girl of about twelve was keeping an eye on the piano, occasionally rewinding it and slipping two sous into the slot.

★　★　★

The evening got going very quickly. No sooner had the new arrivals climbed down from the carriages than they cleared away the tables and started dancing, calling for drinks. Maigret had lost sight of James and found him again at the bar, lost in thought over a Pernod. The waiters were laying the tables outside under the trees.

One of the carriage drivers moaned: 'I hope they don't keep us too late! It's Saturday! . . . '

Maigret was alone. Slowly, he turned full circle. He saw the little house with its plume of smoke, the carriages, the lean-to, the two young lovers, the crowd in fancy dress.

'This is it,' he murmured to himself.

The Two-Penny Bar! The name might refer to the poverty of the establishment, or perhaps to the two coins you had to put into the mechanical piano to make it work.

And somewhere here there was a murderer! Perhaps one of the wedding party! Perhaps the young factory hand! Perhaps one of the bargees!

Where was James? Where was Monsieur Basso? . . .

There was no electric lighting. The lean-to was lit by two oil lamps, and other lamps on the tables and in the garden, so the whole scene was a patchwork of light and dark.

'Come on . . . food's ready!'

But they carried on dancing. A few people must have been knocking back the aperitifs, for within a quarter of an hour there was a distinctly drunken atmosphere in the place.

The old woman from the bistro waited at the tables herself, anxious that the food was going down well — salami, then an omelette, then rabbit — but no one cared much. They hardly noticed what they were eating. And everyone wanted their glass refilled.

A noisy hubbub, drowning out the music. The bargees at the bar watched the goings-on and carried on their meandering conversation about the canals of the North and electric haulage systems.

The two lovers danced cheek to cheek, but they couldn't take their eyes away from the tables where all the merrymaking was going on.

Maigret didn't know anyone. He was sitting next to a woman who had a ridiculous painted moustache and beauty spots dabbed all over her face, who for some reason kept calling him Uncle Arthur.

'Would you pass the salt, Uncle Arthur? . . . '

Everyone was on first-name terms. There was much backslapping and ribbing going on. Was this a group of people who knew each other well? Or just a crowd that had been thrown together by chance?

And what did they do in real life? For example, the grey-haired man dressed as the granny?

Or the woman dressed up as a little girl, who spoke in a falsetto voice?

Were they middle-class like the Bassos? Marcel Basso was sitting next to the bride. They weren't flirting. Occasionally they exchanged a meaningful glance that probably meant:

'This afternoon was good, wasn't it?'

Avenue Niel, in a furnished apartment! Was her husband here too?

Someone let off a firecracker. A Bengal light was lit in the garden, and the young couple watched it tenderly, hand in hand.

'It's just like in a theatre,' said the pretty girl in pink.

And there was a murderer!

'Speech! . . . Speech! . . . Speech!'

Monsieur Basso got to his feet, a beaming smile on his face. He coughed, pretended to be embarrassed and began an absurd speech that was interrupted by rounds of applause.

22

Now and again his eye fell on Maigret. His was the only serious face around the tables. And Maigret sensed the man's discomfort as he turned his head away. Nevertheless, his gaze returned to Maigret twice, three times more, questioning, troubled.

'. . . and I'm sure you'll join me in a toast: to the bride!'

'To the bride!'

Everyone stood up. People kissed the bride, clinked glasses. Maigret saw Monsieur Basso go over to James and ask him a question. No doubt it was:

'Who's that?'

He heard the reply:

'I don't know . . . just a pal . . . He's fine . . . '

The tables had been abandoned. Everyone was dancing in the lean-to. A small group of people, barely distinguishable from the tree trunks in the dark, had gathered to watch the fun.

Corks were popping.

'Come and have a brandy!' said James. 'I guess you aren't a dancer.'

What an odd fellow! He had already drunk enough to lay out four or five normal men, but he wasn't really drunk. He just slouched around, looking sour, not joining in. He took Maigret back into the house. He sat in the landlord's high-backed armchair.

A stooping old woman was doing the washing-up while the landlord's wife, who didn't look far off fifty, and who was no doubt her daughter, busied herself around the kitchen.

'Eugène! . . . Another six bottles of bubbly . . . It might be a good idea to ask the coachman to go and fetch some more from Corbeil.'

A country cottage interior, very poor. A pendulum clock in a carved walnut case. James stretched out his legs, picked up the bottle of brandy he had ordered and poured out two glasses.

'Cheers . . . '

The sound of the voices and the music were now a distant hubbub. Through the open door they could see the fast-moving current of the Seine.

'Little cubby holes for canoodling couples,' said James contemptuously.

He was thirty years old. But it was obvious he wasn't the canoodling type.

'I bet they're at it already at the bottom of the garden . . . '

He watched the old woman bent double over her washing-up.

'Here, give me a tea towel.'

He started drying the glasses and dishes, pausing only to take a swig of cognac.

Now and again someone passed by the door. Maigret took advantage of a moment when James was talking to the old woman to slip away. He'd only gone a few paces out of the door when someone asked him for a light. It was the grey-haired man in the woman's dress.

'Thanks . . . You don't dance either?'

'Never!'

'Not like my wife, then. She hasn't missed a single dance.'

'The bride?'

'Yes . . . And when she does stop, she'll catch her death . . . '

He gave a sigh. He looked grotesque, a serious-looking middle-aged man in an old woman's dress. The inspector wondered what he did in real life, what he normally looked like.

'I feel like we've already met,' he said casually.

'Me too . . . I've seen you somewhere before . . . But where? . . . Maybe you've bought a shirt in my shop . . . '

'You're a haberdasher?'

'On the Grands Boulevards . . . '

His wife was now making more noise than anyone. She was obviously drunk, and was becoming quite over-exuberant. She was dancing with Basso and was clinging to him so tightly that Maigret turned away in embarrassment.

'A funny little girl,' the man sighed.

Little girl! This thirty-year-old, buxom woman with her sensual lips and her come-hither look, now throwing herself at her gentleman partner.

'She's a bit wild once she gets going . . . '

The inspector looked at his companion, unable to tell whether he was being angry or affectionate.

At that moment someone shouted:

'They're off to the bridal chamber! . . . Take your places, everyone! . . . Where's the bridegroom? . . . '

The bridal chamber was a small outhouse at the end of the lean-to. Someone got the door open, someone else went to find the bridegroom at the end of the garden.

Maigret was observing the real husband, who was smiling.

'First the garter!' someone shouted.

It was Monsieur Basso who removed the garter, cut it up into small pieces and distributed them among the crowd. The bride and groom were bundled into the outhouse and the door locked behind them.

'She's enjoying herself . . . ' murmured Maigret's companion. 'Are you married yourself?'

'Oh, yes . . . '

'Is your wife here?'

'No . . . she's on holiday.'

'Does she like being with young people too?'

Maigret couldn't tell if he was being serious or teasing. He took advantage of a lapse in conversation to cross the garden, passing close to the factory worker and his girlfriend, who were pressed up against a tree.

In the kitchen James was talking pleasantly with the old woman while drying glasses, and emptying them.

'What's going on?' he asked Maigret. 'Have you seen my wife?'

'I haven't noticed her.'

'Hard to miss her, surely.'

The night wound down quickly. It must have been around one in the morning. Some people started talking about making a move. Someone was being sick by the river. The bride had regained her freedom. Only the younger members of the group were still dancing.

The carriage driver came up to James.

'Do you think it'll be much longer? The old woman's been waiting for me for an hour . . . '

'You're married too?'

So James rounded everyone up. In the carriages, some people started nodding off to sleep, while others were trying to keep the party spirit going, singing and laughing with varying degrees of conviction.

They passed a line of sleeping barges. A train whistled in the distance. They slowed down when they reached the bridge.

The Bassos got out at their villa. The haberdasher had already left the group at Seine-Port. A woman was whispering to her husband, who was drunk:

'I'll tell you tomorrow what you got up to! . . . Shut up! . . . I'm not listening! . . . '

The sky was sprinkled with stars, which were reflected in the water of the river. At the Vieux-Garçon, everyone was asleep. Handshakes all round.

'Are you coming sailing tomorrow?'

'We're going fishing.'

'Goodnight.'

A row of bedrooms. Maigret asked James:

'Is one of these for me?'

'Take your pick! . . . See if you can find an empty one . . . If not, you can always sleep in my room.'

Lights went on in a few windows. The sound of shoes being dropped on the floor. The squeak of bedsprings. A couple whispered loudly in one of the rooms. Perhaps the woman who had a thing or two to say to her husband?

27

It was eleven o'clock in the morning. Now they all looked like themselves. It was hot and sunny. The waitresses dressed in black and white bustled round the terrace, laying tables.

The group began to reassemble. Some were still in pyjamas, others in sailors' outfits, others still in flannels.

'Hung over?'

'Not too bad . . . And you?'

Some had already set off to go fishing, or had already returned. There were some small sailing-dinghies and canoes.

The haberdasher was wearing a well-tailored grey suit. Clearly a man who liked to appear well-groomed in public. He spotted Maigret and came over.

'Allow me to introduce myself: Monsieur Feinstein . . . I mentioned my shop yesterday . . . My professional name is Marcel.'

'Did you sleep well?'

'No, I didn't! As I thought, my wife had made herself ill . . . It's always the same . . . She knows she doesn't have a robust constitution . . . '

Why did he seem so interested in Maigret's reaction?

'Have you seen her this morning?'

He looked around and finally spotted her in a sailing-boat with four or five people in bathing costumes. Monsieur Basso was at the helm.

'Is this your first visit to Morsang? . . . It's very nice. You'll want to come back, you'll see . . . We'll have the place to ourselves . . . Just the usual crowd, friends . . . Do you play bridge?'

'Oh . . . a bit . . . '

'We'll be having a game later . . . Do you know Monsieur Basso? . . . One of the biggest coal merchants in Paris . . . A splendid chap! . . . That's his dinghy coming in now . . . Madame Basso is very sporty.'

'And James?'

'Already on the booze, I shouldn't wonder. It's all he lives for. And he's still a young man, he could be doing something with his life. He'd rather take it easy. He works for an English bank in Place Vendôme. He's been offered loads of jobs, turned them all down. He insists on finishing work at four so he can hit the bars in Rue Royale.'

'And that young man over there — the tall one?'

'The son of a jeweller.'

'And the man over there fishing?'

'Runs a plumbing business. He's the keenest fisherman in Morsang. Some of us play bridge, others like fishing, others prefer sailing. It all makes for a good crowd. Some people have their own villas out here.'

In the distance, at the first bend in the river, stood the tiny white house. One could just make out the lean-to with its mechanical piano.

'Does everyone go to the Two-Penny Bar?'

'It's been our haunt for the last two years. James was the one who discovered it. Before that it was just used by workers from Corbeil, who came here to dance on Sundays. James used to slip off there for a quiet drink when things got too boisterous around here. One day the gang went with him, had a bit of a dance, and that's how it all started. We've pretty much taken over the place . . . the former clientele has more or less drifted away.'

A waitress walked by with a tray full of aperitifs. Someone dived into the river. A frying smell came from the kitchen.

And there was smoke rising from the chimney of the Two-Penny Bar. A face came to Maigret's mind: thin, dark moustache, pointed teeth, quivering nostrils . . . Jean Lenoir pacing up and down to hide his fear, talking about the Two-Penny Bar.

'*There are others who deserve this, and I wish they were going down with me!*'

But the next day, at the crack of dawn, he was alone. No one from the bar was there with him.

Despite the heat, Maigret felt a sudden chill. And he looked at this dapper haberdasher with his gold-tipped cigarette with fresh eyes. Then he turned to where the Bassos' boat was being moored at the bank, half-naked people leaping ashore to greet their friends with handshakes.

'May I introduce you to our friends?' said Monsieur Feinstein. 'Monsieur . . . ?'

'Maigret. I'm a civil servant.'

The introductions were very proper: short bows, exchanges of 'Pleased to meet you' and 'The pleasure is all mine'.

'You were there yesterday evening, weren't you? I thought the whole thing went splendidly. Are you playing bridge with us this afternoon?'

A thin young man came up to Monsieur

Feinstein, took him to one side and spoke to him in a low voice. None of this was lost on Maigret. He saw Feinstein frown; he looked somewhat alarmed. He inspected Maigret from head to foot before adopting his normal demeanour.

The group went up to the terrace to find a table.

'Pernods all round? Hey, where's James?'

Monsieur Feinstein was edgy, despite his efforts to remain calm. He paid particular attention to Maigret.

'What are you drinking?'

'I don't mind.'

'You . . . '

His sentence tailed off, and he pretended that something else had caught his attention. After a pause, he tried coming from a different angle:

'It's odd that you should have landed up at Morsang . . . '

'Yes, very strange . . . ' the inspector agreed.

The drinks were served. Everyone was talking over each other. Madame Feinstein had placed her foot on Monsieur Basso's, and her bright eyes were fixed on his.

'Such a lovely day. What a shame that the water is too clear for fishing.'

The air was clammy and still. Maigret remembered a shaft of sunlight penetrating a high white cell.

Lenoir walking and walking to forget that he wouldn't be walking for much longer.

And Maigret's gaze rested heavily on each face in turn: Monsieur Basso, the haberdasher, the businessman, James, who had just arrived, the

31

young men and women . . .

He tried to picture each of them in turn, by the Canal Saint-Martin at night, carrying a corpse 'like a shop dummy and trying to make it look like it's your friend walking next to you'.

'Your good health,' said Monsieur Feinstein, maintaining his fixed smile for as long as he could.

# 3

## The Two Boats

Maigret had lunch on his own on the terrace of the Vieux-Garçon. The rest of the group sat at adjoining tables, and the conversation flowed between them.

He had now established the social background of this crowd: tradesmen, owners of small businesses, an engineer, two doctors. They were people who owned their own cars, but who only had Sundays off for unwinding in the country-side.

They all owned boats — either motor-boats or small dinghies. They were all keen on fishing.

They lived here for twenty-four hours every week, dressed in their sailing gear, wandering around barefoot or in sandals. Some of them affected the rolling gait of old sea-dogs.

More couples than young people. They displayed the rather deep familiarity of people who have been spending every Sunday together for years.

James was everyone's favourite, the person who bound them all together. With his casual manner, his ruddy complexion and his dreamy eyes, he only had to make an appearance to put everyone in a good mood.

'How's the hangover, James?'

'I never get hangovers. If I feel queasy, I find a

couple of Pernods usually sort it out.'

They started reliving the night before. They had a laugh about someone who had been sick, and another who had almost fallen into the Seine on the way back. Maigret was part of the group without really belonging. The previous evening, everyone had talked to him like an old friend; now they eyed him a little more cautiously, occasionally involving him in the conversation out of politeness.

'Do you like fishing?'

The Bassos were having lunch at home. The Feinsteins too, and a few others who had their own villas. Thus the group fell into two classes: those who owned villas and those who stayed at the inn.

Around two o'clock the haberdasher came to fetch Maigret; he seemed to have taken him under his wing.

'We're waiting for you to come and play bridge.'

'At your place?'

'At the Bassos'! We were supposed to play at my place today, but the maid is sick, so we'll be better off at the Bassos' . . . Are you coming, James?'

'I'll come in the boat.'

The Bassos' villa was a kilometre upstream. Maigret and Feinstein went on foot, while the rest went by dinghy or canoe.

'Basso's a fine fellow, don't you think?'

Maigret couldn't tell if he was being serious or not. He was a strange one. Neither one thing nor the other: neither old nor young, neither good-looking nor ugly; maybe without a single original thought in his head, yet maybe full of secrets.

'I expect we'll be seeing you every Sunday from now on?'

They came across groups of people picnicking, as well as fishermen every hundred metres or so along the river bank. It was getting hotter. The air was extraordinarily still and oppressive.

In the Bassos' garden wasps buzzed around the flowers. There were three cars parked there already. The young boy was playing by the riverbank.

'You're joining our game?' the coal merchant asked Maigret as he greeted him cordially. 'Excellent! In which case we don't need to wait for James. He'll never get any wind in his sail on a day like today.'

Everything was brand new. The villa was like a city dweller's fantasy: a profusion of red-checked curtains, old Norman furniture and rustic pottery.

The card table was set up in a living room that opened on to the garden through a large bay window. Bottles of Vouvray were chilling in an ice bucket frosted with condensation. Bottles of liqueur were set out on a tray. Madame Basso, dressed in a nautical outfit, did the honours.

'Brandy, *quetsche, mirabelle*? Unless you'd rather have a Vouvray?'

There were vague introductions to the other players, not all of whom had been present the night before, but who were still part of the Sunday crowd.

'Monsieur . . . er . . . '

'Maigret.'

'Monsieur Maigret, who plays bridge . . . '

It was almost like the set of a light opera, so vivid and spruce was the décor. Nothing to remind you of the serious business of life. The child had clambered into a white-painted canoe, and his mother called out:

'Be careful, Pierrot!'

'I'm going to meet James!'

'A cigar, Monsieur Maigret? If you prefer a pipe, there is some tobacco in this pot. Don't worry, my wife is used to it.'

Directly opposite on the other bank stood the Two-Penny Bar.

The first part of the afternoon passed uneventfully. Maigret noticed, however, that Monsieur Basso wasn't playing and that he appeared a little more on edge than this morning.

He didn't look like the nervous type. He was tall and well built and seemed to ooze vitality through every pore. A man who loved life, a rough and ready sort from sturdy working-class stock.

Monsieur Feinstein played bridge like a real aficionado and called Maigret to task on more than one occasion.

At around three o'clock the Morsang crowd began to fill the garden, and then the room where they were playing. Someone put on a record. Madame Basso poured out the Vouvray, and fifteen minutes later there were half a dozen couples dancing around the bridge players.

At that moment Monsieur Feinstein, who had seemed completely absorbed by the game, murmured:

'Hey what's happened to our friend Basso?'

'I think I saw him get into a boat!' someone said.

Maigret followed the haberdasher's gaze to the opposite bank of the river, where a small boat had just arrived right next to the Two-Penny Bar. Monsieur Basso climbed out of it and walked up towards the inn. He returned a short while later, looking preoccupied, despite his ostensible air of good humour.

Another incident which passed almost unnoticed. Monsieur Feinstein was winning at cards. Madame Feinstein was dancing with Basso, who had just come back. James, a glass of Vouvray in his hand, joked:

'Some people couldn't lose if they tried.'

The haberdasher didn't flinch. He dealt out the cards. Maigret was watching his hands, and they were as steady as ever.

Another hour or two went past. The dancers were getting tired. Some of the guests had gone for a swim. James, who had lost at cards, stood up and muttered:

'How about a change of scene? Anyone for the Two-Penny Bar?'

He bumped into Maigret on the way out.

'Come with me.'

He had reached that level of drunkenness that he never went beyond, no matter how much he drank. The others all stood up. A

young man cupped his hands around his mouth
and called out:

'Everyone to the Two-Penny Bar!'

'Careful you don't fall!'

James helped the inspector to climb into his
six-metre sailing boat, pushed off with a
boat-hook and sat down in the stern.

There wasn't a breath of wind. The sail
flapped. They struggled against the current, even
though it was virtually non-existent.

'We're not in any hurry!'

Maigret saw Marcel Basso and Feinstein get
into the same motor-boat, cross the river in no
time and step out in front of the bar.

Then came the dinghies and the canoes.
Though it had set out first, James's boat soon
brought up the rear, because of the lack of wind,
and the Englishman seemed reluctant to use the
oars.

'They're a good bunch,' James suddenly
murmured, as if following his own line of
thought.

'Who?'

'All of them. They have such boring lives. But
what can you do about that? Everyone's life is
boring.'

It was ironic, for as he lolled in the back of the
boat with the sun glinting off his bald pate, he
looked supremely content.

'Is it true you're a policeman?'

'Who told you that?'

'I can't remember. I heard someone mention
it. Hey, it's just a job like any other.'

James tightened the sail, which had caught a

breath of wind. It was six o'clock. The Morsang clock was striking, and was answered by the one at Seine-Port. The bank was obstructed by reeds, which were teeming with insects. The sun was beginning to turn red.

'What do you . . . '

James's question was cut short by a sharp crack. Maigret leapt to his feet, almost overturning the boat.

'Look out!' his companion shouted. He threw his weight over to the other side, then grabbed an oar and started rowing. His brow was furrowed, his eyes wide with anxiety.

'It's not the hunting season yet.'

'It came from behind the bar!' said Maigret.

As they drew closer they could hear the tinkle of the mechanical piano and an anguished voice shouting:

'Turn the music off! Turn the music off!'

There were people running. A couple was still dancing, even after the piano was switched off. The old grandmother was coming out of the house, carrying a bucket in her hand. She stood stock-still, trying to work out what was going on.

Because of the reeds it was difficult to land. In his haste, Maigret stepped into the water up to his knee. James came after him with his supple stride, mumbling to himself inaudibly.

They only had to follow the group of people heading behind the lean-to that served as the dance hall. Round the back of the shed they found a man staring wide-eyed at the crowd, stammering over and over:

'It wasn't me! . . . '

It was Basso. He seemed unaware that he was holding a small, pearl-handled revolver in his hand.

'Where's my wife? . . . ' he asked the people around him, as if he didn't recognize them.

Some people went to look for her. Someone said:

'She stayed at home to prepare dinner . . . '

Maigret had to push his way to the front before he saw a figure lying in the long grass, dressed in a grey suit and a straw hat.

Far from being tragic, the scene had an air of absurdity, with everyone standing around not knowing what to do. They stood there looking in bewildered fashion at Basso, who seemed just as bewildered as they.

To cap it all, one of the members of the group, who was a doctor, was standing right next to the body but hadn't made a move. He was looking at the others, as if waiting for instructions.

There was, however, a small moment of tragedy after all. The body suddenly twitched. The legs seemed to be trying to bend. The shoulders twisted back. A part of Monsieur Feinstein's face came into view. Then, as if in one last effort, he stiffened, then slowly became immobile.

The man had just died.

★ ★ ★

'Check his heart,' Maigret told the doctor curtly.

The inspector, who was not unfamiliar with such events, caught every detail of the scene. He saw everything at once, with an almost unreal clarity.

Someone had fallen to the ground at the back of the crowd, wailing piteously. It was Madame Feinstein, who had been the last to arrive because she had been the last to stop dancing. Some people were bending over her. The landlord of the bar was approaching with the suspicious expression of a distrustful peasant.

Monsieur Basso was breathing quickly, pumping air into his lungs. He suddenly noticed the revolver in his clenched fist. He appeared stupefied. He looked at each of the persons around him in turn, as if wondering to whom he should give the gun. He repeated:

'It wasn't me . . . '

He was still looking round for his wife, despite what he had been told.

'Dead,' said the doctor as he stood up.

'A bullet?'

'Here . . . '

And he pointed to the wound in the side, then looked round for his own wife, who was dressed in only a swimming-costume.

'Do you have a telephone?' Maigret asked the landlord.

'No. You have to go to the station . . . or up to the lock.'

Marcel Basso was wearing white flannel trousers, and his shirt was partly unbuttoned, showing off the broadness of his chest.

He rocked slightly on his feet, reached out a hand as if looking for some support, then suddenly slumped down in the grass less than three metres from the corpse and laid his head in his hands.

The comic note returned. A thin female voice piped up:

'He's crying! . . . '

She thought she was whispering, but everyone heard.

'Do you have a bicycle?' Maigret asked the landlord.

'Of course.'

'Then cycle up to the lock and alert the police.'

'At Corbeil or at Cesson?'

'It doesn't matter!'

Maigret observed Basso, feeling a little troubled. He took the revolver: only one bullet had been fired.

It was a woman's revolver, pretty, like a piece of jewellery. The bullets were tiny, nickel-plated. Yet it had only taken one to end the life of the haberdasher.

There was hardly any blood. A reddish stain on his summer jacket. Otherwise, he was as neat and tidy as usual.

'Mado has taken a turn, back in the house!' a young man cried out.

Mado was Madame Feinstein, whom they had laid on the innkeeper's tall bed. Everyone was watching Maigret. He felt a chill when a voice called out from the riverbank:

'Cooeey! . . . Where are you?'

It was Pierrot, Basso's son, who was getting out of a canoe and was looking for the group.

'Quickly! Don't let him come round!'

Marcel Basso was gathering himself together. He uncovered his face and stood up, confused by his recent show of weakness, and once again seemed to look for the person to whom he should be speaking.

'I'm a policeman,' Maigret told him.

'You know . . . It wasn't me . . . '

'Would you care to follow me?'

The inspector spoke to the doctor:

'I'm relying on you to make sure no one touches the body. And I would like to ask the rest of you to leave me and Monsieur Basso alone.'

The whole scene had been dragged out like a slow, badly directed play in the bright glare and oppressive atmosphere of the afternoon.

Some anglers passed by on the towpath, their catches in baskets slung over their shoulders. Basso walked by Maigret's side.

'I just can't believe it . . . '

There was no spring in his step. When they turned the corner of the lean-to they saw the river, the villa on the opposite bank and Madame Basso rearranging the wicker chairs that had been left out in the garden.

'Mummy wants the key to the cellar,' the little boy shouted from his canoe.

But the man didn't reply. His expression changed to that of a hunted animal.

'Tell him where the key is.'

He summoned up his strength and called out:

'Hanging on a hook in the garage!'

'What's that?'

'On a hook in the garage!'

43

And his words echoed faintly:

'. . . rage!'

'What happened between you?' asked Maigret as they went inside the lean-to with the mechanical piano, empty but for the glasses left on the tables.

'I don't know . . .'

'Whose revolver is it?'

'It's not mine! . . . Mine is still in my car.'

'Did Feinstein attack you?'

A long silence. Then he sighed.

'I don't know! I didn't do anything! . . . I . . . I swear I didn't kill him.'

'You were holding the gun when . . .'

'I know . . . I don't know how that happened . . .'

'Are you saying someone else pulled the trigger?'

'No . . . I . . . You don't know how awful this is for me . . .'

'Did Feinstein kill himself?'

'He . . .'

He sat down on a bench and put his head in his hands once more. He grabbed an unfinished drink from the table and swallowed it in one go, with a grimace.

'What happens next? Are you going to arrest me?'

He stared at Maigret, his brow furrowed:

'But how did you happen to be there? You couldn't have known . . .'

He was struggling to make sense of everything, to tie together his tattered thoughts. He grimaced.

'It's like some sort of trap . . . '

The white canoe was on its way back from the far bank.

'Papa! . . . The key isn't in the garage! . . . Mummy wants to know . . . '

Mechanically, Basso felt his pockets. There was a tinkle of metal. He took out his keys and placed them on the table. Maigret took them across to the towpath and called out to the boy:

'Here! . . . Catch!'

'Thank you, monsieur.'

The canoe moved off again. Madame Basso was laying the table for dinner with the help of the maid. Some of the canoes were heading back towards the Vieux-Garçon. The landlord was cycling back from the lock, where he had made the phone call.

'Are you sure it wasn't you that pulled the trigger?'

Basso shrugged, gave a sigh and didn't reply.

The canoe reached the far bank. They could just make out the child and his mother talking. The maid was sent to fetch something inside the house, and returned almost immediately. Madame Basso took the binoculars from her and trained them on the Two-Penny Bar.

James was sitting in a corner with the landlord and his family, pouring out large glasses of brandy and stroking the cat that had nestled in his lap.

45

# 4

## Meetings in Rue Royale

It had been a dreary, tiring week, full of boring chores, time-consuming tasks and countless petty frustrations. Paris remained oppressive, and around six every evening heavy thunderstorms would turn the streets into rivers.

Madame Maigret wrote from her holiday: '*The weather's lovely, I've never seen such a crop of sloes . . .* '

Maigret didn't like being in Paris without his wife. He ate without appetite in whichever restaurant was nearest to hand; he even stayed over in hotels so as not to go back home alone.

The story had all begun in the sun-filled shop on Boulevard Saint-Michel, where Basso was trying on a top hat. Then came the secret rendezvous in a furnished block in the Avenue Niel. A wedding party in the evening at the Two-Penny Bar. A game of bridge and the unexpected drama . . .

When the police had arrived on the scene, Maigret, who was off duty, left them to do their job. They had arrested the coal merchant. The prosecutor's office had been informed.

One hour later, Monsieur Basso was sitting between two police sergeants in the little railway station at Seine-Port. The Sunday crowd were all waiting for the train. The sergeant on the right offered him a cigarette.

The lamps had been lit. Night had virtually fallen. When the train had arrived in the station and everyone was crowding to get on, Basso shook off his captors, bustled his way through the crowd, ran across the rails and made for the woods on the other side.

The policemen couldn't believe their eyes. Only a few moments earlier he had been sitting there quite calm and apparently docile between the pair of them.

Maigret heard about the escape when he got back to Paris. It was an unpleasant night for everyone. The police searched the countryside around Morsang and Seine-Port, set up roadblocks, kept the railway stations under surveillance and questioned passing motorists. The net spread out over nearly the whole *département*, and weekend ramblers returning home from their walks were astonished to find the gates of Paris manned by police.

Two policemen stood guard outside the Bassos' house in Quai d'Austerlitz; two more in front of the block where the Feinsteins had their private apartment in Boulevard des Batignolles.

On Monday morning Maigret had to go to the Two-Penny Bar with magistrates from the prosecutor's office and got caught up in endless discussions.

By Monday evening, nothing! It was almost certain that Basso had slipped through the cordon and taken refuge in Paris or one of the surrounding towns, like Melun, Corbeil or Fontainebleau.

On Tuesday morning came the forensic report: a bullet fired from a distance of about thirty centimetres. It was impossible to determine whether the shot had been fired by Feinstein himself or by Basso.

Madame Feinstein identified the weapon as belonging to her. She was unaware that her husband had been carrying it in his pocket. Normally the revolver was kept — loaded — in the young woman's bedroom.

She was questioned at her flat in Boulevard des Batignolles. Unremarkable décor, few luxuries, very plain. And none too clean either — one maid to do everything.

And Madame Feinstein wept! She wept and wept! It was more or less her only response, apart from the odd 'If only I'd known!'

She had been Basso's mistress for a few months. She loved him!

'Had you had other lovers before him?'

'Monsieur!'

Of course she'd had other lovers. Feinstein couldn't have kept a live wire like her satisfied.

'How long have you been married?'

'Eight years.'

'Did your husband know about your affair?'

'Oh, no!'

'Didn't he suspect a little?'

'Not at all.'

'Do you think he would have been capable of threatening Basso with the gun if he had found out something?'

'I don't know . . . He was a strange man, very closed in on himself.'

Obviously theirs was not a marriage based on great intimacy. Feinstein occupied with running his business, Mado left to her shopping and her secret liaisons.

And Maigret glumly pursued his investigation, proceeding by the book, questioning the concierge, the suppliers and the manager at Feinstein's shop in Boulevard des Capucines.

The case was depressing in its banality, though there was something about it that didn't feel quite right.

Feinstein had started off with a small haberdasher's on Avenue de Clichy. Then, one year after he got married, he took over a larger concern on the Boulevards, with the help of a bank loan.

From then on it was the age-old story of a small business overstretching itself: unpaid bills, bounced cheques, loans and beating the wolf from the door at the end of the month.

Nothing shady, nothing improper, but nothing solid either.

At home too they owed money to all the local tradesmen.

In the dead man's office behind his shop Maigret spent a good two hours going through his books. He found nothing unusual around the time of the crime Jean Lenoir had talked about the day before his execution.

No large receipts, no out-of-the-ordinary expenses.

Absolutely nothing, a complete blank. The investigation was grinding to a halt.

The most annoying part of it was questioning

Madame Basso at Morsang. The inspector was surprised by her attitude. Although clearly sad, she was hardly in despair. She showed a dignity of which Maigret would not have thought her capable.

'My husband must have had a good reason to run away.'

'You don't think he's guilty?'

'No.'

'But he still ran away . . . Have you heard any word from him at all?'

'No.'

'How much money did he have on him?'

'Not more than ten francs!'

The coal merchant's affairs were the exact opposite of the haberdasher's. The business never made less than 500,000 francs, even in a bad year. The offices and the yard were well organized. There were three barges moored at the quayside. Marcel Basso had inherited the business from his father and had expanded it.

Nor did the weather do much for Maigret's mood. Like all large people he suffered from the heat, and Paris wilted under the hot sun every day until three in the afternoon.

That's when the sky clouded over, the air crackled with electricity and the wind began to gust, suddenly raising swirling plumes of dust from the streets.

By late afternoon it broke: rumbles of thunder, then a deluge of rain pounding the asphalt, seeping through the awnings of the café terraces, forcing people to seek shelter in doorways.

It was on Wednesday that Maigret, caught in a sudden shower, sought shelter in the Taverne Royale. A man stood up and offered him his hand. It was James, who had been sitting alone at a table, nursing a Pernod.

The inspector hadn't seen him before in his weekday clothes. He looked more like a bank clerk now than when he was all dressed up at Morsang, but he still somehow had the air of a circus performer.

'Care for a drink?'

Maigret was exhausted. There would be a couple of hours of rain to sit out. Then he would have to go back to the Quai des Orfèvres to catch up with any news.

'A Pernod?'

Normally he only drank beer. But he didn't raise any protest. He drank mechanically. James wasn't a bad companion, and he had one salient quality: he didn't talk much!

He sat there in his cane armchair with his legs crossed, smoking cigarettes and watching the people scuttling past in the rain.

When a paper boy came by, he bought an evening paper, flicked through it vaguely, then handed it to Maigret, indicating a paragraph with his finger.

Marcel Basso, the murderer of the haberdasher from Boulevard des Capucines, is still at large, despite an extensive search by the police.

'What's your opinion?' Maigret asked.

51

James shrugged his shoulders, made a gesture of indifference.

'Do you think he's gone abroad?'

'I don't think he'll have gone far . . . He's probably lying low in Paris.'

'Why do you say that?'

'I don't know. I think . . . he must have had a reason for running away . . . Waiter, two more Pernods!'

Maigret had three glasses and slipped gently into a state he wasn't familiar with. He wasn't drunk, but he wasn't totally clear in the head either.

He felt agreeably mellow, sitting there on the terrace. He was able to think about the case in a more relaxed manner, almost with a degree of pleasure.

James talked about this and that, without any hint of urgency. At eight o'clock on the dot he stood up and announced:

'Time to go! My wife will be expecting me . . .'

Maigret was a little annoyed with himself for the time he'd wasted and for allowing himself to drink too much. He had dinner, then went back to his office. Neither the local police nor the Paris force had anything to report.

The next day — Thursday — he plodded on with the inquiry with the same lack of enthusiasm.

He waded through files dating back ten years but found nothing relating to the information Jean Lenoir had given.

He looked through the legal registers. He rang

52

around the hospitals and sanatoriums in the vague hope of finding Victor, Lenoir's friend with tuberculosis.

There were lots of Victors, but not the right one!

By midday, Maigret had a splitting head but no appetite. He had lunch in Place Dauphin, in a little restaurant popular with police officers. Then he phoned Morsang, where policemen had been posted outside the Bassos' villa.

No sign. Madame Basso was carrying on with life as normal with her son. She read all the papers. The villa didn't have a telephone.

At five o'clock, Maigret came out of the apartment block on the Avenue Niel. He had come on the off chance of digging something up, but hadn't found anything.

Then mechanically, as if he'd already been doing it for years, he headed off to the Taverne Royale, where he was greeted by James, and sat down beside him.

'What's new?' James asked him, then before he could answer called out: 'Two Pernods!'

The storm was behind schedule today. The streets remained bathed in sunlight. Coachloads of tourists drove past.

'The most straightforward hypothesis,' Maigret murmured, as if to himself, 'the one the newspapers seem to favour, is that Basso was attacked by his companion for some reason or another, grabbed hold of the gun that was pointed at him and shot the haberdasher . . . '

'Which is rubbish.'

Maigret looked at James, who also seemed to

be talking to himself.

'Why do you say it's rubbish?'

'Because if Feinstein had wanted to kill Basso, he'd have been a bit more calculating than that. He was a cool customer, a skilful bridge player.'

The inspector couldn't help smiling at the serious tone in which James said this.

'So what's your theory?'

'I don't exactly have a theory. Just that Basso should never have got involved with Mado. You can tell just by looking at her that she's not the sort of woman who lets a man go easily, once she's got her claws into him.'

'Had her husband shown any signs of being jealous?'

'What, him?'

And James gave Maigret a curious look. There was an ironic twinkle in his eye.

'Don't you know?'

James shrugged his shoulders and murmured:

'It's none of my business. Besides, if he was the jealous type, then most of the Morsang gang would be dead by now.'

'You mean they were all . . . ?'

'Well, not all. Let's not exaggerate. Let's just say that Mado danced with everyone, and when you danced with Mado, you could end up disappearing into the bushes.'

'Including you?'

'I don't dance,' James replied.

'If what you say is true, then Feinstein must have known.'

The Englishman sighed.

'I don't know! But he did owe all of them money.'

At first sight, James came across as a drunken oaf. But there was a lot more to him than met the eye.

Maigret whistled.

'Well, well.'

'Two Pernods! Two!'

'Yes. Mado didn't even have to know. It was all very discreet. Feinstein tapped his wife's lovers for money, without letting on that he knew, but leaving the implication hanging in the air . . . '

They didn't talk much after that. The storm still hadn't broken. Maigret drank his Pernods, his eyes fixed on the crowds flowing past in the street outside. He was comfortably ensconced in his chair, turning over in his mind this new complexion on the case.

'Eight o'clock! . . . '

James shook his hand and set off, just at the moment the storm was beginning to break.

By Friday it had become a daily habit. Maigret headed for the Taverne Royale almost without realizing it. At one point, he couldn't resist asking:

'Don't you ever go home after work? Between five and eight you seem to . . . '

'You have to have a little bolt-hole to call your own,' James sighed.

And James's bolt-hole was a café terrace, a marble-topped table, a cloudy aperitif; his view was the columns of the Madeleine, the waiters' white aprons and the crowds and traffic in the street.

'How long have you been married?'

'Eight years.'

Maigret didn't dare ask him whether he loved his wife. In any case, James would probably say yes. Only after eight o'clock! After the bolt-hole!

Maigret wondered whether they were starting to become friends.

Today they didn't discuss the case. Maigret drank his three Pernods. He needed to blot out the hard day he'd had. His life was clogged up with trivial problems.

It was the holidays, and he was having to fill in for several absent colleagues. And the examining magistrate in the Two-Penny Bar case never gave him a moment's peace. He had sent him to interrogate Mado Feinstein for a second time, told him to examine the haberdasher's books and to question Basso's employees.

The police were already short-handed, and a number of officers were pinned down watching the places where the fugitive was likely to show up. This all put the chief in a bad mood.

'Haven't you got this one sorted out yet?' he had asked that morning.

Maigret agreed with James. He sensed that Basso was in Paris. But how had he been able to get hold of money? And if he hadn't, how was he living? What was he hoping for? What was he expecting to happen? What was he doing with himself?

His guilt had not been proven. If he had stayed in custody and hired a good lawyer he could have hoped, if not for acquittal, then at least a light sentence. After which he could return to his business, his wife and his son. Instead of that, he was running away, in hiding, and thus giving up all his former life.

'He must have his reasons,' James had said in his usual philosophical way.

Don't let us down. Will be at station. Love.

It was Saturday. Madame Maigret had sent an affectionate ultimatum. Her husband wasn't yet sure how to reply. But at five o'clock he was at the Taverne Royale, shaking James's hand. James ordered as usual:

'Pernod!'

As on the previous Saturday, there was a rush to the stations — a continuous stream of taxis piled high with luggage, the bustle of people getting away on holiday.

'Are you going to Morsang?'

'Yes, as usual.'

'It'll be a strange atmosphere.'

The inspector wanted to go to Morsang himself. On the other hand, he wanted to see his wife, to go trout fishing in the rivers of Alsace, to breathe in the lovely smells of his sister-in-law's house.

He couldn't make his mind up. He vaguely observed James get up and head to the back of the bar.

There was nothing unusual in this. He thought nothing of it and barely registered the fact that his companion returned after a few moments

57

and sat down again.

Five, ten minutes went past. A waiter approached.

'Is one of you two gentlemen Monsieur Maigret?'

'That's me. What is it?'

'A phone call for you . . . '

Maigret stood up and went to the back of the bar, frowning; despite his inebriation, he could smell something fishy. When he went into the box, he turned round to see James looking at him from the terrace.

'Strange,' he muttered. 'Hello! . . . Hello! . . . This is Maigret . . . Who's calling? . . . '

He started to snap his fingers impatiently. Finally there was a woman's voice at the other end of the line.

'How can I help you?'

'Hello . . . who's there?'

'This is the operator. Which number do you require?'

'But you called me, mademoiselle.'

'Not so, monsieur. This number hasn't been rung for at least ten minutes. Please hang up.'

He bashed the door open with his fist. Outside, in the shade of the terrace, there was a man standing next to James. It was Marcel Basso. He looked different in new, ill-fitting clothes. He was keeping an anxious eye on the door of the phone box.

He saw Maigret at the same moment the latter spotted him. Maigret saw his lips move — a few quick words — then he dashed off into the crowds outside.

'How many calls?' the cashier asked the inspector.

But Maigret was running. The terrace was crowded, he had to weave his way through, and by the time he reached the street there was no way of knowing in which direction Basso had fled. There were dozens of taxis out on the street — had he hopped into one of them? Or even leaped on to a passing bus? . . .

Maigret returned to his table, scowling. He sat down without a word, without looking at James, who hadn't moved a muscle. A waiter approached.

'The cashier would like to know how many calls you made.'

'Damn!'

He noticed a smile on James's lips and said crossly:

'Congratulations!'

'You reckon?'

'How long did it take you to hatch this little scheme?'

'It was pretty much off the cuff. Waiter, two Pernods! And some cigarettes!'

'What did he say to you? What did he want?'

James leaned back in his chair and merely sighed, as if he couldn't see the point of this conversation.

'Money? And where did he get hold of that suit he was wearing?'

'He can't be expected to walk round Paris in white flannels!'

That was indeed what Basso was wearing

when he ran away at Seine-Port station. James forgot nothing.

'Have you contacted him prior to today?'

'He contacted me!'

'And you have nothing to say?'

'You'd do the same as me. I've been a guest at his house hundreds of times. He's never done me any harm!'

'Did he want money?'

'He's been watching us for half an hour. I thought I saw him yesterday across the road. He just didn't dare come over.'

'So you had me summoned to the phone.'

'He seemed tired.'

'Did he say anything?'

'It's weird how different clothes can change a man . . . ' James sighed, evading the question.

Maigret observed him out of the corner of his eye.

'Are you aware that, by rights, you could be arrested for aiding and abetting?'

'There are lots of things you can do by rights. But rights aren't always right.'

He was clowning around as usual.

'Waiter, where are those Pernods?'

'Coming!'

'Are you coming down to Morsang? Because if you are, we may as well get a taxi. It's only a hundred francs, and the train costs . . . '

'What about your wife?'

'She always comes by taxi, with her sister and her friends. Five of them, that works out at twenty francs a head, whereas the train costs . . . '

'OK.'

'Coming or not?'

'I'm coming. Waiter, how much is that?'

'Excuse me. Separate bills, as usual.'

It was a matter of principle. Maigret paid for his own drinks, James for his. He added ten francs for the 'phone call'.

In the taxi, James appeared preoccupied. When they reached Villejuif, he revealed what was on his mind:

'I wonder where we'll be playing bridge tomorrow afternoon.'

It was time for the storm. The first drops of rain began to streak the windscreen.

# 5

## The Doctor's Car

They might have expected to find a different atmosphere at Morsang. It had only been the previous Sunday that the events had taken place. One of the group was now dead, another was a wanted murderer.

Nevertheless, when James and Maigret arrived, they found a group of people standing around a new car, admiring it. They had exchanged their weekday clothes for their sports gear. Only the doctor was still dressed in a suit.

It was his car, and he was giving it its first outing. Everyone was asking questions, and he was extolling its special features.

'Yes, it does guzzle more gas, but . . . '

Almost everyone had a car. The doctor's was brand new.

'The engine purrs, just listen to this . . . '

His wife was sitting contentedly inside the car, happy to let the confab take its course. Doctor Mertens was about thirty, skinny as a rake, as limp-wristed as a sickly young girl.

'Is that your new car?' James asked, bursting into the conversation.

He strode around it, muttering to himself inaudibly.

'I wouldn't mind taking it for a spin tomorrow. Is that all right with you?'

One would have thought that Maigret's presence would disturb them. They hardly noticed he was there! They all felt so at home at the inn, they came and went as they pleased.

'Your wife not with you, James?'

'She's coming with Marcelle and Lili.'

They took their canoes out of the garage. Someone was repairing a fishing-rod with some silk cord. They all did their own thing until dinnertime. There wasn't much conversation during the meal, just the odd exchange here and there.

'Is Madame Basso at home?'

'What a week she must have had!'

'What are we doing tomorrow?'

Maigret was like a spare part. Everyone avoided him, without making it too obvious. When James wasn't with him, he would wander the terrace or the riverbank alone. When night fell he slipped off to check with the officers who were guarding the Bassos' villa.

There were two of them on duty. They took it in turn to take their meals in a bistro in Seine-Port, two kilometres away. When the inspector arrived, the one who was off duty was fishing.

'Anything to report?'

'Not a thing. She keeps herself to herself. Every now and again she takes a tour round the garden. The tradesmen have been calling as usual: the baker at nine, the butcher a short while later, then the greengrocer comes by with his cart around eleven.'

There was a light on on the ground floor. They

could make out the silhouette of the boy drinking his soup with a serviette tied around his neck. The policemen were stationed in a little wood on the riverbank. The one who was fishing said:

'This place is teeming with rabbits. If we weren't on a job . . . '

Opposite, the Two-Penny Bar, where two couples — probably workers from Corbeil — were dancing to the strains of the mechanical piano.

★   ★   ★

A Sunday morning like any other at Morsang, with anglers all along the banks, others sitting immobile in green-painted dinghies anchored at both ends, canoes, a couple of sailing-boats.

It was a well-ordered routine that nothing was going to disrupt.

The countryside was pretty, the sky was clear, everyone was at peace. Perhaps that's why the scene was as sickly as an overly sweet dessert.

Maigret found James dressed in a blue-and-white-striped sweater, white trousers and espadrilles, with an American sailing cap perched on his head. He was sipping a large glass of brandy and water by way of breakfast.

'Did you sleep well?'

Maigret noticed one amusing detail: in Paris, he always addressed Maigret with the formal *vous*. Here in Morsang, he used the familiar *tu* for everyone, including the inspector, without even realizing.

'What are you up to this morning?'

'I think I'll drop in on the Two-Penny Bar.'

'I'll see you there. Apparently we've arranged a get-together there for pre-lunch drinks. Do you want to borrow a canoe?'

Maigret was the only one in dark city clothes. He was given a small flat-bottomed boat which he had great trouble keeping steady. When he arrived at the Two-Penny Bar, it was ten o'clock in the morning, and there wasn't a customer in sight.

Or rather, there was one, in the kitchen munching on a hunk of bread and a fat sausage. The old woman was saying to him:

'You want to take better care. One of my lads didn't look after himself properly and it killed him. And he was bigger and stronger than you!'

At that moment the customer had a coughing fit and couldn't swallow his mouthful of bread. As he was coughing, he noticed Maigret standing at the door and he frowned.

'A bottle of beer!' said the inspector.

'Wouldn't you prefer to sit out on the terrace?'

No, he preferred the kitchen, with its table scored by knife marks, its rush chairs and its stove on which a large pot was bubbling away.

'My son has gone off to Corbeil to chase up some bottles of soda water they forgot to deliver. Would you help me open the trapdoor?'

The trapdoor in the middle of the kitchen was opened to reveal the gaping hole of a damp cellar. The stooping old woman went down into it while the customer never took his eyes off Maigret.

He was a pale, thin young man of about twenty-five with blond stubble on his cheeks. He had deep-set eyes and thin, colourless lips.

But what was most striking about him was what he was wearing. He wasn't dressed in rags, like a vagabond. Nor did he have that insolent look of the professional tramp.

No, he displayed a strange mixture of shyness and self-confidence. He was humble and aggressive at the same time. He was both clean and dirty.

His clothes were neat and well kept, even though he looked as if he had been on the road for days.

'Show me your papers, please.'

Maigret had no need to identify himself as a policeman. The boy had grasped that straight away. He took a grubby army identity card from his pocket. The inspector read the name under his breath:

'Victor Gaillard!'

He calmly closed the card and returned it to its owner. The old woman came back up from the cellar and closed the trapdoor.

'Nice and cold,' she said, opening the bottle of beer.

And she went back to peeling potatoes while the two men began talking in a steady, dispassionate tone.

'Last address?'

'The municipal sanatorium in Gien.'

'When did you leave?'

'A month ago.'

'And since then?'

'I've been broke, on the road. You could arrest me for vagrancy, but they'd just put me back in a sanatorium. I've only got one lung left.'

There was nothing self-pitying in his tone. On the contrary, it was as if he were presenting his credentials.

'Did you get a letter from Lenoir?'

'Who's Lenoir?'

'Stop messing about. He told you you'd find your man at the Two-Penny Bar.'

'I'd had enough of the sanatorium.'

'And thought you'd squeeze a bit more out of the guy from the Canal Saint-Martin!'

The old woman listened without understanding, without showing any surprise. It was as if they were having an everyday conversation in this rundown country kitchen, where a hen had wandered in and was pecking away around their feet.

'Have you got nothing to say?'

'I don't know what you're talking about.'

'Lenoir told me everything.'

'I don't know any Lenoir.'

Maigret shrugged his shoulders, lit his pipe and repeated:

'Stop messing about! You know I know what you're up to.'

'What's the worst they can do? Send me back to the sanatorium.'

'I know, I know . . . you've only got one lung.'

Some canoes glided past on the river.

'What Lenoir told you is true. Your man is here.'

'I'm not saying anything.'

'So much the worse for you. If you haven't changed your mind by this evening, I'll have you locked up for vagrancy. After that, we'll see . . . '

Maigret looked him in the eye. He could read him like a book. He'd met his sort before.

A different kettle of fish entirely from Lenoir. Victor was the sort who rode on the back of the bigger villains, the one who's always put on lookout duty and gets the smallest share of the loot.

He was one of those types who is easily led astray and doesn't have the strength of character to get back on the rails. He had started hanging around the streets and the dance halls at the age of sixteen. With Lenoir, he had landed on his feet that night at the Canal Saint-Martin, and had managed to live off the proceeds of his blackmail as if it were a regular salary.

But for his tuberculosis, he would probably have become a stooge in Lenoir's gang. But his ill health meant he ended up in the sanatorium. He must have driven the doctors and nurses to despair with his thieving and petty misdemeanours. Maigret guessed that he had faced the courts on more than one occasion and had been in and out of various sanatoriums, hospitals, hospices and young offenders' institutions.

He wasn't afraid. He had the same answer to everything: his lung. He'd be living off it until the day it killed him.

'What do I care?'

'Are you refusing to tell me the name of the man at the Canal?'

'Don't know what you're talking about.'

There was an ironic twinkle in his eyes as he said this. He bit off a large chunk of sausage and started chewing it assiduously.

'I know Lenoir wouldn't have said anything,' he murmured, after a pensive pause. 'Not like that, right at the end . . . '

Maigret stayed cool. He knew he had the upper hand. What's more, he now had a new means of getting to the truth.

'Another beer, please, madame.'

'A good thing I brought three bottles up.'

She gave Victor a curious look, as if trying to work out what crime he could have committed.

'To think you were well taken care of in the sanatorium and you left. Just like my son! He'd rather have his freedom than . . . '

Maigret watched the canoes row past in the bright sunlight outside. It was nearly time for drinks. A sailing-boat containing James's wife and two of her friends pulled in at the riverbank outside. The three women beckoned to a canoe, which followed close behind. Other boats followed. The old woman sighed:

'My son hasn't got back yet. I won't be able to manage on my own. My daughter has gone to fetch the milk.'

Nevertheless, she gathered up some glasses, which she took out to the tables on the terrace, then she dug some loose change out of a pocket concealed under her petticoat.

'They'll need some pennies for the piano.'

Maigret stayed where he was, one eye on the new arrivals and the other on his sickly companion, who continued to munch away unperturbed. And he noticed the Bassos' villa in the background, with its blooming garden, its diving-board next to the river, its two boats moored at the bank, the child's swing.

He gave a sudden start when he heard what sounded like a shot being fired in the distance. The people next to the river looked up too. But there was nothing to be seen. Nothing happened. Ten minutes went by. The guests from the Vieux-Garçon took their seats around the tables. The old woman came out, carrying several bottles of aperitif.

Then a dark figure ran down the Bassos' lawn. Maigret recognized one of the police officers. He fumbled with the chain of one of the boats, got in and started rowing towards them with all his might.

Maigret stood up and turned to Victor.

'You . . . stay put.'

'Happy to oblige.'

Outside, everyone had stopped ordering drinks, intent on the sight of the officer rowing across. Maigret walked down to the reeds by the river and waited impatiently.

'What's happened?'

The officer was out of breath.

'Get in . . . I swear it wasn't my fault.'

With Maigret on board, he started rowing back across to the villa.

'It was all quiet. The greengrocer had just been round. Madame Basso was walking in the garden with the child. I don't know why, I just had this feeling something was up — like they were expecting something. Then a car pulled up,

70

a brand-new car. It parked just outside the gate, and a man got out.'

'Balding, in his thirties?'

That's right! He came into the garden and started walking with Madame Basso and the boy. You know where my observation post is . . . it's a fair distance away. They shook hands. The woman walked the man back to the gate. He climbed in and turned on the ignition. And before I could make a move, Madame Basso jumped in with the boy, and the car sped off.'

'Who fired the shot?'

'I did. I was trying to puncture a tyre.'

'Was Berger with you?'

'Yes. I sent him to Seine-Port to phone around everyone.'

This was the second time they'd had to alert all the police stations in Seine-et-Oise. The boat reached the far bank. Maigret went into the garden. But what could they do there now? There was nothing to do but phone around and alert the other stations.

Maigret bent over to pick up a woman's handkerchief, embroidered with Madame Basso's initials. She had pulled it to ribbons as she had nervously waited for James to appear.

What upset the inspector the most was the thought of all those hours he had whiled away drinking Pernod with the Englishman on the terrace of the Taverne Royale. Now he resented that. He was annoyed that he had let down his guard and allowed himself to be sucked in.

'Shall I carry on keeping an eye on the villa?'

'In case the bricks run off? No, go and find

Berger. Then the two of you help with the search. Try and get hold of a motorbike, and bring me hourly updates.'

On the kitchen table, next to the vegetables, there was an envelope bearing James's writing:

To be delivered without fail to Madame Basso.

Obviously the greengrocer had delivered the letter. It told the young woman what was going to happen. That's why she was nervously patrolling the garden with her son.

Maigret rowed back to the Two-Penny Bar. He found the group gathered round the vagrant. Someone had given him an aperitif, and the doctor was asking him questions. Victor had the cheek to give the inspector a look as if to say:

'I'm busy. Leave me alone . . . '

And he continued with his explanation:

'He was an important professor, apparently. They filled my lung with oxygen, right, and then they sealed it like a balloon . . . '

The doctor smiled at the way he described it, but nodded to his companions to show that what he was saying was true.

'Now they have to do the same thing with the half-lung on the other side, because you've got two lungs, see, or in my case one and a half.'

'And you drink alcohol?'

'Yeah. Cheers.'

'Do you get cold sweats at night?'

'Sometimes. When I sleep in draughty barns.'

'What are you drinking, inspector?' someone

asked. 'Has something happened that they had to come and fetch you like that?'

'Tell me, doctor, did James borrow your car this morning?'

'He asked if he could take it for a spin. He'll be back soon . . . '

'I very much doubt it.'

The doctor gave a start, then tried to smile as he stammered:

'You're joking, of course . . . '

'I assure you I'm quite serious. He's just used it to abduct Madame Basso and her son.'

'What . . . James?' the doctor's wife asked, unable to believe her ears.

'Yes, James.'

'It must have been a joke. He really likes a good hoax.'

Victor was greatly amused by this. He sipped his drink and looked at Maigret with a sardonic smile.

The landlord returned from Corbeil in his little pony and trap. As he was unloading the bottles of soda water, he happened to say:

'What a palaver! You can't go down the road now without being stopped by the police. Luckily they know who I am.'

'Was this on the road to Corbeil?'

'Yes, just a few minutes ago. There are ten of them next to the bridge. They're stopping cars and asking everyone to show their papers. So there's a tailback of about thirty cars.'

Maigret turned away. It was nothing to do with him. It had to be done, but it was an extremely crude and heavy-handed method. And it was a lot for people to put up with two Sundays in a row, in the same *département*, especially for a small-scale crime that had had very little coverage in the newspapers.

Had he lost track of the case? Had he been left floundering in the wake of events? Once again the memory of the hours spent drinking with James in the Taverne Royale came back to haunt him.

'What are you drinking?' he heard a voice ask. 'A large Pernod?'

The very word was enough to remind him of the week gone by, the Sunday get-togethers of the Morsang crowd, the whole disagreeable case.

'A beer,' he replied.

'At this hour?'

The well-meaning waiter who had offered him the aperitif was taken aback at the fury of Maigret's response:

'Yes, at this hour!'

Victor, too, received a bad-tempered look. The doctor was talking about him to the fishermen:

'I've heard of the treatment, but I've never seen such a thoroughgoing application of the technique of pneumothorax . . . '

Then, in a whisper:

'Not that it'll make much difference. I'd give him a year at most . . . '

★ ★ ★

Maigret had lunch at the Vieux-Garçon, ensconced in a corner like a wounded beast, growling if anyone came near. Twice the police

74

officer came on his motorbike to report in.

'Nothing. The car was spotted on the road to Fontainebleau, but hasn't been seen since.'

Marvellous! A traffic jam on the Fontainebleau road! Hundreds of cars held up!

Two hours later, it was reported that a car matching the description of the doctor's car had filled up at a petrol station at Arpajon. But was it the right one? The petrol-pump attendant had sworn there was no woman in the car.

Finally, at five o'clock, a message from Montlhéry. The car had been seen doing circuits of the racetrack, as if on a time trial, when it blew a tyre. By sheer chance a policeman had asked the driver for his licence. He didn't have one.

It was James, and he was on his own. They were waiting for Maigret's instructions whether to let him go or lock him up.

'They were brand-new tyres,' the doctor moaned. 'And on its first time out! I'm beginning to think he's mad. Or else he's drunk, as usual.'

And he asked Maigret if he could come with him.

# 6

## Haggling

They made a detour to the Two-Penny Bar to pick up Victor. Once he was in the car, he turned and gave the landlord a look which meant something like 'You see the special treatment I'm getting?'

He was sitting on the fold-down seat, facing Maigret. The window was wound down, and he had the impudence to ask:

'Do you mind if I close it? It's because of my lung, you know.'

At the track there were no races on today. There were a few drivers doing practice laps in front of the empty stands. The emptiness of the place, if anything, made it seem more vast.

A short distance away, a parked car; a police officer was standing next to a man in a leather helmet who was on his knees tinkering with his bike.

'Over there,' the inspector was told.

Victor was fascinated by a racing-car hurtling round the track at around 200 kilometres an hour. Now he opened the window so he could lean out to get a better view.

'It's my car all right,' said the doctor. 'I hope it isn't damaged . . .'

Then they saw James, standing quite calmly next to the motorcyclist, stroking his chin, giving

advice on how to fix the engine. When he saw
Maigret and his companions approach, he
murmured:

'That was quick!'

Then he looked at Victor from head to toe, as
if wondering what he was doing there.

'Who's this?'

If Maigret had been hoping for something
from this meeting, he was disappointed. Victor
scarcely noticed the Englishman, he was too
interested in watching the racing-car. The doctor
was already inspecting the inside of his car for
any signs of damage.

'Have you been here long?' the inspector
growled.

'I'm not sure . . . quite long, yes.'

He was so self-possessed, it was unbelievable.
You wouldn't think to look at him that he had
just whisked away a woman and her child from
under the noses of the police, and because of
him the entire Seine-et-Oise force was on a state
of alert.

'Don't worry,' he said to the doctor. 'Nothing
worse than a puncture. The rest of the car is
intact. It's a good machine . . . the clutch is a
little sticky, perhaps . . . '

'Did Basso ask you yesterday to pick up his
wife and child?'

'You know very well I can't answer questions
like that, my dear Maigret.'

'And I don't suppose you will tell me where
you dropped them off?'

'I'm sure if you were in my shoes . . . '

'I'll give you credit for one thing, something

even a professional criminal wouldn't have thought of.'

James was modestly surprised.

'What's that?'

'The racetrack. Having delivered Madame Basso safely, you didn't want the police to find the car straight away. And since there were roadblocks everywhere, you thought of the racetrack. You could have driven round and round for hours.'

'I'd always fancied having a go at it, you know.'

But the inspector wasn't listening. He dashed over to the doctor, who was attempting to fit the spare tyre.

'I'm sorry, the car stays put until we receive the order to release it.'

'What? But this is *my* car! I haven't done anything . . . '

It was no use protesting. The car was put into a lock-up, and Maigret took away the key. The policeman awaited instructions. James smoked a cigarette. Victor was still watching the racing-cars.

'Take him away,' said Maigret, indicating Victor, 'and put him in a cell.'

'What about me?' James asked.

'Do you still have nothing to say to me?'

'Not really. Put yourself in my shoes!'

Maigret sulkily turned his back on him.

★   ★   ★

Maigret was delighted when it began to rain on the Monday. The grey weather chimed in better with his mood and the tedious tasks of the day.

Among them, he had to write a report on the events of the day before, in which he had to justify his deployment of the officers under his command.

At eleven o'clock, two officers from Criminal Records came to collect him from his office, and all three of them took a taxi to the racetrack, where Maigret was able to do little except watch his colleagues at work.

They knew that the doctor had clocked up only sixty kilometres since buying the car. The dial now showed 210 kilometres. They reckoned that James must have done about fifty kilometres at the racetrack.

That left about a hundred kilometres to account for. The distance between Morsang and Montlhéry was barely forty kilometres by the most direct route.

Using this information, they were able to mark a circle on a route map showing the maximum area the car could have reached.

The two experts worked meticulously. They carefully scraped the tyres, gathered up the dust and other debris and examined it under a magnifying glass, putting some of it aside for further analysis.

'Fresh tar,' one of them said.

And the other examined a special map provided by the transport department, looking for places within their circle where there were current roadworks. There were four or five, all in different directions. The first expert said:

'Chalk deposits.'

Now they consulted a military map. Maigret walked up and down glumly, smoking his pipe.

'No calcareous soil in the Fontainebleau area, but between La Ferté-Allais and Arpajon . . .'

'I've found some grains of wheat in the tread . . .'

And so the evidence accumulated. The maps became covered in blue and red lines.

At two o'clock they rang the town hall at La Ferté-Allais to find out whether any firm in the town was currently using Portland cement in such a way that some of it could have found its way on to the road. They didn't get their answer until three o'clock:

'There's building work going on at the Essonne mills. There's cement on the main road from La Ferté to Arpajon.'

They had pinned down one thing. The car had definitely passed through there. The experts took away a few other objects to examine more closely in the laboratory.

Maigret checked off all the towns and villages within the circle on the map, and rang round the relevant police stations and municipal offices.

At four o'clock, he left his office intending to interrogate Victor, whom he had not seen since the previous day and who was now held in the temporary cell at the foot of the stairs at the police headquarters. As he descended the stairs, however, he had an idea. He returned to his office and telephoned the accountant of Basso's firm.

'Hello! Police! Could you tell me the name of your bank? . . . The Banque du Nord, Boulevard

80

Haussmann. Thank you.'

He had himself driven to the bank, where he asked to see the manager. Five minutes later, Maigret had another lead in his inquiry. At ten o'clock that morning, James had cashed a cheque for 300,000 francs drawn up by Marcel Basso.

The cheque was dated four days previously.

★ ★ ★

'Boss, the guy downstairs wants to see you. Says he has something important to tell you.'

Maigret walked ponderously downstairs and entered the cell, where Victor was sitting on a bench, leaning on the table with his head in his hands.

'I'm listening.'

The prisoner stood up briskly. He had a cunning look on his face. Shifting from one foot to the other, he said:

'You haven't found anything yet, have you?'

'Still pursuing our inquiries.'

'See, you haven't found anything yet. I'm not stupid . . . Anyway, last night I had a bit of a think.'

'You've decided to talk?'

'Hold on! We need to reach an understanding. I don't know if Lenoir talked or not. If he did, he didn't tell you everything. Without me, you won't get anywhere. That's a fact. You're stuck, and you're going to stay that way. So, this is what I've got to say. Information like that's got to be worth something. Got to be worth a lot. Let's say I went and found the murderer and told him I was going to tell the police everything. Don't you think he'd cough up whatever I asked for?'

Victor had that triumphant look of the underdog who suddenly finds himself in a position of power. All his life the police had hassled him, and now he felt that he had the upper hand. He was strutting around looking very pleased with himself.

'So there it is. Why would I talk? Why would I harm someone who hasn't done me any wrong? You think you can put me away for vagrancy? You're forgetting my lung. They'll send me to a hospital, then to a sanatorium.'

Maigret looked at him steadily, but didn't say a word.

'How's about 30,000 francs? It's not a lot. Just enough to see me through to the end, which can't be long now. Thirty grand — what's a piddling amount like that to the government?'

He imagined he already had the money in his hands. He was exultant. He was interrupted by a coughing fit, which brought tears to his eyes, but they were like tears of triumph. Wasn't he smart? Wasn't he in the driving seat?

'That's my final offer. Thirty thousand francs and I tell you everything. You'll get your man. There'll be a promotion in it for you. You'll have your name in the papers. Otherwise, nothing! You can do what you like with me. Just remember, it all took place six years ago, and there were only two witnesses: Lenoir, who won't be saying any more, and yours truly . . . '

'Is that it?' asked Maigret, who had remained

standing the whole time.

'You think it's too much?'

Victor felt a pang of disquiet at Maigret's calm, inscrutable reaction.

'I'm not scared of you, you know.' He gave a forced laugh. 'I know the score. You could rough me up a bit, but I'd tell the papers how the police beat up a poor invalid with one lung . . . '

'Are you finished?'

'Don't think you'll find the truth on your own. If you ask me, 30,000 francs is not much to pay . . . '

'Are you finished?'

'And if you think I'm stupid enough to go after the guy if you let me go, you've got another think coming. I won't write to him, I won't ring him . . . '

His tone had changed now. He felt the ground slipping under him, but he was still trying to put on a brave face.

'Anyway, I want to see a lawyer. You can't keep me here more than twenty-four hours.'

Maigret blew out a little puff of smoke, thrust his hands in his pockets and left the cell. On the way out he said to the warder:

'Lock him in.'

He was angry, and now he was on his own he could let it show in his face. He was angry because he had this idiot in his grasp, at his mercy, but he couldn't get anything out of him.

And that was because he was an idiot, because he thought he was cunning and tough!

He thought he could use his lung as a form of blackmail!

Three or four times during this interview, the inspector had almost struck him across the face, to knock some sense into him, but had managed to restrain himself.

In truth, his hand was not a strong one. Legally, he had nothing on Victor.

He had plenty of previous form, for sure; he'd led his whole life going from one petty crime to the next. But there was nothing new, except a vagrancy charge, that Maigret could get him on.

And he was right about the lung. He'd have everyone on his side. The newspapers would devote several column inches to portraying the police as monsters.

Dying man beaten by police!

So he stood there calm as you like, demanding to be paid 30,000 francs! And he was right when he said they would soon have to release him!

'Let him out tonight at around one o'clock. Tell Sergeant Lucas to follow him and not to let him out of his sight.'

And Maigret clenched his teeth round the stem of his pipe. Victor knew, and he only had to say one word. Now Maigret was stuck with having to concoct theories out of diverse, and sometimes contradictory, evidence.

He hailed a taxi and barked at the driver:

'To the Taverne Royale!'

★ ★ ★

James wasn't there. Eight o'clock came and he still hadn't turned up. The doorman at the bank confirmed that he had left at five as usual.

Maigret had a meal of *choucroute*, then phoned his office around 8.30.

'Has the prisoner asked to see me?'

'Yes. He says he's given the matter more thought and he's willing to come down to 25,000. That's his final offer. And he wants it put on the record that a man in his condition shouldn't be fed bread without butter and be forced to stay in a cell where the temperature never gets above sixteen degrees.'

Maigret put down the receiver. He went for a short walk in the Boulevards, then caught a taxi to Rue Championnet, where James lived. His block was enormous, like a barracks. It contained small apartments inhabited by office workers, commercial travellers and small investors.

'Fourth, on the left.'

There was no lift, so the inspector slowly climbed the stairs, catching a whiff of cooking or hearing children's voices from behind the doors on each landing.

James's wife answered the door. She was dressed in a pretty royal-blue dressing gown — it wasn't particularly luxurious, but it didn't look that cheap either.

'You wish to speak to my husband?'

The entrance hall was barely wider than a dining-table. On the walls were pictures of sailing-boats, bathers, young men and women in sporting garb.

'It's for you, James!'

She pushed open a door, ushered Maigret through and sat back down in her armchair next to the window, where she picked up her crochet.

The other apartments in the block were still decorated in the style of the last century, with their Henry II and Louis-Philippe furniture.

This apartment, however, felt more like Montparnasse than Montmartre. It owed more to the decorative arts in style, but seemed to be the work of an amateur.

Plywood partitions had been erected at odd angles, and most of the furniture had been removed to make way for shelving painted in bright colours.

The carpet was in a single colour, a rather lurid green. The lampshades were meant to resemble parchment.

It all looked smart and fresh, but seemed to lack solidity; you felt that the walls might give way if you leaned on them and that the paintwork was not quite dry.

Above all, especially when James stood up, you felt that the apartment was too small for him, that he was boxed in and had to be careful not to bash into things when he moved around.

An open door to the right revealed the bathroom, where there was only just enough space for the bath. The kitchen was no more than a galley, with a spirit stove on a bench.

James was sitting in a small chair with a cigarette in his mouth and a book in his hands.

Maigret had the distinct impression that there was no contact at all between these two people.

They each sat in their own corner, James reading, his wife crocheting, with only the sound of the cars and trams outside the window to break the silence.

No hint of intimacy whatsoever.

He stood up, offered Maigret his hand, smiling awkwardly, as though he were embarrassed to be seen in such a place.

'How are you, Maigret?'

But his familiar cordiality had a different ring in this doll's house of an apartment. It seemed to clash with the furnishings, the carpet, the modern ornaments arranged on the shelves, the wallpaper, the fancy lampshades . . .

'I'm fine, thank you.'

'Take a seat. I was just reading an English novel.'

And his expression was saying:

'Don't mind all this. It's none of my doing. I don't feel at home here.'

His wife listened in, without interrupting her work.

'Do we have anything to drink, Marthe?' he asked her.

'You know we don't!'

Then to the inspector:

'It's his fault. If we ever get any bottles of liquor in, they get drunk within a couple of days. He has enough to drink when he's out.'

'Inspector, what do you say we go down to the bistro?'

But before Maigret could respond, James frowned as he looked at his wife, who must have been making urgent signals to him.

'If you'd like to . . . '

He closed his book with a sigh and started fidgeting with a paperweight lying on a low table next to him.

The room was not more than four metres long, and yet it felt like two rooms, as if two people lived their lives here without ever crossing each other's path.

The wife, who had decorated the flat entirely to her own taste, spent her time sewing, embroidering, cooking, making dresses, while James would come home every evening at eight and eat his dinner without saying a word, then read until bedtime, when that sofa covered with brightly coloured cushions was pulled out to form a bed.

It was easier now to understand James's need for his 'little bolt-hole' on the terrace of the Taverne Royale, with his glass of Pernod in front of him.

'Sure. Let's go.'

And James leaped to his feet with a sigh of relief.

'Could you wait a moment while I get my shoes?'

He was wearing slippers. He squeezed between the bath and the wall. The bathroom door was still open, but his wife didn't bother lowering her voice:

'Don't pay any attention. He's not like other people.' And she started counting her stitches: 'Seven . . . eight . . . nine . . . Do you think he knows something about the business at Morsang?'

'Where is the shoehorn?' James muttered as he rummaged noisily through a cupboard.

She looked at Maigret as if to say 'You see what I mean?'

James finally emerged from the bathroom, once more looking too large for the room, and said to his wife:

'I'll be back soon.'

'I've heard that before.'

He motioned to the inspector to get a move on, no doubt fearing his wife might change her mind. Even in the stairwell he seemed too big, as if he didn't match the décor.

The first building on the left was a bar frequented by taxi drivers.

'It's the only one around here.'

The dim lighting glinted off the zinc counter. There were four men playing cards at the back of the bar.

'Ah, Monsieur James, the usual?' said the landlord, rising from his seat. He already had a bottle of brandy in his hand.

'And what would you like, sir?'

'The same.'

James rested his elbows on the bar and asked:

'Did you go to the Taverne Royale? I thought so. I couldn't get there today . . . '

'Because of the 300,000 francs.'

James's face displayed neither surprise nor embarrassment.

'What would you have done in my place? Basso is a friend. We've drunk together hundreds of times. Cheers!'

'I'll leave you the bottle,' said the landlord. He

was obviously used to James and was anxious to get back to his card game. James didn't seem to hear but continued:

'Basically he didn't have a chance. A woman like Mado. Talking of whom, have you seen her recently? She came by my office earlier to ask if I'd seen Marcel. Can you believe that? It's like that guy with his car. He's supposed to be a friend, but now he rings me to say that he's going to have to ask me to pay for the repairs and the charge for releasing his car from police custody. Your good health! What do you think of my wife? She's nice, isn't she?'

And James poured himself another glass of brandy.

# 7

## The Second-Hand Dealer

There was something about James that Maigret found very interesting. As he drank, instead of becoming glassy-eyed, like most people, his gaze became more and more acute, until it acquired a sharpness that was almost penetrating.

He never removed his hand from his glass, except to refill it. His voice was slurred, faltering, lacking in conviction. He looked at no one in particular. He seemed to be melting into the background.

The card players at the back of the bar hardly spoke. The lights reflected dully off the zinc counter.

And James's voice was also dull when he sighed:

'It's weird. A man like you — strong, intelligent — and others too. Uniformed cops, judges, loads of people. How many are there involved in this? A hundred, maybe, if you include the clerks typing up the case notes, the telephonists passing on the orders . . . Let's call it a hundred people working day and night all because Feinstein got plugged by one tiny little bullet.'

He looked at Maigret, and the inspector was unable to tell whether he was being sincere or ironic.

'Cheers! It's all worth it, isn't it? And all this time poor old Basso is being hunted like an animal. Last week, he was rich. He had his business, his car, his wife and son. Now he can't stick his head out of his hole.'

James shrugged his shoulders. His voice slurred even more. He looked round the room with an expression of weariness or disgust.

'And what's it all about, eh? A woman like Mado with an appetite for men. Basso lets himself get snared — let's face it, you don't knock back opportunities like that when they come along. She's a good-looking girl. Spirited. You tell yourself it's just a bit of fun. You get together and spend an hour or two in a furnished apartment . . . '

James took a large swig then spat on the floor.

'Stupid, isn't it? One man ends up dead. A family is ruined. And the whole machinery of the law swings into action. Even the papers come along for the ride.'

The strangest thing was that there was no vehemence in his voice. He seemed to be talking aimlessly, gazing round the room at nothing in particular.

'And that's trumps,' the landlord said triumphantly from the back of the room.

'And Feinstein, who has spent his whole life chasing after money, trying to sort out his finances. Because that's what his life has been — one long nightmare of unpaid bills and invoices. To the point where he has to put the squeeze on his wife's lovers. And that's obviously worked well, now that he's dead . . . '

'Now that he's been killed,' Maigret corrected him dreamily.

'Do we really know which of the two actually killed the other?'

There was a heavy, morbid quality to James's words that fitted in with the growing gloom inside the bar.

'It's stupid! It's so obvious what happened. Feinstein needs money. He has been watching Basso since the previous evening, waiting for his chance. Even during the mock wedding, when he is dressed up as an old woman, he is still thinking about his debts! He watches Basso dancing with his wife. You see what I'm saying? So the next day he makes a move. Basso's been tapped for money before. He doesn't play ball. Feinstein won't give up that easily, pulls out his sob story: ruin, shame, he'd rather end it all now . . . the full works. I'd lay money on it being something like that. Just what you want on a fine Sunday afternoon by the river!

'Of course, it's all for effect. Feinstein is making it very clear that he is not as blind to his wife's peccadilloes as he likes to make out.

'Anyway, there they are behind the lean-to. Basso's thinking about his nice villa, his wife and kid across the river. He has to hush this whole thing up. He tries to stop him pulling the trigger, it's all getting out of hand, he makes a grab for the gun . . . then bang! That's it. One bullet from a tiny little revolver . . . '

James finally looked at Maigret.

'So I ask you. What the hell does any of this matter?'

93

He laughed. A laugh of contempt.

'And now we have hundreds of people scuttling around like ants who've just had their ant-hill set alight. The Bassos are being hunted like animals. And to cap it all, Mado still can't give up on her lover. Landlord!'

The landlord reluctantly put down his cards.

'What do I owe you?'

'But now Basso has 300,000 francs at his disposal.'

James merely shrugged his shoulders as if to reiterate his earlier question: 'What the hell does any of this matter?'

Then suddenly, he exclaimed:

'Wait! I remember how all this started. It was a Sunday. Some people were dancing in the garden of the villa. Basso was dancing with Madame Feinstein, and someone bumped into them, knocking them to the ground. They were lying there in each other's arms. Everyone laughed, including Feinstein.'

James picked up his change, but didn't seem to want to leave. Finally, he sighed:

'Another glass, landlord.'

He had downed six glasses, but he wasn't drunk. He must have had a bit of a sore head. He frowned and wiped his brow with his hand.

'Well, you've got to get back to the chase.'

He sounded like he felt sorry for Maigret.

'Three poor devils; a man, a woman and a child, all being hounded simply because the man slept with Mado.'

Was it his voice, his physical presence, the

94

atmosphere of the bar? Whatever it was, he wove a fascinating spell, and Maigret was struggling to regain his objective view of the events that had taken place.

'Cheers, drink up. I'd better be getting back. I wouldn't put it past my wife to stick a bullet in me. It's stupid, stupid . . . '

He opened the door with a tired movement. Outside, in the badly lit street, he looked Maigret in the eyes and said:

'A strange occupation.'

'What? The police?'

'Just being a man . . . When I get home my wife will count the change in my pocket to see how much I've been drinking. Goodnight. See you in the Taverne Royale tomorrow?'

James went off, leaving Maigret with a sense of unease, which it took him a long time to shake off. It was as if all his thoughts had been unravelled and all his values had been turned on their head. Even the street looked distorted, the passers-by were a blur, and the long, thin trams were like brightly glowing worms.

It was like the ant-hill James had talked about. An anthill in a turmoil because one ant had been killed!

In his mind's eye, Maigret saw the haberdasher lying in the long grass behind the Two-Penny Bar. Then he saw all the police out manning the roadblocks. The ant-hill all stirred up!

'Drunken fool!' he murmured as he thought of James with a bitterness not altogether devoid of affection.

95

He made a fresh effort to look at the case objectively. He had forgotten what he had come to James's apartment to do — to find out where James had taken the 300,000 francs. But then he thought of the Basso family — the father, the mother and the child — skulking in their hideaway, jumping at the slightest noise from outside.

'That damn fellow gets me drinking every time we meet!'

He wasn't drunk, but he did feel out of sorts and went to bed in a bad mood, dreading the next day, when he would wake up with a thumping headache.

'You have to have a little bolt-hole to call your own,' James had said, talking of the Taverne Royale.

He didn't just have a bolt-hole, he inhabited a whole world of his own, totally self-contained, created in a haze of Pernod or brandy, in which he wandered around totally indifferent to the real world. It was a formless world, a teeming ant-hill of flitting shadows where nothing mattered, nothing had any purpose, where it was possible to wander aimlessly, effortlessly, feeling neither joy nor sadness, cocooned in a thick mist.

A world into which James, with his clownish manner and his apathetic way of talking, had sucked Maigret without seeming to do so.

So much so that the inspector found himself thinking about the Bassos — the father, the mother and the son — cowering in the cellar where they had sought refuge, listening anxiously to the footsteps coming and going over their heads.

When he got up he was even more conscious of the absence of his wife, from whom the postman delivered a postcard.

We are starting to make the apricot jam. When will you be coming to taste it?

He sat down heavily at his desk, causing the pile of letters in his in-tray to topple over. He called out, 'Come in!' to the clerk who was knocking at the door.

'What is it, Jean?'

'Sergeant Lucas has phoned asking for you to come to Rue des Blancs-Manteaux.'

'Which number?'

'He didn't say. He just said Rue des Blancs-Manteaux.'

Maigret checked that there wasn't anything in his mail that required urgent attention, then went on foot to the Jewish quarter, of which Rue des Blancs-Manteaux was the main shopping street, with a number of second-hand dealers huddled in the shadow of the large pawnshop.

It was 8.30 in the morning. It was quite quiet. At the corner of the street Maigret spotted Lucas, who was walking up and down with his hands in his pockets.

'Where's our man?' asked Maigret anxiously, for Lucas had been given the task of following Victor Gaillard after the latter's release the previous night.

With a movement of the head the officer

97

pointed out the figure of a man standing in front of a shop window.

'What's he doing there?'

'I've no idea. Last night he wandered round Les Halles. He ended up dossing on a bench. At five o'clock this morning a policeman moved him on, and he made his way straight here. Ever since then he's been strolling round this house — occasionally wandering off then coming back again — pressing his nose against the window, all obviously for my benefit.'

Victor noticed Maigret and wandered off, his hands in his pockets, whistling ironically. He found a doorway and sat down in it, as if he had nothing better to do. The sign on the shop window read:

Hans Goldberg. Articles Bought and Sold.
All Types of Bargains.

In the semi-darkness inside the shop sat a small man with a little goatee beard, who looked perturbed at the unusual activity outside his window.

'Wait here,' said Maigret.

He crossed the road and went inside the shop, which was stuffed with old clothes and a variety of other junk that gave off a musty odour.

'Are you looking for any item in particular?' the little Jew asked, not sounding terribly convinced that Maigret was a customer.

At the back of the shop there was a glass door leading into a room where a very fat woman was washing the face of a child of about two or three.

The washbasin was placed on the kitchen table next to the cups and the butter dish.

'Police,' said Maigret.

'I suspected as much.'

'Do you know that person who's been hanging around in front of your shop all morning?'

'The tall thin chap with the cough? I've never seen him before. But his presence has been bothering me, and I asked my wife just earlier, but she didn't recognize him either. He's not an Israelite.'

'And do you recognize this man?'

Maigret held out a photo of Marcel Basso, which the man scrutinized intently.

'He's not an Israelite either!' he said.

'And this one?'

This time it was a picture of Feinstein.

'Yes!'

'You know him?'

'No, but he is one of us.'

'You've never seen him before?'

'Never. We don't go out much.'

His wife kept glancing at them through the door. She lifted another child out of a cradle, which began to howl when she started washing it.

The shopkeeper seemed quite sure of himself. He slowly rubbed his hands together as he awaited the inspector's next question and he looked round his shop with the satisfied expression of an honest tradesman with nothing to hide.

'How long have you owned this shop?'

'A little over five years. In that time I've

established a reputation for fair dealing.'

'Who was here before you?' Maigret asked.

'You don't know? It was old Ulrich, the one who disappeared.'

The inspector gave a sigh of satisfaction. Finally he was on to something.

'Was Ulrich a second-hand dealer?'

'You should know better than I. Don't the police have records? I can't tell you anything definite. But I have heard people say that he didn't just buy and sell, he was also in the moneylending business.'

'He was a loan shark?'

'I don't know what his rate of interest was. He lived alone. He didn't have an assistant. He opened and closed up his shop himself. One day he disappeared, and the shop stayed closed for six months. I took it over. And I gave it a much better reputation altogether.'

'So you didn't know old Ulrich?'

'I didn't live in Paris at that time. I moved here from Alsace when I took over the shop.'

The baby was still crying in the other room; his brother had opened the door and was looking at Maigret and gravely sucking his finger.

'That's all I can tell you. Believe me, if I knew any more . . . '

'All right. That's fine.'

And Maigret went out after one last look around. He found Victor sitting in the doorway.

'Is this where you wanted to lead me?'

Victor feigned innocence:

'What do you mean?'

'I mean this business with old Ulrich?'

'Old Ulrich?'

'Stop messing about.'

'Don't know what you're talking about, honest.'

'Is he the one who took the plunge into the Canal Saint-Martin?'

'Dunno.'

Maigret shrugged his shoulders and walked away As he passed Lucas, he said:

'Carry on keeping an eye on him, just in case.'

Half an hour later, he was searching through the old files. Finally he found what he was looking for. He summarized the details on a piece of paper:

Jacob Ephraïm Lévy, known as Ulrich, sixty-two years old, originally from Haute-Silésie, second-hand dealer in Rue des Blancs-Manteaux, suspected of usury.

Disappeared 20 March, though his neighbours did not alert the police until the 22nd.

No clues found at his house. Nothing was missing. A sum of 14,000 francs was discovered under his mattress.

As far as can be ascertained, he left home on the evening of the 19th. Nothing unusual in that.

No information on his private life. Inquiries in Paris and the provinces unsuccessful. The authorities in Haute-Silésie are informed, and one month later the sister of the missing man turns up in Paris to claim ownership of the property. She has to wait six months before he is officially declared missing presumed dead.

At midday Maigret, his head now aching, finally found some information in the heavy old registers of the police station at La Villette, the third he had visited that morning.

He transcribed the relevant passage:

On 1 July a body was pulled out of the Canal Saint-Martin, near the lock, by some bargees. The corpse was in an advanced state of decomposition.

The body was taken to the Forensic Institute, but it was not possible to make an identification.

Height: 1.55 m. Probable age: sixty to sixty-five.

Most of the clothing had been torn away on the canal bed and by boat propellers. Nothing found in the pockets.

Maigret heaved a sigh. He was finally emerging from the clouds of obfuscation that James seemed able to summon up at will to obscure the case.

Now he had something solid to work on. It was old Ulrich who was murdered six years ago and thrown into the Canal Saint-Martin.

Why? And by whom?

That was what he was going to find out. He filled his pipe and lit it slowly with pleasure. He took his leave of his colleagues at La Villette and stepped out into the street, smiling, sure of himself, feeling solid on his sturdy legs.

# 8

## James's Mistress

The chartered accountant came into Maigret's office rubbing his hands and looking pleased with himself.

'Got it!'

'What's that?'

'I've quickly gone through the haberdasher's books for the last seven years. It was easy. Feinstein didn't keep the books himself, but had a bank clerk come round two or three times a week to do them. Nothing out of the ordinary: just the usual tricks to minimize tax. But it's as plain as the nose on your face what was going on: the business would have been no worse than any other but for the lack of underlying capital. Suppliers paid on the 4th and 10th of every month, debts rescheduled two or three times, frequent sales to get some money in the tills at whatever cost. Finally, Ulrich!'

Maigret didn't react. He knew it would be better to let the voluble little man carry on talking, as he paced up and down the room.

'The classic story! Ulrich's name first appears in the books seven years ago. A loan of 2,000 francs to pay bills that had become due. Repaid a week later. The next billing date, a further loan of 5,000 francs. You see? He had found a way to get hold of cash when he needed it. He got into the habit. From that initial loan of 2,000, within six months he was borrowing 18,000. And this 18,000 cost him 25,000 to repay — old Ulrich liked to exact a price! I should say that Feinstein always honoured his debts, he always paid up on time. But he was paying off his debts by getting further into debt. For example, he repaid 15,000 francs on the 15th and borrowed another 17,000 on the 20th. He repaid this the following month, only to borrow 25,000 straight afterwards. By March, Feinstein owed Ulrich 32,000 francs.'

'Did he repay it?'

'I beg your pardon? From that date on Ulrich is never mentioned in the books again.'

And there was a very good reason for that: the old Jew from Rue des Blancs-Manteaux was dead, a death that left Feinstein the richer by 32,000 francs.

'Who took over from Ulrich?'

'No one, for a time. A year later, Feinstein was in trouble again and asked a small bank for credit, which he received. But the bank soon lost patience with him.'

'And Basso?'

'His name crops up in the later books — not under loans this time, but bills of exchange.'

'What was his situation like at the time of his death?'

'No better or worse than usual. He needed twenty grand to bale him out — at least until the next payment date! There are thousands of small traders in Paris in exactly the same situation — constantly chasing the exact sum they need to stop themselves tipping over the brink into bankruptcy.'

Maigret stood up and reached for his hat.

'Thank you, Monsieur Fleuret.'

'Do you want me to do a more in-depth analysis?'

'Not just yet.'

It was all going well. The inquiry was now running like clockwork. Paradoxically, Maigret was feeling down, as if he thought it was all falling into place rather too easily.

'Any news from Lucas?' he asked the clerk.

'He's just phoned. He said your man had gone to a Salvation Army hostel to ask for a bed. He's now sleeping.'

Of course Victor didn't have a single sou on him. Was he still hoping to receive 30,000 francs in return for the name of old Ulrich's murderer?

Maigret walked along the river. He hesitated in front of a post office, then went in and wrote a telegram:

Will probably arrive Thursday, stop. Love.

It was Monday. He hadn't been able to go and join his wife since the start of the holiday. He stuffed his pipe as he re-emerged on the street. He seemed to hesitate again, then he hailed a taxi and told the driver to take him to Boulevard des Batignolles.

He had handled hundreds of cases in his time, and he knew that they nearly always fell into two distinct phases. Firstly, coming into contact with a new environment, with people he had never even heard of the day before, with a little world which some event had shaken up.

He would enter this world as a stranger, an enemy; the people he encountered would be hostile, cunning or would give nothing away.

This, for Maigret, was the most exciting part. He would sniff around for clues, feel his way in the dark with nothing to go on. He would observe people's reactions — any one of them could be guilty, or complicit in the crime.

Suddenly he would get a lead, and then the second period would begin. The inquiry would be underway. The gears would start to turn. Each step in the inquiry would bring a fresh revelation, and nearly always the pace would quicken, so the final revelation, when it came, would feel sudden.

The inspector didn't work alone. The events worked for him, almost independently of him. He had to keep up, not be overtaken by them.

This was how it had been since the Ulrich discovery. Only this morning, Maigret had no clue as to the identity of the body in the Canal Saint-Martin.

Now he knew he was a second-hand dealer who doubled as a loan shark, to whom the haberdasher owed money.

Now he had to follow this thread. A quarter of an hour later, he was ringing the bell at the Feinsteins' apartment on the fifth floor of a building in Boulevard des Batignolles. A rather dim-looking maid with unkempt hair came to answer the door and seemed unsure whether she should let him in or not. But at that same moment Maigret spotted James's hat hanging in the hallway.

Was this the wheels of the case turning relentlessly onwards, or was it a spanner in the works?

★ ★ ★

'Is your mistress at home?'

The maid looked as if she was fresh up from the country, and he took advantage of her uncertainty to enter. He went to a door behind which he could hear voices, knocked and entered immediately.

He already knew the apartment. It was indistinguishable from most of the other lower-middle-class apartments in the area — a narrow sofa and rickety-looking armchairs with gilt feet. The first person he saw was James, who was standing in front of the window, staring out at the street.

Madame Feinstein was dressed to go out — all in black with a fetching little crêpe hat. She seemed extremely animated.

Despite this, she displayed no sign of annoyance when she saw Maigret, unlike James, who seemed put out, even embarrassed.

'Come in, inspector. You're not disturbing anything. I was just about to tell James how stupid he is.'

'Ah.'

It had all the appearance of a domestic tiff. James pleaded, with no great hope:

'Please, Mado . . .'

'No! Be quiet! I'm talking to the inspector.'

Resigned, James turned back to look at the street, where he could have seen little more than the heads of the passers-by.

'If you were an ordinary policeman, inspector, I wouldn't be talking to you like this. But as you were our guest at Morsang, and as you are clearly a man who is capable of understanding these things . . . '

And she was a woman who was capable of talking nonstop for hours, capable of calling the whole world as her witness, capable of reducing even the most talkative person to complete silence!

She wasn't especially beautiful. But she had a seductive quality, particularly in her mourning dress which, rather than giving her a sad appearance, made her look even more alluring. She was curvy, vivacious; she would have made an excellent mistress.

There couldn't be a greater contrast with the phlegmatic James, with his lugubrious face and his wandering gaze.

'Everyone knows I am Basso's mistress, don't they? I'm not ashamed of it. I've never made any secret of it. At Morsang, no one had any problem with it. If my husband had been a different sort of man . . . '

She barely paused for breath.

'If he'd been able to sort out his financial problems. Look at this dump. I have to live here. He was never around. Or when he was, in the evening after dinner, all he ever talked about was money problems, the business, his staff, stuff like

108

that. But what I say is, if you can't give your wife the life she deserves, you can't complain if she goes off with someone else . . .

'Anyway, Marcel and I planned to get married one day. You didn't know? Naturally we didn't shout it from the rooftops. But for his son, he'd have started divorce proceedings already. I'd have done the same.

'You've seen his wife, haven't you? Not at all the sort of woman a man like Marcel needs.'

In the corner, James sighed. He was now staring at the carpet.

'Where do you think my duty lies? Marcel is in trouble, he's wanted by the police, he may have to go abroad. Don't you think that I should be there by his side? Tell me, just say what you think.'

'Hmm . . . well,' Maigret mumbled in a non-committal fashion.

'Exactly! You see, James? The inspector agrees with me. Never mind the gossip. I don't care what people think. But James won't tell me where I can find Marcel. He knows, I'm sure he does. He won't even deny it.'

Luckily Maigret had come across women like her before, otherwise he could have been suffocated by this tirade. He was not surprised by her complete lack of conscience.

It was less than two weeks since Feinstein had been killed, apparently by Basso.

And here was his wife, in their dreary apartment, with her husband's picture on the wall and his cigarette holder still in the ashtray, talking about her 'duty'.

109

James's face spoke volumes. Not just his face! His whole slumped posture seemed to be saying: 'Can you believe this woman?'

She turned towards him.

'You see, the inspector . . . '

'The inspector said no such thing.'

'I hate you! You're not a real man. You're afraid of everything. Suppose I tell him why you came here today . . . '

This took James so by surprise that his face went bright red. He was blushing like a child, to the roots of his hair. He tried to speak, but the words didn't come out. He tried to regain his composure, but only managed to emit a strained laugh.

'Go on, you may as well tell him now.'

Maigret was watching the woman. She was a little thrown by what James had said.

'I didn't mean to . . . '

'No, you never mean to do anything! But you always end up doing it anyway!'

The room seemed smaller, more intimate. Mado shrugged her shoulders as if to say: 'Fine, I will. On your head be it.'

'Excuse me,' the inspector interjected, trying to keep a straight face as he spoke to James, 'I noticed you addressed her as *tu*. As I recall, in Morsang you were more formal . . . '

He could scarcely disguise his amusement, so great was the contrast between the James he knew and the sorry figure now standing in front of him. James had the look of a naughty schoolboy waiting outside the headmaster's study.

At his apartment, with his wife crocheting in the other corner, he had maintained a certain aloof demeanour.

Here, he seemed a stammering wreck.

'You must have worked it out by now. Yes, Mado and I were lovers too.'

'Luckily not for long,' she sneered.

He seemed disconcerted by this remark. He looked to Maigret for help.

'There you have it. It was a long time ago. My wife never knew about it.'

'And wouldn't she let you know about it if she did!'

'Knowing her as I do, I would never hear the last of it as long as I lived. So I came to ask Mado not to say anything if she was questioned.'

'And did she agree?'

'Only on the condition that I gave her Basso's current address. Can you believe that? He's with his wife and child. He's probably already left the country.'

He said that last bit less decisively. He was lying.

Maigret sat down in one of the armchairs, which gave a creak under his weight.

'Were you lovers for long?' he asked, like some friend of the family.

'Too long!' Madame Feinstein snapped.

'Not long . . . a few months,' James sighed.

'Did you meet in a furnished apartment like the one in the Avenue Niel?'

'No! James rented a place in Passy.'

'Were you already going to Morsang at the weekend?'

111

'Yes.'

'And Basso?'

'Yes. It's been the same gang for the last seven or eight years, with one or two exceptions.'

'Did Basso know you were lovers?'

'Yes. He wasn't in love with me then. He only became interested about a year ago.'

In spite of himself, Maigret felt jubilant. He looked round the little apartment, with its useless and rather hideous ornaments, and remembered James's rather more modern and pretentious studio, with its doll's house plywood partitions.

Then he thought of Morsang, the Vieux-Garçon, the canoes and sailing-boats, the rounds of drinks on the shady terrace, in a gentle, beautiful landscape.

For the last seven or eight years, every Sunday, the same group of people had been drinking aperitifs together, and playing bridge and dancing to records in the afternoon.

But in the beginning it was James who slipped off into the bushes with Mado. It was also he, no doubt, who first drew Feinstein's sarcastic gaze, he who had midweek rendezvous with her in Paris.

Everyone knew. Everyone turned a blind eye and was complicit in covering for Mado's affairs.

Among them her affair with Basso, who one day fell for her charms himself.

And now Maigret was enjoying this little scene in the apartment, what with James standing there looking pitiful and Mado forging on regardless.

It was to the latter that Maigret said:

'How long is it since you were James's mistress?'

'Let's see . . . five . . . no, six years, more or less.'

'And how did it end? Did he break it off or did you?'

James tried to speak, but she cut him off:

'It was mutual. We realized that we weren't right for each other. Despite his airs and graces, James is as petit bourgeois as they come. Perhaps even more so than my husband.'

'Did you remain good friends?'

'Of course, why not? It wasn't that we stopped liking each other . . . '

'One question for you, James. Did you lend any money to Feinstein around this time?'

'Me?'

But Mado answered his question:

'What are you driving at? Lend my husband money? Why?'

'No reason. Just idle curiosity. However, Basso did lend your husband money . . . '

'That's different. Basso is a wealthy man. My husband had financial problems. He was talking about taking me to America. Basso wanted to avoid any complications, so he lent him money . . . '

'That's all very well. But mightn't your husband have mentioned the possibility of going to America six years ago?'

'What are you insinuating?'

She was about to get on her high horse. Rather than face her blustering outrage, Maigret changed his tack:

113

'I'm sorry, I must have been thinking aloud. I assure you I didn't mean to insinuate anything. You and James were free agents. That's what a friend of your husband told me, a Monsieur Ulrich . . . '

Through half-closed eyes he observed both their reactions. Madame Feinstein looked surprised.

'A friend of my husband?'

'Or a business associate.'

'That's more likely. I've never heard that name mentioned. What did he say to you? . . . '

'Oh, nothing. We were discussing men and women in general.'

And James also looked surprised, but in the manner of a man who smells a rat and is trying to work out where this is all leading.

'This is all very well, but it doesn't get away from the fact that he knows where Marcel is and won't tell me,' said Madame Feinstein, rising from her chair. 'No matter, I'll find him myself. Anyway, he's bound to write to me to ask me to join him. He can't get by without me . . . '

James couldn't resist a sideways glance at Maigret, a look that was as mournful as it was ironic. It could be translated as: 'Do you think he's going to write to her? Do you think he wants a woman like her on his back all over again?'

She spoke to him:

'Is that your final word, James? Is that all the thanks I get, after everything I've done for you?'

'Have you done a lot for him?' Maigret asked.

'Why . . . he was my first lover! . . . Before he

came along I'd never have dreamed of cheating on my husband. He was different then. He didn't drink. He looked after himself. He still had hair.'

And so the scales continued to oscillate between tragedy and complete farce. It was hard to hold on to the reality of the case: that Ulrich was dead, that someone had carried him to the Canal Saint-Martin, that six years later, behind the lean-to of the Two-Penny Bar, Feinstein had been shot dead and that Basso and his family were on the run from the police.

'Do you think he could have left the country inspector?'

'I don't know . . . '

'If he needed your help you'd give it, wouldn't you? You've been his guest. You've seen what sort of man he is.'

'I have to get to the office! I'm already running late,' said James, searching each of the chairs for his hat.

'I'll come out with you,' Maigret added hastily. He certainly had no desire to be left alone with Madame Feinstein.

'Are you in a hurry?'

'I, er, have things to do, yes. But I'll be back.'

'Marcel will be grateful for your support. He knows how to show his appreciation.'

She was proud of her diplomatic skills. She could now envisage Maigret driving Basso to the border and being given a wad of banknotes for his pains.

When Maigret came to shake her hand, she held it for a long time, meaningfully. Indicating

James, she murmured:

'We can't be too hard on him, what with his drinking and all.'

★ ★ ★

The two men didn't speak as they walked along Boulevard des Batignolles. James strode ahead, staring at the ground in front of him. Maigret puffed contentedly on his pipe and seemed to be enjoying the spectacle of the street.

It was only when they reached the corner of Boulevard Malesherbes that the inspector casually asked:

'Is it true that Feinstein never asked you for money?'

James shrugged his shoulders:

'He knew that I didn't have any.'

'Weren't you working at the bank in Place Vendôme?'

'No. At that time I was working as a translator for an American oil company in Boulevard Haussmann. I was earning less than a thousand francs a month.'

'Did you have a car?'

'I used the metro . . . as I still do, incidentally.'

'Did you have your apartment then?'

'No. We lived in a rented place on Rue de Turenne.'

He was tired. There was an expression of disgust on his face.

'Do you want a drink?'

And, without waiting for a reply, he went into the bar on the street corner and ordered two

116

brandies and water.

'Personally, I couldn't give a damn. But I just don't want my wife to be bothered. She has enough troubles as it is.'

'Is she not well?'

Another shrug of the shoulders.

'You don't imagine she has much of a life, do you? Apart from Sundays at Morsang, where she can have a bit of fun.'

He threw a ten-franc note on to the counter, then changed the subject abruptly:

'Are you coming to the Taverne Royale tonight?'

'Maybe.'

As he came to shake Maigret's hand, he hesitated, looked away and murmured:

'What about Basso . . . have you discovered anything?'

'Classified information, I'm afraid,' said Maigret with a smile, full of bonhomie. 'You like him, don't you?'

But James was already on his way. He hopped on to a passing bus heading towards Place Vendôme.

Maigret stood there on the kerb for at least five minutes, quietly smoking his pipe.

# 9

## Twenty-Two Francs of Ham

At Quai des Orfèvres they were looking for Maigret everywhere, for he had been sent a telegram from the police station at La Ferté-Allais:

Basso family found. Await your instructions.

It had been a combination of scientific deduction and sheer luck.

The scientific part was the tests on the car that James abandoned at Montlhéry tests which narrowed down the field of inquiry to a small sector centred on La Ferté-Allais.

Then the luck came into it. The police had searched all the inns and kept watch on the streets without success. They had even questioned a hundred or so people in the town, but had drawn a blank.

Then, on this same day, a policeman named Piquart came home for lunch as usual. His wife was feeding the baby, so she said to him:

'Could you nip down to the grocer's for some onions? I forgot to buy them earlier.'

A small-town grocer's shop on the market square. There were four or five shops in total. The policeman, who didn't much like these errands, stood by the door, looking uninterested,

118

while the grocer served an old woman known in the town as old Mathilde. He overheard the grocer say to her:

'You're pushing the boat out. Twenty-two francs' worth of ham! Are you going to eat that all by yourself?'

Automatically Piquart looked at the old woman, who was obviously very poor. And as the ham was being sliced, his brain began to whirr. Even at his house, where there were three of them, they never bought twenty-two francs' worth of ham at one go.

He followed the woman when she left the shop. She lived in a little house on the Bellancourt road, with hens pecking round in the small garden out the front. He let her go inside, then he knocked and asked to be let in in the name of the law.

Madame Basso was working at the kitchen stove, an apron tied round her waist. In the corner, sitting on a rush chair, Basso was reading the newspaper that the old woman had just brought him. The child was sitting on the floor, playing with a puppy.

★   ★   ★

The police had phoned Maigret's apartment in Boulevard Richard-Lenoir, then a few other places where he might have been found. They hadn't thought to try Basso's offices on the Quai d'Austerlitz.

For that is where he had gone after he had left James. He was in good humour. With his pipe in

119

his mouth and his hands in his pockets he chatted and joked with the firm's employees, who, in the absence of instructions to the contrary, had carried on with business as usual. The barges were loaded and unloaded every day as normal.

The offices weren't especially up-to-date. But they weren't old-fashioned either. A quick look around was enough to get a sense of how the place was run.

The boss didn't have his own office, but had a desk in the corner, next to the window. The chief accountant sat opposite him, and his secretary was at a desk nearby.

Obviously, this wasn't a hierarchical place. People seemed free to chat, and many of them worked with a pipe or a cigarette in their mouth.

'An address book?' the accountant responded to the inspector's request. 'Yes, of course we have one, but it only contains the addresses of our customers in alphabetical order. If you wish to see it . . . '

Maigret had a quick look at the letter U, but, as he had expected, the name of Ulrich wasn't there.

'Are you sure Monsieur Basso doesn't have a private address book? . . . Hold on, who was working here when his son was born?'

'I was,' the secretary replied, a little reluctantly, for she was a thirty-five-year-old who wanted to pass herself off as twenty-five.

'Good. Monsieur Basso must have sent out announcements.'

'He did. I took care of that.'

120

'Then he must have given you a list of his friends' names.'

'Yes, that's right, he gave me a little notebook! I filed it away with his personal items.'

'Where is the file?'

She hesitated, looked to her colleagues for guidance. The chief accountant shrugged as if to say: 'I don't see that we have any choice.'

'It's up at the house,' she said. 'Would you care to follow me?'

They walked across the yard. On the ground floor of the house, there was a simply furnished study that looked as if it was never used. In fact, it was known as the library.

The library of a family for whom reading came well down the list of distractions. A family library, used as the dumping-ground for a whole host of disparate objects.

For example, on the lower shelves were the prizes Basso had won at school. Then some bound volumes of *Magazine des Families* dating back fifty years.

Some books for young girls that Madame Basso must have brought with her when she got married. Then a number of serious novels bought on the strength of favourable newspaper reviews.

Finally some brand-new picture books belonging to the child and some toys stored on the remaining empty shelves.

The secretary opened the drawers of the desk, and Maigret noticed a fat yellow envelope that was sealed.

'What's that?'

'Monsieur's letters to madame when they were engaged.'

'Have you found the notebook?'

She discovered it at the bottom of a drawer that contained a dozen or so old pipes. It looked at least fifteen years old. It was in Basso's hand, though his writing had changed over time, and the ink had faded.

It was like the lines of seaweed on a beach, showing which tide had washed them up by how dried out they were.

The addresses were fifteen years old, addresses of friends now no doubt forgotten. A few had been crossed out, perhaps because of some falling out, or because the person in question had died.

There were a number of addresses of women, such as:

Lola, Bar des Églantiers, 18, Rue Montaigne.

But Lola had been erased from Basso's life by a blue pencil.

'Have you found what you're looking for?' the secretary asked.

He had indeed! A name the coal merchant was ashamed of, for he hadn't written it out in full:

Ul. 13 bis, Rue des Blancs-Manteaux.

The ink and the handwriting suggested this was an old entry It was one of those addresses with a blue line through it, though it was still legible underneath.

'Can you tell me approximately when these words were written?'

The secretary bent over to take a closer look.

'It was when Monsieur Basso was a young man, and his father was still alive.'

'How can you tell?'

'Because it is written in the same ink as the woman's address on the other page. He once told me he had a fling with her in his younger days.'

Maigret closed the notebook and slipped it into his pocket, despite the disapproving look he received from the secretary.

'Do you think he will come back?' she asked, after a slight hesitation.

The inspector gave a non-committal shrug.

When he got back to the Quai des Orfèvres, Jean, the office clerk, ran up to meet him.

'We've been looking for you for the last two hours. They've found the Bassos.'

'Ah!'

He gave a mighty sigh, which almost sounded like a sigh of regret.

'Has Lucas phoned?'

'He calls in every three or four hours. Your man is still at the Salvation Army hostel. They wanted to turf him out after they had fed him, but he offered to sweep up around the place.'

'Is Janvier here?'

'I believe he's just got back.'

Maigret went to Janvier's office.

'I've got just the sort of awkward job you like, my friend. I want you to track down a certain Lola, who gave her postal address as the Bar des

Églantiers, Rue Montaigne, about ten to fifteen years ago.'

'And since then?'

'Who knows? She could have died in hospital. She could have married an English lord . . . Get cracking.'

On the train journey to La Ferté-Allais he examined the address book, smiling every now and again at certain entries that seemed so evocative of how it felt to be young, free and single.

★ ★ ★

A police lieutenant was waiting for him at the station. He drove the inspector to old Mathilde's house, where they found Piquart gravely standing guard in the small front garden.

'We've made sure that there is no way of escape at the back,' the lieutenant explained. 'It's just so small inside that my officer has to stand out the front. Do you want me to come in with you?'

'Perhaps it would be better if you stayed out here.'

Maigret knocked at the door, which opened immediately. It was late. It was still light outside, but the window was so narrow that inside the house he could see little more than moving shadows.

Basso was straddling a chair in the pose of a man who had been waiting for a long time. He got to his feet. His wife and child must have been in the adjoining room.

'Could we have some light?' Maigret asked the old woman.

'I'll have to see if there's any oil in the lamp,' she replied tartly.

It turned out that there was. The glass was replaced with a clink, the wick began first to smoke, then to burn with a yellow flame that gradually filled the corners of the room with light. It was quite hot inside the house. A smell of the countryside, of poverty.

'Do sit down,' Maigret told Basso. 'If you wouldn't mind leaving us alone, madame.'

'What about my soup?'

'Off you go. I'll keep an eye on it.'

She went away grumbling to herself and shut the door behind her. In the adjoining room she could be heard speaking in a low voice.

'Are there just the two rooms?' the inspector asked.

'Yes. The room at the back is the bedroom.'

'Is that where the three of you have been sleeping?'

'The two women and my son. I've been sleeping in here on a straw bale.'

There were bits of straw still lodged in the cracks between the uneven floor tiles. Basso was calm, but it was the sort of calm that follows on from several days of fever. It was as if he were somehow relieved to be arrested. Indeed, the first thing he said was:

'I was going to turn myself in.'

He was probably expecting Maigret to be surprised by this, but the latter showed no reaction. The inspector didn't even say a word.

He merely looked at Basso from head to toe.

'Isn't that one of James's suits?'

It was a grey suit, too tight. Basso had broad shoulders and was as sturdily built as Maigret. Nothing can diminish a man in the prime of his life as much as a set of ill-fitting clothes.

'Obviously you know already . . . '

'I know lots of things besides . . . But do you think we should take this soup off the stove?'

The pan was belching out steam, and the lid was rattling under the pressure. Maigret removed the pan from the heat, and his face was momentarily lit up by the red flames.

'You knew old Mathilde before?'

'I wanted to talk to you about her. I don't want her to get into trouble because of me. She used to be my parents' servant. She's known me since I was a boy. When I came here looking for a place to hide, she couldn't turn me away.'

'Of course not. It's just a shame she made the mistake of buying twenty-two francs' worth of ham at one go.'

Basso had lost a lot of weight. He hadn't shaved for four or five days. In all, he looked a bit of a mess.

'I also trust that my wife has nothing to answer for . . . ' he sighed.

He stood up, looking stiff and awkward, like someone trying to find the right way to broach a weighty topic.

'I was wrong to run away, to stay in hiding for so long. But maybe that shows that I am not a real criminal. Do you understand? I lost my head. I saw my life in ruins because of this stupid affair. I thought I would go abroad, have my wife and child come out to join me and try to start a new life.'

'And you got James to bring your wife here, to withdraw 300,000 francs from the bank and to bring you a change of clothes.'

'Yes.'

'Only, you realized that you were being pursued.'

'Old Mathilde told me there were policemen at every crossroads.'

There was still some noise coming from next door. The child must have been moving about. Madame Basso was probably listening at the door because every now and again they heard her say 'Shush!' to the child.

'Today I came to the only possible conclusion: I had to give myself up. But fate decreed otherwise, and the policeman turned up . . . '

'Did you kill Feinstein?'

Basso looked Maigret straight in the eye.

'I did,' he said quietly. 'It would be mad to deny it, wouldn't it? But I swear on my son's life that I will tell you the whole truth.'

'Just a moment.'

Maigret now got to his feet. And they stood there, both more or less the same build, under the low ceiling, in a room that was too small for them.

'Did you love Mado?'

Basso's lip curled in bitterness.

'You're a man, you should understand. I've known her for six or seven years, maybe more. I'd never given her a second glance before. Then

127

one day, about a year ago, I don't know what happened. It was a party, like the one you came to. We were drinking, dancing . . . I ended up kissing her . . . then we slipped off to the bottom of the garden.'

'And then?'

He gave a tired shrug.

'She took it all seriously. She swore she'd always been in love with me, that she couldn't live without me. I'm no saint. I admit that I started it. But I didn't want to get that involved, I didn't want to jeopardize my marriage.'

'So you've been seeing Madame Feinstein in Paris two or three times a week for the last year . . . '

'And she's been phoning me every day! I've pleaded with her to be more careful, but it's no use. She's always come up with some ridiculous excuse. I was sure we'd be discovered any day. You can't imagine what that was like . . . If only she wasn't so sincere. But no! I think she really did love me.'

'And Feinstein?'

Basso looked up suddenly.

'Oh yes,' he groaned. 'That's why I couldn't bear the thought of having to defend myself in court. There are limits in these compromising situations. There's only so much the public will swallow. Can you see me, Mado's lover, standing up in court, accusing her husband of . . . '

' . . . of blackmailing you.'

'I don't have any proof. He was and he wasn't. He never explicitly said that he knew anything was going on. He never threatened me directly.

You know what he was like — an inoffensive little man, wouldn't hurt a fly. A weedy-looking chap, always smartly dressed, always polite — too polite. That hangdog smile of his . . . The first time he came to me with a problem concerning a protested bill and begged me to lend him some money. He offered me all sorts of assurances. I did as he asked. I would have done anyway, even without Mado.

'However, this turned into something of a routine. I realized it was quite calculated. I tried to refuse. That's when the blackmail began. He took me into his confidence. He said his wife was his only consolation. It was because of her that he had taken on expenses he couldn't afford and had got himself into this bind, etcetera. And he'd rather kill himself than refuse her anything she wanted. And if he did, what would become of her?

'Can you believe it? He always managed to show up just after I had left Mado. I was afraid he would be able to smell her perfume on my clothes. One time he picked a woman's hair — one of hers — off the collar of my jacket.

'He was never threatening. More whining, which is worse! At least you can defend yourself against threats. But what do you do with a man who cries? Yes, I've actually had him in my office in tears.

'And the things he came out with: 'You're young, you're strong, you're good-looking, you're rich . . . A man like you has no trouble finding someone to love him . . . But what about me? . . . ' It made me sick. And yet I could never be absolutely certain that he knew.

'That Sunday, he had already spoken to me before we played bridge and had asked me to lend him 15,000 francs. It was too much. I wouldn't play ball. I'd had enough. So I just said no, straight out. And I said I wouldn't see him again if he continued to harass me in this way.

'So that's how it all blew up, the whole stupid, sordid little mess. If you recall, he arranged it so that we sailed across the river at the same time. He dragged me behind the bar. Then, suddenly, he pulled a small revolver from his pocket and pointed it at his own head, saying, 'This is what you've brought me to . . . I ask just one thing of you. Take care of Mado when I'm gone . . . ''

Basso ran his hand across his brow, as if trying to wipe away this wretched memory.

'It was just bad luck. I felt light-headed that day Perhaps it was the sun. I went up to him to try to grab the gun.

''No, no!' he cried. 'You're too late. It's you who have brought me to this!''

'Naturally, he had no intention of pulling the trigger,' Maigret muttered.

'I know. That's why the whole thing is so tragic. I lost my head. I should have left well alone and nothing would have come of it. He'd have burst into tears again, or extricated himself some other way. But no! I was a naive fool. Like I was with Mado. Like I've always been.

'I tried to grab the revolver off him. He retreated, but I went after him. I grabbed him by the wrist. Then it happened. The gun went off. Feinstein fell, without a word, without a sound.

130

Dropped like a stone . . .

'Not that a jury will believe me. Nor will the judges be any less hard on me. I'll be the man who killed his mistress's husband and then accused the dead man of blackmail.'

He was becoming quite animated.

'I wanted to run away And I did. I also wanted to tell my wife everything, ask her whether, in spite of everything, she still wanted me as her husband. I wandered round Paris, hoping to find James. He's a friend, probably my only real friend in the Morsang crowd.

'You know the rest. My wife knows too. I'd rather we'd got away abroad and avoided this trial, which will be very painful for all concerned. I have the 300,000 francs here. What with that and my head for business, I'd have been able to start afresh somewhere — in Italy, for example, or Egypt.

'But . . . do you believe what I've just told you?'

He faltered all of a sudden. But the doubt was merely momentary, so caught up was he in what he was saying.

'I believe you didn't mean to kill Feinstein,' Maigret replied, slowly, articulating each word carefully.

'You see! . . . '

'Wait a minute. What I want to know is whether or not Feinstein had a stronger card to play than his wife's infidelity. In short . . . '

He paused while he took the little address book from his pocket and opened it at the letter U.

131

'In short, I would like to know who killed a certain Monsieur Ulrich, a second-hand dealer of Rue des Blancs-Manteaux, six years ago, and subsequently threw his body into the Canal Saint-Martin.'

He almost didn't finish his sentence, so violent was the change in Basso's demeanour. So violent, in fact, that he almost lost his balance and, in seeking to grab hold of something, placed his hand on the stove and then withdrew it with an oath.

'My God!'

He stared at Maigret, wide-eyed with horror. He recoiled until he bumped into his chair, and he collapsed into it, looking completely drained of strength.

'My God!'

The door burst open and Madame Basso rushed into the room screaming:

'Marcel! . . . Marcel! . . . It can't be true! . . . Tell me it's not true!'

He looked at her uncomprehendingly, perhaps not even seeing her. Suddenly he choked; he put his head in his hands and started sobbing.

'Papa! . . . Papa!' the child yelped, dashing in to add to the confusion.

Basso didn't hear anything. He pushed away his wife and son. He was totally crushed, unable to control his tears. He sat bent over in his chair, his shoulders heaving in time with his racking sobs.

The child was crying too. Madame Basso bit her lip, sending Maigret a look of pure hatred.

And old Mathilde, who hadn't dared to come

in, but who had witnessed everything through the open door, also cried, the way old women cry: short, regular sobs, wiping her eyes with the corner of her checked apron.

Yet despite her tears and sniffles, she managed to put her soup pan back on the stove, stoking the flames to life with a poker.

# 10

## Inspector Maigret's Absence

Scenes like this don't last long. The nervous system can only take so much. Once the crisis has reached its pitch, a sudden flat calm sets in, a calm as numb as the preceding fever was manic.

We are then supposed to feel shame, shame for the frenzy, the tears, for the things we said, as if such emotion were somehow not human.

Maigret waited, feeling awkward, looking out of the little window at the policeman's cap silhouetted against the darkening sky. He was conscious nonetheless of what was going on behind him — Madame Basso going up to her husband, grabbing him by the shoulders and pleading in her hoarse voice:

'Just tell me it isn't true!'

Basso sniffed, got to his feet, pushed his wife away and looked around him with the glassy-eyed gaze of a drunk. The door of the stove was open. The old woman was feeding it with coal. It threw a large circle of red light on to the ceiling, causing the beams to stand out.

The boy looked at his father and, in copycat fashion, stopped crying also.

'I'm done now . . . I'm sorry for all that,' said Basso, now standing in the centre of the room.

He seemed poleaxed. His voice dwindled away. He didn't have an ounce of strength left in him.

'Do you confess?'

'No, I've got nothing to confess. Listen . . . '

He looked at his family with a wounded expression, his brow furrowed deeply.

'I didn't kill Ulrich. The reason I broke down just now was because I . . . I realized that . . . '

He was so drained he could hardly find the words.

'That you couldn't prove your innocence?'

He nodded. Then he said:

'I didn't kill him.'

'You said those same words right after Feinstein was killed. Yet you have just confessed to that.'

'That's different . . . '

'Did you know Ulrich?'

A bitter smile.

'Look at the date on the first page of the notebook. Twelve years ago. It was about ten years ago that I saw Ulrich for the last time.'

He had recovered some of his composure, but his voice still displayed the same despair.

'My father was still alive. Talk to anyone who knew him and you'll hear what a hard man he was. Strict on himself and on others. I was given a smaller allowance than even the poorest of my friends. So someone took me to see old Ulrich in Rue des Blancs-Manteaux, who had some experience of these matters.'

'And you didn't know he was dead?'

Basso said nothing. Maigret repeated his

question without drawing breath:

'You didn't know he had been killed, driven in a car to the Canal Saint-Martin and thrown into the lock?'

Basso didn't reply. His shoulders became even more hunched. He looked at his wife, his son and the old woman, who were laying the table despite their tears, simply because it was dinnertime.

'What are you going to do?'

'I'm arresting you. Madame Basso and your son can stay here, or go home.'

Maigret opened the front door and said to the policeman:

'Bring a car round.'

A crowd of onlookers had gathered in the road, but like the prudent peasants they were, they kept their distance. When Maigret turned round, Madame Basso was in her husband's arms. He was mechanically patting her back, while staring into space.

'Promise me you'll take care of yourself,' she murmured. 'And don't do anything stupid.'

'Yes.'

'Swear!'

'Yes.'

'Think of your son, Marcel!'

'Yes,' he repeated with a trace of annoyance in his voice, as he disentangled himself from her embrace.

Was he afraid of being overcome by emotion again? He waited impatiently for the car he had heard Maigret order. He didn't want to say anything, listen to anything, look at anything.

His fingers trembled constantly.

'You didn't kill this man, did you? Listen to me, Marcel. You have to listen to me. They won't condemn you for . . . for the other business. You didn't mean to do it. And we can prove that this man was a wicked person. I'll find a good lawyer straight away. The best . . . '

She was speaking vehemently. She wanted to make sure she was heard.

'Everyone knows you're a good man. We can probably get you out on bail. Just don't let it get on top of you. Just remember . . . that other crime wasn't anything to do with you.'

She looked at Maigret defiantly.

'I'll see a lawyer tomorrow. I'll get my father up from Nancy, to give me some advice. Come on, we can get through this . . . '

She didn't realize that she was hurting him, by threatening to remove the last shred of composure he possessed. He was trying to ignore her, straining to hear the sounds from outside. He was aching for the car to arrive.

'I'll come and see you. I'll bring the boy.'

Finally there was the sound of the car pulling up. Maigret brought the scene to a conclusion.

'Let's go.'

'You promised, Marcel!'

She couldn't let him go. She pushed their son towards him, to melt his heart further. Basso was already walking down the three steps outside the house.

Then she grabbed Maigret's arm so firmly she pinched it.

'Watch him!' she panted. 'Watch him carefully.

137

Make sure he doesn't kill himself. I know what sort of man he is.'

She noticed the group of onlookers but gave them a bold, unrepentant look.

'Wait! Your scarf!'

She ran back inside the house to fetch it, and handed it through the window of the car as it was pulling away.

In the car, Basso, now he was in the company of men, seemed to relax slightly. He sat there with Maigret for a good ten minutes without either of them saying a word. It was only when they reached the main road that Maigret spoke, his words seeming to bear no relation to the drama that had just taken place.

'You have an admirable wife.'

'Yes, she understood. Perhaps it is because she is a mother. I don't know that I'd be able to explain why I got involved with . . . with that woman.'

There was a pause. Then he continued in a confidential tone:

'At the time, you don't think. It's a game, and you don't quite have the courage to break it off. You're afraid there'll be a scene, you're scared of the recriminations. And so this is where you end up.'

There was nothing to see out of the window except the trees flashing past, illuminated by the car's headlights. Maigret filled his pipe and offered Basso his tobacco pouch.

'No, thank you. I only smoke cigarettes.'

It helped somehow to have some ordinary conversation.

'I noticed you had a dozen or so pipes in your drawer at home.'

'Yes. At one time I used to be a keen pipe-smoker. My wife asked me to stop . . .'

His voice faltered. Maigret noticed his eyes filling with tears. He hastily changed the subject:

'Your secretary seems very loyal too.'

'She's a good girl. She looks after me really well. She must be devastated.'

'I'd say she was fairly optimistic. She was asking when you would be coming back. All in all, you seem to be well liked.'

They fell silent again. They were now passing through Juvisy. At Orly, they saw the airfield searchlights raking the sky.

'Was it you who gave Feinstein Ulrich's address?'

But Basso refused to answer.

'Feinstein had lots of dealings with him. His name crops up in the accounts, along with the sums involved. At the time that Ulrich was murdered, Feinstein owed him at least 30,000 francs.'

No, Basso wouldn't reply. He sat there in obstinate silence.

'What is your father-in-law's profession?'

'He is a teacher in a school in Nancy. My wife trained as a teacher also.'

And so the conversation proceeded, drifting close to the trauma of recent events, then receding to the safety of small talk. At times Basso spoke quite normally, as if he had forgotten his situation. Then came tense silences, pregnant with unspoken thoughts.

'Your wife is right. In the Feinstein case you have a good chance of being acquitted. At worst you may get a year in prison. As for the Ulrich case, however . . . '

Then, abruptly, he went on:

'I'm going to put you in the cell at police headquarters tonight. Tomorrow we can get you transferred to a remand prison.'

Maigret tapped out his pipe and wound down the glass screen to speak to the driver:

'Quai des Orfèvres! Go straight into the courtyard.'

Then without further ado, the inspector led Basso to the cell where Victor had been locked up.

'Goodnight,' said Maigret, after checking that he had everything he needed in the cell. 'I'll see you tomorrow. Have a think. Are you sure that you have nothing to say to me?'

Basso was perhaps too full of emotion to speak. He merely shook his head.

Confirm will arrive Thursday, stop. Will stay
a few days, stop. Love.

It was Wednesday morning when Maigret wrote the telegram to his wife. He was in his office at the Quai des Orfèvres and he gave it to Jean to take to the post office.

A short while later, the examining magistrate in charge of the Feinstein case phoned him. Maigret told him:

'I hope to be able to give you my completed case report by this evening . . . Yes, of course, the guilty party too . . . No, no, not at all. Just a standard, open-and-shut case . . . Yes! Talk to you this evening. Goodbye.'

He got up and went into the operations room, where he found Lucas typing up a report.

'How's our vagrant?'

'I've handed over to Dubois. Nothing much to report. You know Victor started doing some work at the Salvation Army hostel. He seemed to get well into it. He'd told them about his lung, of course, so they were especially keen to help him out. I think they'd started to regard him as a potential recruit. Who knows, we could have been seeing him in his uniform in a month or so.'

'What happened?'

'It's quite amusing. Yesterday evening a Salvation Army lieutenant asked him to do something or other. He refused and started kicking up a fuss about how he was being made to work like a dog despite all his afflictions. They asked him to leave, and it ended up in fisticuffs. He had to be thrown out by force. He spent the night kipping under the Pont Marie. Now he's hanging about down by the river. Dubois will be ringing in soon to bring you up to date.'

'I won't be here, so tell him to bring him in and lock him in the cell with the other person who's in there.'

'OK.'

Maigret went home and spent the rest of the morning packing. He had lunch in a brasserie near Place de la République, checked the railway timetable and found that there was a handy train to Alsace at 10.40 in the evening.

These leisurely activities kept him occupied until four o'clock in the afternoon, when he set off for the Taverne Royale. He had barely taken his place on the terrace when James turned up. They shook hands, and James looked round for a waiter as he asked Maigret:

'Pernod?'

'Why not?'

'Waiter, two Pernods!'

James crossed his legs, sighed and looked straight ahead like a man with nothing to say and nothing on his mind. It had clouded over. Unexpected gusts of wind swept the street, raising plumes of dust.

'There's going to be a storm,' James sighed. Then abruptly: 'Is it true what I read in the papers? You've arrested Basso?'

'Yes. Yesterday afternoon.'

'Cheers. It's stupid.'

'What's stupid?'

'What he did. A solid, respectable man like him losing his head like that. He'd have been better advised to turn himself in at the start and defend himself. What did he really have to lose?'

Maigret had already heard Madame Basso give the same speech and he smiled to himself.

'Your good health. Maybe you're right, maybe you're wrong.'

'What do you mean? It wasn't premeditated murder, was it? You can hardly even call it a crime.'

'Quite. If Basso had only the death of Feinstein to answer for, then we could say he simply lost his head in a moment of weakness.'

Then, with a suddenness that made James jump, he called out:

'Waiter! What do I owe you?'

'Six-fifty.'

'You're leaving?'

'I have to go and see Basso.'

'Ah.'

'Would you like to see him? You can come too.'

In the taxi they made small talk.

'How's Madame Basso bearing up?'

'She's a very brave woman. And very cultured too. I wouldn't have thought that, seeing her that Sunday at Morsang in her sailing clothes.'

And Maigret asked him:

'How is your wife?'

'Fine, as usual.'

'Not too upset by recent events?'

'Why would she be? She's not the worrying sort. She takes care of the housework, she sews, she does her embroidery, she goes shopping, likes looking for bargains.'

'We're here. This way.'

Maigret steered his companion across the courtyard. He asked the officer guarding the cell:

'Are they here?'

'Yes.'

'Everything peaceful?'

'Apart from the new one Dubois brought in this morning. Says he's going to appeal to the League of Human Rights.'

Maigret barely smiled. He opened the door of the cell and let James go in first.

★ ★ ★

There was only one bunk, and Victor was occupying it. He had taken off his jacket and sandals.

Basso was walking up and down with his hands behind his back when they came in. He looked at them both, questioningly then fixed his eyes on Maigret.

Victor stood up grumpily, then sat down again, muttering inaudibly to himself.

'I bumped into James and I thought you'd like to see him.'

'Hello, James,' said Basso, shaking his hand.

But there was something missing. It was difficult to pinpoint. There was a certain reserve, a certain chill in the atmosphere. Maigret realized he would have to force the pace.

'Gentlemen,' he began, 'please take a seat, for we may be some time. You, make some room on the bunk. And please try to refrain from coughing for the next quarter of an hour. It cuts no ice in here.'

Victor merely sneered, like a man who was happy to bide his time.

'Take a seat, James. You too, Monsieur Basso. Excellent. Now, if you're sitting comfortably, I would like to take a few moments to recap the story so far.

'Some time ago, a man named Lenoir was sentenced to death. Before his execution he made an accusation against a certain individual whom he refused to name. It concerned an old case whose perpetrator no doubt felt was now safely gathering dust. Briefly, around six years ago a car drove away from an address in Paris and headed towards the Canal Saint-Martin. There, the driver lifted a body from the car and dropped it into the water.

'No one would have known a thing about it but for the fact that the whole scene was witnessed by two young villains by the name of Lenoir and Victor Gaillard. It didn't cross their minds to inform the police. They preferred to profit from their discovery, and so they traced the murderer and extorted various sums of money from him over a period of time.

'However, being still novices, they failed to take adequate precautions. One fine day they discovered that their cash cow had upped and left.

'And there we have it. The victim was called Ulrich. He was a Jewish second-hand dealer who lived on his own and consequently was missed by no one.'

Maigret slowly lit his pipe without looking at his audience. Nor did he look at them when he started talking again, but rather stared at his feet the whole time.

'Six years later, Lenoir came across the murderer again quite by chance, but he was unable to resume his lucrative business because he was caught for a crime of his own and sentenced to death.

'Now, listen carefully. Before he died, as I mentioned, he said a few things that narrowed down the field to a very select group of people. He also wrote to his former colleague to inform him of the discovery, and he hot-footed it to the Two-Penny Bar.

'And so we come, as it were, to the second act. Don't interrupt, James! Same goes for you, Victor. We come to the Sunday when Feinstein was killed. Ulrich's murderer was at the Two-Penny Bar that day. It could have been you, Basso, or me, or you, James, or Feinstein, or someone else. Only one person can tell us for certain, and that's Victor Gaillard, here present.'

Victor opened his mouth to speak, and Maigret literally shouted:

'Silence!'

Then, in a quieter tone, he continued:

'Now the said Victor Gaillard, who is a cunning little lowlife, doesn't want to give up the information for free. He wants 30,000 francs in return for the name. Let's say he'll settle for twenty-five. Silence, I say! Let me finish! Now the police are not in the habit of doling out such large sums of money, so all they can do for Gaillard is to pursue him on a charge of blackmail.

'Let us consider the various suspects. As I said earlier, all the people who were at the Two-Penny Bar on the Sunday in question could be under suspicion. Some more than others, however. For example, it is a fact that Basso once knew Monsieur Ulrich. It is also a fact not only that Feinstein knew him, but that the moneylender's death meant he didn't have to repay the considerable sum of money he owed him.

'Feinstein is dead. From what we have gathered, it is clear he was not a nice person to know. If he killed Ulrich, then the case is closed and no further action is required. Victor Gaillard

146

could confirm this, but I am not in a position to accept his blackmail . . . Silence! You will have a chance to speak when you are questioned.'

Victor was getting quite worked up and was trying to interrupt the inspector at every opportunity. Maigret still did not look at any of them. He had been speaking in a monotonous tone, as if reciting a lesson. Suddenly he went to the door, murmuring:

'I'll be back in a minute. I have an important phone call to make.'

The door opened, then closed behind him. Then the sound of his steps faded away up the stairs.

# 11

## Ulrich's Murderer

Maigret was talking to the examining magistrate on the phone.

'Hello! Yes! Just give me another ten minutes . . . His name? I don't know yet . . . Yes, of course I'm serious. Do I ever joke about these things?'

He put down the receiver and started walking up and down his office. He went over to Jean.

'By the way, I'll be away for a few days. Here is the address for forwarding my mail.'

He kept looking at his watch, then finally decided to go back down to the cell where he had left the three men.

When he came in, the first thing he saw was Victor's hate-filled face. He was no longer sitting on the bed, but was pacing angrily round the cell. Basso was sitting on the edge of the bunk with his head in his hands.

As for James, he was leaning against the wall with his arms folded, and he looked at Maigret with a strange smile.

'I'm sorry for keeping you waiting. I . . . '

'It's over,' said James. 'You didn't need to pull that stunt with the phone call.'

And his smile grew broader the more Maigret looked discomfited.

'Victor Gaillard will not earn his 30,000 francs, either by talking or by keeping his mouth shut. I killed Ulrich.'

The inspector opened the door and called to an officer who was passing:

'Lock this man up somewhere until I'm ready for him.'

He indicated Victor, who was still shouting:

'Don't forget it was me who led you to Ulrich! Without me, you'd be nowhere. And that's worth . . . '

Maigret now found this obstinate persistence in trying to extract a profit from the case not so much contemptible as pathetic.

'Five thousand! . . . 'he shouted as he was hauled up the stairs.

★   ★   ★

Now there were three of them in the cell. Basso was the most downcast of the three. He remained sitting a good while before standing up and facing Maigret.

'I swear I was willing to pay the 30,000 francs, inspector. What is that to me? But James wouldn't let me.'

Maigret looked from one to the other with an astonishment coloured by a growing sympathy.

'You knew about this, Basso?'

'I've known for a long time,' he murmured.

James filled in the details:

'He was the one who gave me the money those two tykes were extorting from me. So I told him the whole story.'

149

'This is crazy. For just 30,000 francs we could have . . . '

'No! No,' James sighed. 'You don't understand. Nor does the inspector.'

He looked round as if he was searching for something.

'Anyone got a cigarette?'

Basso gave him his cigarette case.

'I suppose a Pernod's out of the question? No matter. I'll have to get used to it. All the same, it would have made this easier.'

He licked his lips like a drinker suffering withdrawal.

'Actually, there's not much to say. I was married. Nice peaceful little marriage, a quiet life. I met Mado. And stupidly I thought I'd hit the jackpot. Just like in the novels. *My life for a kiss . . . Live life like there's no tomorrow . . . Leave the world behind . . . '*

The phlegmatic way he said all this made his confession sound dispassionate, not quite human, as if he was performing in a burlesque.

'When you're at that age it's all very exciting. Secret trysts in rented rooms, glasses of port and petits fours. But that all costs money. I was earning a thousand francs a month. And therein lay the roots of the whole sorry, sordid mess. I couldn't talk to Mado about money. I couldn't tell her that I couldn't afford the apartment in Passy. It was her husband, quite by chance, who put me on to Ulrich.'

'Did you borrow a lot?'

'Less than seven thousand. But that's a lot when you're only on a thousand a month. One evening, when my wife was away visiting her sister in the Vendôme, Ulrich came to see me. He started threatening me. If I didn't pay at least the interest he would tell my employers, just for starters, then he'd send round the bailiffs. Can you see what a disaster that would have been? My bosses and my wife finding out at the same time?'

His tone was still calm and ironic.

'I was an idiot. I only wanted to smash his face in to teach him a lesson. But once he'd got a bloodied nose, he started screaming. I grabbed him round the neck. I felt strangely calm. It's not true that you lose your head at times like this. Quite the contrary. I don't think I've ever been as lucid in my life. I went to hire a car. I propped up the body to make it look as if I was carrying a friend who'd drunk too much. You know the rest.'

He almost reached out a hand to pick up a non-existent drink.

'So there it is. After that, you see life differently. Mado and I dragged on for another month or so. My wife got into the habit of having a go at me for my drinking. I had to give money to those two crooks. I told Basso everything. They say it's good to talk. That's just more fiction. The only thing that could help would be to start your life again from the beginning, right from the cradle.'

It was a droll remark, drolly expressed, and Maigret couldn't help smiling. He noticed Basso was smiling too.

'Stupid, I know, but it would have been even

more stupid to have gone to the police and confessed that I'd killed a man.'

'So you made a little bolt-hole for yourself,' said Maigret.

'You have to survive somehow.'

It was a dismal story rather than a tragic one, perhaps because of James's strange personality. It was a point of honour for him not to lose his cool. He shied away from the slightest hint of emotion.

So much so that he was the calmest person in the room, and seemed puzzled by the long faces of the other two.

'We men are such fools. Basso got himself into the same tangle — and with Mado again! Not even someone different! And of course it all went wrong. If I could have, I'd have confessed to killing Feinstein. Then we'd have been quits. But I wasn't even there. He behaved like an idiot right to the end. He ran away. I did what I could to help him.'

In spite of himself, there was a quaver in James's voice, so he stopped talking for a moment, until he was able to carry on in his familiar monotone:

'He should have told the truth from the start! Even now, he still wanted to hand over the 30,000 francs.'

'It would have been easier,' Basso grumbled. 'But now . . . '

'Now I'm free of it at last,' James interrupted him. 'Free of everything. This filthy mess of an existence, the office, the café, my . . . '

He was about to say 'my wife', his wife with

whom he had not the slightest thing in common. His flat in Rue Championnet, where he sat reading any old thing just to pass the time. Morsang, where he would round up his companions for another drinking session.

He continued:

'I will be at peace.'

In prison! Somewhere he wouldn't be waiting for something that wasn't going to happen.

At peace in his little bolt-hole, eating, drinking and sleeping at the prescribed hour, breaking rocks on a chain gang or sewing up mailbags.

'What do you think, about twenty years?'

Basso was looking at him. He could hardly see him through the tears that welled up in his eyes and flowed down his cheeks.

'Stop it, James!' he cried out, his hands tensed into fists.

'Why?'

Maigret wiped his nose and tried mechanically to light his pipe, which was empty.

He felt he had never experienced such dark despair.

Not even dark. It was a dull, grey despair. A despair with no words of lament, no grimaces of pain.

A drinker's despair without the drunkenness — James never got drunk!

The inspector now understood what it was that brought them together every evening on the terrace of the Taverne Royale.

They would sit there together drinking, chatting aimlessly. And deep down James would hope that his companion would arrest him. He saw the suspicion emerging in Maigret and he nourished this suspicion, watched it grow. He waited.

'Another Pernod, old chap?'

He loved him like a friend who he hoped would one day deliver him from himself.

*     *     *

Maigret and Basso exchanged unreadable glances. James stubbed out his cigarette on the white table top.

'I just wish I could have done with it straight away. But there's the trial, all the questions, the tears, the sympathy.'

A police officer opened the door.

'The examining magistrate is here,' he announced.

Maigret hesitated, not quite knowing how to bring things to an end. He came forward and offered his hand with a sigh.

'Look, would you put in a good word for me? Just ask him if he can push it through quickly. I'll confess to everything. I just want to get in my bolt-hole as soon as possible.'

Then, as if to lighten the atmosphere, he added a parting remark:

'I'll tell you who'll be most upset. The waiter at the Taverne Royale. Will you go there and have one for me, inspector?'

Three hours later, Maigret was sitting on a train on his way to Alsace. Along the banks of the Marne he saw lots of bars just like the Two-Penny Bar, with their mechanical pianos in their wooden lean-tos.

He woke up early the next morning as the train pulled in. He saw a green-painted barrier in a little station bedecked with flowers.

Madame Maigret and her sister were anxiously scanning all the train doors.

And everything — the station, the countryside, his in-laws' house, the surrounding hills, even the sky — looked as fresh as if it had been scrubbed clean every morning.

'I bought you some varnished wood clogs yesterday in Colmar.'

Handsome yellow clogs that Maigret wanted to try on even before he had taken off his dark city clothes.

# The Shadow Puppet

Translated by
ROS SCHWARTZ

# 1

## The Shadow Puppet

It was ten p.m. The iron gates of the public garden were locked and Place des Vosges was empty. Glistening tyre tracks on the asphalt, the continuous play of the fountains, leafless trees and the regular shapes of identical rooftops silhouetted against the sky.

There were few lights under the splendid arcades encircling the square. Only three or four shops. Inspector Maigret could see a family eating inside one of them, cluttered with beaded funeral wreaths.

He was trying to read the numbers above the doors, but he had barely passed the wreath shop when a diminutive form stepped out of the shadows.

'Is it you I just telephoned?'

She must have been watching out for a long time. Despite the November cold, she had not slipped on a coat over her apron. Her nose was red, her eyes anxious.

Less than 400 metres away, on the corner of Rue de Béarn, a uniformed police officer stood guard.

'Didn't you inform him?' grumbled Maigret.

'No! Because of Madame de Saint-Marc, who's about to give birth . . . Oh look! There's the doctor's car, he was asked to come straight away.'

There were three cars drawn up alongside the

159

pavement, headlamps on, red rear lights. The sky, with its drifting clouds against a moonlit backdrop, had an ambiguous paleness. It felt as if the first snows were in the air.

The concierge turned under the archway at the building's entrance, from which hung a twenty-five-candlepower bulb covered in a film of dust.

'Let me explain. This is the courtyard — you have to cross it to get to all parts of the building, except for the two shops. This is my lodge on the left. Take no notice, I didn't have time to put the children to bed.'

There were two of them, a boy and a girl, in the untidy kitchen. But the concierge didn't go inside. She pointed to a long building, at the far end of the vast and beautifully proportioned courtyard.

'It's there. You'll see.'

Maigret was intrigued by this curious little woman, whose restless hands betrayed her febrility.

'There's someone on the phone asking for a detective chief inspector!' he had been told earlier at Quai des Orfèvres.

The voice on the other end was muffled. Several times he had repeated, 'Please speak up, I can't hear you.'

'I can't. I'm calling you from the tobacconist's. So — '

And a garbled message followed.

'You must come to 61, Place des Vosges right away . . . Yes . . . I think it's a murder, but don't tell anyone yet!'

160

And now the concierge was pointing at the tall first-floor windows. Behind the curtains, shadows could be seen coming and going.

'It's up there.'

'The murder?'

'No! Madame de Saint-Marc who's giving birth . . . Her first . . . She's not very strong. You understand?'

And the courtyard was even darker than Place des Vosges. It was illuminated by a single lamp on the wall. A staircase could just be made out on the other side of a glazed door, and there was the occasional lighted window.

'What about the murder?'

'I'm coming to that! Couchet's workers left at six o'clock — '

'Wait a moment. What is Couchet?'

'The building at the far end. A laboratory where they make serums. You must have heard of Doctor Rivière's Serums.'

'And that lighted window?'

'Wait. Today's the 30th, so Monsieur Couchet was there. He's in the habit of staying behind on his own after the offices have closed. I saw him through the window, sitting in his armchair. Look — '

A window with frosted-glass panes. A strange shadow, like that of a man slumped forward on his desk.

'Is that him?'

'Yes. Around eight o'clock, when I was emptying my rubbish bin, I glanced over in that direction. He was writing. You could clearly see the penholder or pencil in his hand.'

'What time did the murder — '

'Just a minute! I went upstairs to see how Madame de Saint-Marc was doing. I glanced over again when I came back down, and there he was, as he is now. Actually I thought he'd dozed off.'

Maigret was beginning to lose patience.

'Then, fifteen minutes later — '

'Yes! He was still in the same position! Get to the point.'

'That's all. I decided to check. I knocked on the office door. There was no answer so I went in. He's dead. There's blood everywhere.'

'Why didn't you go to the police? The police station is round the corner, in Rue de Béarn.'

'And they'd all have arrived in uniform! They'd have turned the place upside down! I told you that Madame de Saint-Marc — '

Maigret had both hands in his pockets, his pipe between his teeth. He looked up at the first-floor windows and had the impression that the birth was imminent, as there was even more to-ing and fro-ing. He heard a door opening, and footsteps on the stairs. A tall, broad shape appeared in the courtyard and the concierge, touching the inspector's arm, murmured reverentially, 'Monsieur de Saint-Marc. He's a former ambassador.'

The man, whose face was in shadow, paused, started walking again and stopped once more, constantly glancing up in the direction of his own windows.

'He must have been sent outside to wait. Already, earlier on . . . Come . . . Oh no! There they go again with their gramophone! And right above the Saint-Marcs, too!'

A smaller window, on the second floor, not so brightly lit. It was closed, and you could imagine, rather than hear, the music from a gramophone.

The concierge, all obsequious, jittery, red-eyed, her fingers twitching, walked to the far end of the courtyard, pointed to a short flight of steps, a half-open door.

'You'll see him, on your left. I'd rather not go in there again.'

★   ★   ★

An ordinary office. Light-coloured furniture. Plain wallpaper.

And a man in his mid-forties, sitting in an armchair, his head on the scattered papers in front of him. He'd been shot in the chest.

Maigret listened attentively: the concierge was still outside, waiting for him, and Monsieur de Saint-Marc was still pacing up and down the courtyard. From time to time, an omnibus rumbled past and the racket made the ensuing silence seem all the more absolute.

The inspector touched nothing. He simply made sure that the gun had not been left lying around the office, stood surveying the scene for three or four minutes, puffing on his pipe, then he left, with a determined air.

'Well?'

The concierge was still there. She spoke in hushed tones.

'Nothing! He's dead!'

'Monsieur de Saint-Marc has just been called upstairs.'

There was a commotion in the apartment. Doors were slamming. There was the sound of running footsteps.

'She's so frail!'

'Yes!' muttered Maigret, scratching the back of his neck. 'Only that's not the issue. Do you have any idea who could have entered the office?'

'Me? How would I . . . ?'

'Excuse me, but from your lodge at the entrance to the building, you must see the residents coming and going.'

'I ought to! Now if the landlord gave me a decent lodge and put in proper lighting . . . I can only just hear footsteps and, yes, at night I see shadows . . . There are some footsteps I'm able to recognize.'

'Have you noticed anything unusual since six o'clock?'

'Nothing! Nearly all the residents came down to empty their rubbish. The bins are here, to the left of my lodge. Do you see the four dustbins? They're not allowed to come down before seven p.m.'

'And nobody came in via the archway?'

'How would I know? It's obvious you don't know this building. There are twenty-eight residents. Not counting the Couchet laboratory, where people are coming and going all the time.'

Footsteps in the entrance. A man in a bowler hat entered the courtyard, turned left and, going over to the dustbins, grabbed an empty bin.

164

Despite the darkness, he must have spotted Maigret and the concierge, since he froze for a second, and then said, 'Nothing for me?'

'Nothing, Monsieur Martin.'

And Maigret asked, 'Who's that?'

'Monsieur Martin, a Registry Office official who lives on the second floor with his wife.'

'How come his rubbish bin — ?'

'Nearly all of them do that when they have to go out. They bring the bin down on the way out and pick it up when they come back. Did you hear that?'

'What?'

'It sounded like . . . like a baby crying. If only those two up there would turn off that wretched gramophone! They know perfectly well that Madame de Saint-Marc's giving birth.'

She hurried over to the staircase, which someone was descending.

'Well, doctor? Is it a boy?'

'A girl.'

And the doctor left. He could be heard starting up his car and driving off.

Day-to-day life went on. The dark courtyard. The archway and its feeble bulb. The lighted windows and the vague sound of music from a gramophone.

The dead man was still in his office, all alone, his head resting on scattered papers.

Suddenly there was a scream from the second floor. A piercing shriek, like a desperate call for help. But the concierge didn't react. She sighed as she pushed open the door to her lodge, 'There goes the madwoman again.'

165

Then it was her turn to shout, because one of her kids had broken a plate. The light revealed the concierge's thin, tired face, her ageless body.

'When will all the formalities begin?' she asked.

★  ★  ★

The tobacconist's opposite was still open, and a few minutes later Maigret shut himself inside the telephone booth. He issued instructions in hushed tones.

'Yes, the public prosecutor . . . 61 . . . Almost on the corner of Rue de Turenne . . . and inform the forensics department . . . Hello! . . . Yes, I'm remaining at the scene.'

He walked a few steps and mechanically passed under the archway and ended up standing glumly in the middle of the courtyard, hunching his shoulders against the cold.

One by one the lighted windows went dark. The silhouette of the dead man could still be seen through the frosted glass like a Chinese shadow puppet.

A taxi pulled up. It wasn't the public prosecutor yet. A young woman crossed the courtyard with hurried steps, leaving a whiff of perfume in her wake, and pushed open the door to Couchet's office.

# 2

## A Good Man

There was a whole succession of unfortunate moves that resulted in a comical situation. On discovering the body, the young woman wheeled round and caught sight of Maigret's tall form in the doorway. Automatically she associated two images: a dead man and a murderer.

Wide-eyed, her body tensed, she opened her mouth to scream for help, dropping her handbag.

Maigret had no time to argue. He seized her arm and put his hand over her mouth.

'Ssssh! You're mistaken! Police.'

Before his words sank in, she struggled and, being highly strung, tried to bite, kicking back with her heels.

There was a sound of silk ripping: her dress strap.

Finally, Maigret managed to reassure her. 'Hush,' he repeated, 'I'm from the police. We don't want to disturb the entire building.'

Silence, unusual in such situations, was the characteristic of this murder, as was the calmness, the twenty-eight residents all going about their ordinary business oblivious of the body.

The young woman adjusted her clothing and her hair.

'Were you his mistress?'

She shot Maigret a furious look as she rummaged for a pin to fix her strap.

'Had you arranged to meet him this evening?'

'At eight o'clock, at the Select. We were supposed to be having dinner together and then going to the theatre.'

'When he didn't turn up at eight, didn't you telephone him?'

'Yes! But the phone was off the hook.'

They both saw it at the same time, on the desk. The man must have knocked it over when he fell forward.

Footsteps in the courtyard, where that evening the slightest sounds were amplified, as if under a bell. The concierge called out from the threshold, to avoid seeing the body.

'Detective Chief Inspector ... The local police — '

She did not like them. They arrived in groups of four or five, making no attempt to be discreet. One of them was telling a funny story. Another asked, on reaching the office, 'Where's the body?'

Since the local police chief was away, his deputy was standing in for him, so Maigret felt even more comfortable taking charge of operations.

'Leave your men outside. I'm waiting for the public prosecutor. It is preferable for the residents not to have any idea — '

And, while the deputy inspected the office, he turned once more to the young woman.

'What is your name?'

'Nine, Nine Moinard, but everyone calls me by my first name.'

'How long have you known Couchet?'

'Six months maybe.'

There was no need to ask her many questions. It was enough to watch her. A fairly pretty girl, still at the beginning of her career. Her outfit was from a quality fashion house, but her make-up, the way she held her bag and gloves and the aggressive look in her eyes gave away her music-hall background.

'Dancer?'

'I was at the Moulin Bleu.'

'What about now?'

'I'm with him.'

She hadn't had time to cry. Everything had happened too fast and the facts hadn't properly sunk in yet.

'Did he live with you?'

'Not exactly, because he was married. But — '

'Your address?'

'Hôtel Pigalle, Rue Pigalle.'

The police station deputy commented, 'In any case, no one can claim it was a burglary!'

'Why not?'

'Look! The safe's behind him! It's not locked, but the body is blocking the door!'

Nine, who had taken a small handkerchief out of her bag, sniffed and dabbed at her nostrils.

A moment later, the atmosphere changed. Cars screeching to a stop outside. Footsteps and voices in the courtyard. Then handshakes, questions, noisy discussions. The public prosecutor and his investigating team had arrived. The pathologist examined the body and the photographers set up their equipment.

For Maigret, it was an unpleasant wait. After exchanging the obligatory pleasantries, he went outside, his hands in his pockets, lit his pipe and bumped into someone in the dark. It was the concierge, who could not stand by and let strangers run around her building without finding out what they were up to.

'What's your name?' Maigret asked her kindly.

'Madame Bourcier. Are these gentlemen going to be here long? Look! The light's gone out in Madame de Saint-Marc's bedroom, she must have gone to sleep, poor thing.'

Looking up at the building, the chief inspector noticed another light, a cream-coloured curtain and, behind it, a woman's silhouette. She was small and thin, like the concierge. You couldn't hear her voice, but even so, you could tell she was angry. Sometimes she would remain stock still, staring at an unseen person, then abruptly she would start speaking, gesticulating, taking a few steps forward.

'Who is that?'

'Madame Martin. You saw her husband return earlier, you know, the man who picked up his rubbish bin, the Registry Office official.'

'Are they in the habit of arguing?'

'They don't argue. She's the one who shouts. He doesn't dare open his mouth.'

From time to time, Maigret took a look inside the office where ten or so people were busy at work. Standing in the doorway, the prosecutor called the concierge.

'Who is Monsieur Couchet's second-in-command?'

'The manager, Monsieur Philippe. He doesn't live far away, he's on the Ile Saint-Louis.'

'Does he have a telephone?'

'He's bound to.'

There was a sound of voices speaking on the phone. Upstairs, Madame Martin's silhouette could no longer be seen against the curtain. However, a nondescript individual came down the stairs, furtively crossed the courtyard and went out into the street. Maigret recognized Monsieur Martin's bowler hat and putty-coloured overcoat.

It was midnight. The girls playing the gramophone switched off their lights. Apart from the office, the only light left on was on the first floor, in the Saint-Marcs' sitting room, where the former ambassador and the midwife were conversing in low voices, a faint odour of disinfectant in the air.

★　★　★

Despite the late hour, when Monsieur Philippe arrived, he was impeccably turned out, his dark, well-kempt beard, his hands gloved in grey suede. He was in his forties, the epitome of the serious-minded, well-brought-up intellectual.

He was certainly astonished, devastated even, by the news. But he seemed somehow to be holding back in his reaction.

'With the life he led,' he sighed.

'What life?'

171

'I refuse to speak ill of Monsieur Couchet. Besides, there's no ill to speak of. He was master of his own time — '

'Just a minute! Did Monsieur Couchet manage his company himself?'

'Neither hands-on nor hands-off. It was he who started it up. But once it was up and running, he left me to handle everything. To the extent that sometimes I didn't see him for a fortnight. Take today, I waited for him till five o'clock. It's payday tomorrow. Monsieur Couchet was supposed to bring me the money to pay the staff's wages. Around 300,000 francs. At five o'clock, I had to go and I left a report for him on the desk.'

The typed report was still there, beneath the dead man's hand. A mundane report: a suggested rise for one worker and the sacking of one of the delivery men; a draft advert for the Latin American companies and so on.

'So the 300,000 francs should be here?' inquired Maigret.

'In the safe. The fact that Monsieur Couchet opened it proves it. He and I are the only two people who have the key and the code.'

But to open the safe, the body had to be moved, which could not be done until the photographers had finished their job. The pathologist was making his verbal report. Couchet had been hit by a bullet in the chest, which had severed the aorta, and death had been instantaneous. The distance between the killer and his victim was estimated at three metres. And lastly, the bullet was of the most common calibre: 6.35mm.

Monsieur Philippe explained some things to the examining magistrate.

'Here in Place des Vosges, we only have our laboratory, which is behind this office.'

He opened a door. They glimpsed a vast room with a glazed roof where thousands of test tubes stood in rows. Behind another door, Maigret thought he heard a noise.

'What's in there?'

'The guinea pigs. And to the right are the offices of the typists and the clerical staff. We have other premises in Pantin, from which most of the dispatching is done, for you probably know that Doctor Rivière's Serums are renowned world-wide.'

'Was it Couchet who launched them?'

'Yes! Doctor Rivière had no money. Couchet financed his research. Ten years ago he opened a laboratory which wasn't as big as this one yet.'

'Is Doctor Rivière still involved?'

'He died five years ago, in a road accident.'

At last Couchet's body was removed. But, the moment the safe was opened, there was consternation: all the money it had contained had vanished. Only business documents remained. Monsieur Philippe explained, 'Not only the 300,000 francs that Monsieur Couchet would definitely have brought, but another 60,000 francs held by a rubber band that had been cashed that afternoon and which I myself put in the safe!'

In the dead man's wallet, nothing. Or rather two numbered tickets for a theatre near Madeleine, the sight of which made Nine cry.

'They were for us! We were supposed to be

173

going to the theatre.'

The forensics team was done. There was mounting chaos as the photographers folded up their unwieldy tripods, the pathologist washed his hands at a basin he'd come across in a closet, and the prosecutor's clerk yawned.

Despite all the goings-on around him, for a few moments Maigret had a sort of tête-à-tête with the dead man.

A vigorous man, on the short side, tubby. Like Nine, he had doubtless never entirely shed a certain vulgarity despite his well-cut clothes, manicured nails and bespoke silk underwear.

His fair hair was thinning. His eyes were probably blue and had a slightly childlike expression.

'A good man!' sighed a voice behind him.

It was Nine, who was crying piteously and who took Maigret as witness, not daring to address the public prosecutor's more formal men.

'I swear to you he was a good man! Whenever he thought something would make me happy — and not just me, anybody — I've never seen a man give such generous tips. I even used to scold him, I told him people took him for a ride. And he'd reply, 'So what?''

Maigret asked gravely, 'Was he a cheerful man?'

'He seemed cheerful, but not deep down, if you know what I mean. It's hard to explain. He needed to be moving, doing something. If he sat still, he'd become broody or anxious.'

'What about his wife?'

174

'I only saw her once, from a distance. I don't have anything bad to say about her.'

'Where did Couchet live?'

'Boulevard Haussmann. But most of the time he'd go to Meulan, where he has a villa.'

Maigret abruptly turned his head, saw the concierge, who did not dare come in. She was signalling to him, looking more unhappy than ever.

'Listen! He's coming down.'

'Who?'

'Monsieur de Saint-Marc. He must have heard all the commotion. Here he is. Just think! On a day like today!'

The former ambassador, in his dressing gown, was loath to approach. He had realized this was an investigation by the public prosecutor's office. Besides, the body on the stretcher passed close to him.

'What's going on?' he asked Maigret.

'A man's been murdered. Couchet, the owner of the serums laboratory.'

The chief inspector sensed that Monsieur de Saint-Marc had suddenly been struck by a thought, as if recalling something.

'Did you know him?'

'No. I mean, I knew of him.'

'And?'

'Nothing! I know nothing. What time did — '

'The murder must have been committed between eight and nine p.m.'

Monsieur de Saint-Marc sighed, smoothed his silver hair, nodded to Maigret and headed for the staircase leading up to his apartment.

The concierge had kept her distance. Then she went over to someone who was pacing back and forth under the archway, bent forward. When she came back to Maigret, he asked her, 'Who is that?'

'Monsieur Martin. He's looking for a glove he dropped. He never goes out without his gloves, even to go and buy cigarettes fifty metres from here.'

Now searching around the dustbins, Monsieur Martin lit a few matches but eventually gave up and resigned himself to going backup to his apartment.

People were shaking hands in the courtyard. The public prosecutor left. The examining magistrate spoke briefly with Maigret.

'I'll leave you to get on with your job. Naturally you'll keep me posted.'

Monsieur Philippe, still looking as though he'd stepped out of the pages of a fashion magazine, bowed to the detective chief inspector.

'You no longer need me?'

'I'll see you tomorrow. You'll be at your office, I suppose?'

'At nine on the dot, as usual.'

Suddenly there was a moving scene, even though nothing particular happened. The court-yard was still plunged in shadow. A single lamp. And then the archway with its dusty light bulb.

Outside, cars revved up and glided over the asphalt, briefly picking out the trees of the Place des Vosges with their headlamps.

The body was no longer there. The office looked as if it had been ransacked. Nobody had thought to switch off the lights, and the laboratory was lit up as if in anticipation of a hard night's work.

And now there were three of them left in the middle of the courtyard, three very different people who an hour earlier had not known each other and who now seemed to be drawn to each other by an inexplicable kinship.

Or rather, they were like the family members who remain behind after a funeral when the rest of the guests have left.

At least this was Maigret's fleeting impression as he looked from Nine's exhausted face to the concierge's drawn features.

'Have you put your children to bed?'

'Yes, but they're not asleep. They're anxious, it's as if they can sense what's going on.'

Madame Bourcier had a question she wanted to ask, a question she was almost ashamed of, but which, for her, was capital.

'Do you think . . . '

Her gaze swept the courtyard and seemed to pause at each of the dark windows.

' . . . that . . . it's one of the residents?'

And now she was staring at the entrance, at the vast archway with its door constantly open, except after eleven p.m., which led from the courtyard to the street and gave the entire unknown world outside access to the building.

Nine meanwhile was looking uncomfortable, shooting the inspector covert glances.

'The investigation will doubtless answer your question, Madame Bourcier. For the time being, one thing seems certain, and that is that the person who stole the 360,000 francs is not the murderer. At least that is probable, since Monsieur Couchet's body was blocking the safe. By the way, were the lights on in the laboratory this evening?'

'Wait! Yes, I think so. But it wasn't as brightly lit as now. Monsieur Couchet must have switched on a light or two on his way to the toilet, which is right at the back of the building.'

Maigret went back to Couchet's office and switched off all the lights, while the concierge remained in the doorway, even though the body was no longer there. In the courtyard, the inspector found Nine waiting for him. He heard a noise somewhere above his head, the sound of an object swishing against a window pane.

But all the windows were shut, all the lights out.

Someone had moved, someone was watching from the shadows of a room.

'See you tomorrow, Madame Bourcier. I'll be here before the office opens.'

'I'll follow you. I have to lock the main door.'

★  ★  ★

Nine, standing on the edge of the pavement, remarked, 'I thought you had a car.'

She seemed reluctant to leave him. Looking at her feet, she added, 'Whereabouts do you live?'

'Very close by, Boulevard Richard-Lenoir.'

'The last Metro's gone, hasn't it?'

'I think so.'

'I'd like to tell you something.'

'Go ahead.'

She still did not dare meet his eye. Behind them, they could hear the concierge bolting the door and then her footsteps echoing as she went back to her lodge. There was not a soul in the square. The fountains were babbling. The town hall clock struck one.

'You're going to think that I'm imposing on . . . I don't know what you'll think. I told you that Raymond was very generous. He wasn't aware of the value of money. He used to give me anything I wanted. Do you understand?'

'And?'

'It's stupid, I asked for as little as possible. I'd wait until he thought of it. In any case, since he was with me nearly all the time, I didn't need anything. Tonight I was supposed to be having dinner with him. Well — '

'Broke?'

'It's not even that!' she protested. 'It's even more stupid! I was thinking of asking him for some money this evening. At lunchtime I paid a bill.'

This was excruciating for her. She kept an eye on Maigret, ready to clam up at the slightest hint of amusement.

'It never occurred to me that he wouldn't show up. I had a little money left in my bag. While I was waiting for him, at the Select, I ate oysters, and then lobster. I telephoned. It was only when I got here that I realized I only had enough to pay my taxi fare.'

'And at home?'

'I live in a hotel.'

'I'm asking if you have any money saved up.'

'Me?'

A nervous little laugh.

'What for? How could I have known? Even if I had, I wouldn't have wanted — '

Maigret sighed.

'Walk with me to Boulevard Beaumarchais. That's the only place you'll find a taxi at this hour. What are you going to do?'

'Nothing. I — '

She shivered. True, she was dressed only in silk.

'Had he not made a will?'

'How would I know? Do you think people worry about such things when everything's fine? Raymond was a good man. I — '

She wept silently as she walked. The inspector slipped a 100-franc note into her hand, flagged down a passing car and, thrusting his fists in his pockets, muttered, 'See you tomorrow. You did say Hôtel Pigalle didn't you?'

When he got into bed, Madame Maigret woke up only long enough to murmur, sleepily, 'Did you at least have dinner?'

# 3

## The Couple at Hôtel Pigalle

Leaving home at around eight a.m., Maigret had to choose between three pressing tasks: revisiting the premises at Place des Vosges and questioning the staff, paying a visit to Madame Couchet, who had been apprised of events by the local police, and lastly questioning Nine again.

On waking, he had telephoned police headquarters and given them the list of residents at number 61, as well as all the people connected either closely or remotely with the tragedy, so that when he went to his office, detailed information would be waiting for him.

The market on Boulevard Richard-Lenoir was in full swing. The weather was so cold that the inspector turned up the velvet collar of his overcoat. Place des Vosges was close by, but he had to walk there.

A tram going to Place Pigalle rumbled past and that prompted Maigret to make up his mind. He would see Nine first.

Of course, she was not up yet. The hotel receptionist recognized Maigret and expressed concern.

'She's not mixed up in any trouble, I hope? Such a quiet girl!'

'Does she have many visitors?'

'Only her friend.'

'The old one or the young one?'

'She only has one. He's neither young nor old.'

It was a comfortable hotel with a telephone in each room and a lift. Maigret was deposited on the third floor. He rapped on the door of room 27, heard someone thrashing around in bed, and then a voice stammer, 'What is it?'

'Open the door, Nine!'

A hand must have emerged from under the blankets and unbolted the door. Maigret entered the damp gloom, glimpsed the young woman's tired face, and went to draw the curtains.

'What time is it?'

'Not yet nine. Don't get up.'

She half-closed her eyes, because of the harsh light. In that state, she wasn't pretty and looked more like a country girl than a coquette. She ran her hand over her face a couple of times, eventually sat up in bed and placed a pillow behind her. Finally she picked up the telephone.

'Bring my breakfast!'

And, to Maigret, 'What a business! You're not too mad at me for scrounging off you last night? It's stupid! I'll have to sell my jewellery.'

'Have you got a lot?'

She gestured towards the dressing table, where a few rings, a bracelet and a watch lay in a promotional ashtray. Their combined value was around five thousand francs.

There was a knock at the door of the next room and Nine pricked up her ears, gave a vague smile as the knocking began again, more insistent this time.

'Who is that?' asked Maigret.

182

'My neighbours? I don't know! But if anyone manages to wake them up at this hour — '

'What do you mean?'

'Nothing! They're never up before four o'clock in the afternoon. That's when they wake up!'

'Do they take drugs?'

Her eyelashes fluttered a yes, but she hastened to add, 'You're not going to use what I tell you, are you?'

The door eventually opened. As did Nine's, and a chambermaid brought in the tray with the coffee and croissants.

'May I?'

There were dark circles under her eyes and her nightdress revealed scrawny shoulders and small, not very firm breasts like those of a stunted child. As she dunked pieces of croissant in her *café au lait*, she continued to listen out, as if despite everything she did take an interest in what was going on next door.

'Will I be mixed up in all this?' she asked nevertheless. 'It would be awkward if they wrote about me in the newspapers! Especially for Madame Couchet.'

And, as someone was knocking on her door with urgent little taps, she shouted, 'Come in!'

A woman in her early thirties, who had slipped a fur coat over her nightdress and was barefoot, entered. She almost retreated on catching sight of Maigret's broad back, then she plucked up her courage and stammered, 'I didn't know you had company!'

Maigret shuddered at the sound of the languid voice that seemed to be struggling out of a furred mouth. He looked at the woman who was closing the door behind her and saw a face drained of colour, with puffy eyelids. A glance at Nine confirmed his guess. She was the drug addict from next door.

'What's happened?'

'Nothing! Roger has a visitor, so I took the liberty — '

She sat down on the end of the bed, dazed, and sighed as Nine had done, 'What time is it?'

'Nine o'clock!' said Maigret. 'Hmm, someone's been at the cocaine!'

'It's not cocaine, it's ether. Roger says it's better and that — '

She was cold. She got up to go and huddle by the radiator, gazing out of the window.

'It's going to rain again.'

The whole scene was gloomy, depressing. The comb on the dressing table was full of broken hairs. Nine's stockings lay on the floor.

'I'm in the way, aren't I? But apparently it's important. It's about Roger's father, who's just died.'

Maigret watched Nine and saw her suddenly knit her brow like someone who has just had an idea. At the same time, the woman who had just spoken raised her hand to her chin, thought for a moment and muttered, 'Oh my goodness!'

And the inspector asked, 'Do you know Roger's father?'

'I've never seen him. But . . . Hold on! Nine, nothing happened to your friend, did it?'

Nine and the inspector exchanged a glance. 'Why?'

'I don't know. It's all a bit muddled. I've just remembered that Roger once told me that his father was a visitor here. It amused him, but he preferred not to bump into him and one time, when he heard someone coming up the stairs he rushed back into the room. I seem to recall that the person in question came in here.'

Nine stopped eating. The tray on her knees hindered her and her face betrayed her anxiety.

'His son?' she said slowly, staring at the dull glass rectangle of the window.

'Oh my goodness!' exclaimed the other woman. 'Then it's your friend who's dead! They say he was murdered.'

'Is Roger's surname Couchet?' asked Maigret.

'He's Roger Couchet, yes!'

Disconcerted, all three fell silent.

'What does he do?' continued the inspector after a long pause, during which a murmur of voices in the next room could be heard.

'Pardon?'

'What is his profession?'

The young woman snapped, 'You're from the police, aren't you?'

She was flustered. She might hold it against Nine for having lured her into a trap.

'The inspector's very kind!' said Nine, poking one leg out of the bed and leaning forward to pick up her stockings.

'I should have guessed! So then you already knew, before I came in.'

'I hadn't heard anything about Roger!' said Maigret. 'Now, I'll need you to give me some information about him.'

'I don't know anything. We've been together for barely three weeks.'

'What about before?'

'He was with a tall redhead who claimed to be a manicurist.'

'Does he work?'

The word 'work' created further discomfiture.

'I don't know.'

'In other words, he does nothing. Is he wealthy? Does he live extravagantly?'

'No! We nearly always have a six-franc set menu.'

'Does he often talk about his father?'

'I told you, he only mentioned him once.'

'Could you describe his visitor? Have you met him before?'

'No! He's a man . . . how can I say? To start with I thought he was a bailiff, that he'd come because Roger was in debt.'

'Is he well-dressed?'

'Hold on. I saw a bowler hat, a beige overcoat, gloves — '

Between the two rooms there was a communicating door concealed behind a curtain and probably locked. Maigret could have pressed his ear to it and overheard everything, but he was loath to do so in front of the two women.

Nine got dressed, contenting herself with wiping her face with a moistened towel by way of a wash. She was on edge. Her movements were jerky. It was clear that she was out of her depth and now she was expecting all sorts of trouble; she didn't have the strength to react or even to grasp the situation.

The other woman was calmer, perhaps because she was still under the influence of ether, perhaps because she had more experience of this sort of thing.

'What is your name?'

'Céline.'

'Do you have a profession?'

'I was a hairdresser doing home visits.'

'And on the vice squad's books?'

She shook her head, without showing annoyance. A murmur of voices could still be heard coming from next door.

Nine, who had slipped on a dress, gazed around the room and suddenly burst into tears, exclaiming, 'Oh God! Oh God!'

'It's a funny business!' said Céline slowly. 'And, if it really is a murder, they're going to keep pestering us.'

'Where were you last night at around eight p.m.?'

She cast her mind back.

'Hold on . . . Eight o'clock . . . Well, I was at the Cyrano.'

'Was Roger with you?'

'No. We can't be together all the time. I met him at midnight, at the tobacconist's in Rue Fontaine.'

'Did he tell you where he'd been?'

'I didn't ask.'

Through the window, Maigret could see Place Pigalle, its tiny garden, the nightclub signs. Suddenly, he straightened up and marched towards the door.

'Wait here for me, both of you!'

And he went out, knocked at the neighbouring door and turned the handle.

A man in pyjamas was sitting in the only armchair in the room, which reeked of ether despite the open window. Another man was pacing up and down, gesticulating. It was Monsieur Martin, whom Maigret had met twice the previous evening, in the courtyard at Place des Vosges.

★　★　★

'Ah, so you found your glove!'

Maigret was looking at the two hands of the official from the Registry Office, who turned so pale that the inspector thought for a moment that he was about to faint. His lips quivered. He attempted to speak but failed.

'I . . . I — '

The young man had not shaved. He had a pasty complexion, red-rimmed eyes and soft lips that were a sign of his spinelessness. He gulped water out of the tooth mug.

'Get a grip on yourself, Monsieur Martin! I hadn't expected to meet you here, especially at this hour when your office must have opened some time ago.'

Maigret studied him from head to toe. He had to make an effort not to take pity on him, such was the poor man's visible confusion.

From his shoes to his tie and his detachable white collar, Monsieur Martin was like a caricature of the archetypal civil servant. A dignified, neat and orderly official with a waxed moustache, not a speck of dust on his clothes, who no doubt deemed it shameful to go out without gloves.

Right now, he didn't know what to do with his hands, and his gaze searched the corners of the untidy room as if he hoped to find inspiration there.

'May I ask you a question, Monsieur Martin? How long have you known Roger Couchet?'

It was no longer fear, it was sheer terror.

'Me?'

'Yes, you!'

'Since . . . since my marriage!'

He said this as if it were self-evident.

'I don't understand!'

'Roger is my stepson, my wife's son.'

'And Raymond Couchet was his father?'

'Well yes . . . As — '

He grew more assured.

'My wife was Couchet's first wife. She has a son, Roger. After she got divorced, I married her.'

This had the effect of a gust of wind sweeping an overcast sky. The building in Place des Vosges was transformed by it. The nature of the events changed. Some points became clearer. Others, on the contrary, became muddier, more worrying.

To such an extent that Maigret no longer dared speak. He needed to muster his thoughts. He looked from one man to the other with mounting concern.

That very night, the concierge had asked him, looking up at all the windows that could be seen from the courtyard, '*Do you think it's one of the residents?*'

And her eyes finally came to rest on the archway. She hoped that the murderer had come in that way, that it was someone from outside.

Well it wasn't! The drama was indeed an internal affair! Maigret couldn't have said why, but he was convinced of it.

What drama? He hadn't the faintest idea!

Only he had a hunch that there were invisible threads linking points far apart in space, stretching from Place des Vosges to this hotel in Rue Pigalle, from the Martins' apartment to Couchet's laboratory, from Nine's room to that of the couple in an ether-induced stupor.

Perhaps the most disturbing thing was seeing Monsieur Martin tossed like a hapless spinning-top into this maze. He always wore gloves. His putty-coloured overcoat alone was an orderly, dignified statement. And his anxious look sought to alight somewhere without success.

'I came to tell Roger . . . ' he stammered.

'Yes.'

Maigret looked him in the eyes, calmly, deeply, and almost expected to see Monsieur Martin shrink with fear.

'My wife told me that it would be best if we were the ones to . . . '

'I understand.'

'Roger is very — '

'Very sensitive.' Maigret took the words out of his mouth. 'An anxious boy.'

The young man, who was on his third glass of water, glared at him venomously. He must have been twenty-five, but his features were already careworn, his eyelids withered.

And yet he was still attractive, with a dark complexion and looks capable of seducing some women; everything about him was tinged with romanticism, even his weary, slightly nauseated air.

'Tell me, Roger Couchet, did you see your father often?'

'Sometimes.'

'Where?'

And Maigret's eyes bored into him.

'At his office, or at a restaurant.'

'When did you see him for the last time?'

'I don't know, a few weeks ago.'

'And did you ask him for money?'

'As always!'

'In other words, you were sponging off him?'

'He was wealthy enough to — '

'Just a moment! Where were you at around eight p.m. last night?'

There was no hesitation.

'At the Select,' he said with an ironic smile that meant, *Don't you think I can't see where this is leading!*

'What were you doing at the Select?'

'I was waiting for my father.'

'So, you needed money! And you knew that he'd be coming to the Select?'

'He was there nearly every evening with his mistress. And anyway, that afternoon I overheard her talking on the telephone. You can hear everything through these walls.'

'When you realized that your father wasn't

coming, did it occur to you to go to his office in Place des Vosges?'

'No.'

Maigret picked up a photograph of the young man from the mantelpiece. It was surrounded by portraits of different women. He put it in his pocket, mumbling, 'May I?'

'If you wish.'

'You don't think — ?' began Monsieur Martin.

'I don't think anything at all. Which reminds me I'd like to ask you some questions. How were relations between your household and Roger?'

'He didn't come often.'

'And when he did come?'

'He only stayed for a few minutes.'

'Is his mother aware of his lifestyle?'

'What do you mean?'

'Don't pretend to be stupid, Monsieur Martin. Does your wife know that her son lives in Montmartre and is a layabout?'

And the civil servant looked at the floor, embarrassed.

'I have often tried to persuade him to get a job,' he sighed.

This time, the young man started drumming impatiently on the table.

'You can see that I'm still in my pyjamas and that — '

'Would you tell me if you saw anyone you knew at the Select last night?'

'I saw Nine!'

'Did you say anything to her?'

'What? I have never spoken to her.'

'Where was she sitting?'

'The second table to the right of the bar.'

'Where did you find your glove, Monsieur Martin? If my memory serves me correctly, you were looking for it last night in the courtyard, near the dustbins.'

Monsieur Martin gave a strained little laugh.

'It was at home! Can you believe it, I had gone out with only one glove on and I hadn't noticed.'

'When you left Place des Vosges, where did you go?'

'I went for a walk along the embankment. I had a very bad headache.'

'Do you often go out for a walk at night without your wife?'

'Sometimes.'

This was agony for him. And he still didn't know what to do with his gloved hands.

'Are you going to your office now?'

'No! I telephoned to ask for the day off. I can't leave my wife in — '

'Well, go back to her, then!'

Maigret stayed put. The man was casting around for a dignified way of making his exit.

'Goodbye, Roger,' he gulped. 'I . . . I think you should go and see your mother.'

But Roger merely shrugged and gave Maigret an irritated look. Monsieur Martin's footsteps could be heard fading on the stairs.

The young man said nothing. His hand automatically picked up a bottle of ether from the bedside table and set it down further away.

'You have nothing to say?' the inspector asked slowly.

'Nothing!'

'Because, if you do want to make a statement, you'd better do so now rather than later.'

'I won't have anything to say to you later. No, actually I will! One thing I'll tell you right now, is that you're barking up the wrong tree.'

'By the way, since you didn't see your father last night, you must be short of money?'

'Too true!'

'Where are you going to find some?'

'Oh please don't worry about me. Do you mind?'

And he ran some water into the basin and started washing.

Maigret, to keep his countenance, took a few more steps and then left the room. He went next door, where the two women were waiting. Now it was Céline who was the most anxious. Nine was sitting in the wing chair slowly nibbling at a handkerchief and staring at the blank window with her big dreamy eyes.

'Well?' asked Roger's mistress.

'Nothing! You can go back to your room.'

'Is it really his father who — ?'

And suddenly, she frowned.

'So does that mean he's going to inherit?'

Looking pensive, she left.

★ ★ ★

Outside on the pavement, Maigret asked Nine, 'Where are you going?'

A vague, dismissive wave, then, 'I'm going to the Moulin Bleu to see if they'll take me back.'

He watched her with avuncular interest.

194

'Were you fond of Couchet?'

'I told you yesterday, he was a good man. And there aren't many of those around, I can assure you! To think that some bastard — '

There were a couple of tears, then nothing.

'It's here,' she said pushing open a little door that was the stage entrance.

Maigret was thirsty and went into a bar for a beer. He had to go to Place des Vosges. The sight of a telephone reminded him that he hadn't yet dropped into Quai des Orfèvres and that there might be urgent post waiting on his desk.

He called the office boy.

'Is that you, Jean? Nothing for me? What? A lady who's been waiting for an hour? In mourning? It's not Madame Couchet? What? Madame Martin? I'm on my way.'

Madame Martin *in mourning*! And she'd been waiting for him at police headquarters for an hour!

All Maigret had seen of her so far was a shadow puppet, the comical, gesticulating shadow on the second-floor curtain the previous evening, whose mouth opened and shut, emitting a furious invective.

*It happens all the time!* the concierge had told him.

And the poor civil servant, who'd forgotten his glove and gone for a solitary walk along the dark banks of the Seine.

And when Maigret had left the courtyard, at one a.m., he'd heard a noise at a window.

He slowly climbed the dusty stairs, shook hands with a few colleagues in passing and put his head around the half-open door of the waiting room.

Ten green velvet armchairs. A table like a billiards table. On the wall, the roll of honour: 200 portraits of inspectors killed in the line of duty.

In the centre chair a lady in black sat very stiffly, one hand clutching her handbag with its silver clasp, the other resting on the handle of an umbrella.

Thin lips. A steady gaze staring straight ahead.

She did not move a muscle on sensing that she was being watched.

She sat and waited with a set expression.

# 4

## The Second-Floor Window

She walked ahead of Maigret with that aggressive dignity of those for whom mockery is the worst calamity.

'Please sit down, madame!'

It was a clumsy friendly Maigret, with a slightly vague look in his eyes who showed her into his office, indicating a chair bathed in light streaming in through the pale oblong window. She sat down, adopting exactly the same pose as in the waiting room.

A dignified pose, naturally! A fighting posture too. Her shoulders did not touch the back of the chair. And her black-gloved hand was poised to gesticulate without letting go of the handbag, which would swing through the air.

He, on the other hand, sat in an armchair. It was tilted back, and he sprawled in a rather crude position, puffing avidly on his pipe.

'I imagine, Detective Chief Inspector, that you are wondering why I — '

'No!'

It wasn't malice that made Maigret throw her off balance like that the minute they met. It wasn't a coincidence either. He knew it was necessary.

Madame Martin jumped, or rather her chest stiffened.

'What do you mean? I don't imagine you were expecting — '

'Oh yes, I was!'

And he smiled at her good-naturedly. Suddenly, her fingers were ill at ease in her black woollen gloves. Her sharp gaze swept the room and then something occurred to Madame Martin.

'Have you received an anonymous letter?'

It was a statement as much as a question, with a false air of certainty, which made the inspector smile all the more, because this again was a characteristic trait that fitted in with everything he already knew about the woman sitting in his office.

'I've not received any anonymous letter.'

She shook her head dubiously.

'You won't have me believe — '

She was straight out of a family photo album. Physically she was a perfect match for the Registry Office official she had married.

It was easy to imagine them strolling up the Champs-Élysées on Sunday afternoons: Madame Martin's black, twitchy back, her hat always skew-whiff because of her bun, walking with the hurried pace of an active woman and that jerk of her chin to underline her emphatic words; Monsieur Martin's putty-coloured overcoat, his leather gloves and walking stick, and his peaceful, assured gait, his attempts at a leisurely promenade, stopping to gaze at the window displays.

'Did you have mourning clothes at home?' murmured Maigret snidely, exhaling a big cloud of smoke.

'My sister died three years ago . . . I mean my

sister in Blois, the one who married a police inspector. You see that — '

'That — ?'

Nothing. She was warning him. It was time to make him aware that she wasn't just anyone!

She was on edge, because the entire speech she had rehearsed was pointless, and it was the fault of this burly inspector.

'When did you hear about the death of your first husband?'

'Why . . . this morning, like everyone else! It was the concierge who told me you were handling this case and, seeing as my situation is rather awkward . . . You can't possibly understand.'

'I think I can! By the way, didn't your son visit you yesterday afternoon?'

'What are you insinuating?'

'Nothing. It's a simple question.'

'The concierge will tell you that he hasn't been to see me for at least three weeks.'

She spoke sharply. The look in her eyes more aggressive. Had Maigret perhaps been wrong not to let her make her speech?

'I'm delighted that you've come to see me, as it shows great delicacy and — '

The mere word 'delicacy' caused something in the woman's grey eyes to change, and she bowed her head by way of thanks.

'Some situations are very painful,' she said. 'Not everybody understands. Even my husband, who advised me not to wear mourning! Mind you, I'm wearing it without wearing it. No veil. No crape band. Just black clothes.'

He nodded his chin and put his pipe down on the table.

'Just because we're divorced and Raymond made me unhappy, it doesn't mean that I must — '

She was regaining her assurance and imperceptibly launching into her prepared speech.

'Especially in a large building like ours, where there are twenty-eight households. And what households! I'm not talking about the people on the first floor. And even then! Although Monsieur de Saint-Marc is well-bred, his wife's something else, she wouldn't say hello to her neighbours for all the gold in the world. When one has been properly brought up, it's distressing to — '

'Were you born in Paris?'

'My father was a confectioner in Meaux.'

'How old were you when you married Couchet?'

'I was twenty. Of course, my parents wouldn't let me serve in the shop. In those days, Couchet used to travel. He stated that he earned a very good living, that he could make a woman happy.'

Her gaze hardened as she sought reassurance that there was no threat of mockery from Maigret.

'I'd rather not tell you how much he made me suffer! All the money he earned he lost in ridiculous gambles. He claimed he was growing rich, we moved home three times a year, and by the time my son was born, we had no savings at all. It was my mother who had to pay for the layette.'

Finally she rested her umbrella against the desk. Maigret mused that she must have been speaking with the same sharp vehemence the previous evening when he'd seen her shadow against the curtain.

'When a man isn't capable of feeding a wife, he has no business getting married! That's what I say. And especially when he has no pride left. I hardly dare tell you all the jobs Couchet's had. I told him to look for a proper position, with a pension attached, in the civil service, for example. At least if anything happened to him, I wouldn't be left destitute. But no! He even ended up following the Tour de France as some sort of dogsbody. His job was to organize food for the cyclists, or something of the sort. And he came back without a *sou*! That's the man he was. And that's the life I had.'

'Where did you live?'

'In Nanterre. Because we couldn't even afford to live in the city. Did you know Couchet? He wasn't worried, oh no! He wasn't ashamed! He wasn't anxious! He said he was born to make lots of money and that's what he would do. After bicycles, it was watch chains. No! You'll never guess! Watch chains which he sold from a stall at funfairs, monsieur! And my sisters no longer dared go to the Neuilly fair for fear of coming across him selling his watch chains.'

'Were you the one who asked for a divorce?'

She modestly bowed her head, but her features remained tense.

'Monsieur Martin lived in the same apartment block as us. He was younger then. He had a good job in the civil service. Couchet left me on my own all the time while he went off gallivanting. Oh! It was all very above-board! I gave my husband a piece of my mind. The divorce was requested by mutual consent for incompatibility of temperaments. All Couchet had to give me was maintenance for the boy. And Martin and I waited a year before getting married.'

Now she was fidgeting on her chair. Her fingers plucked at the silver clasp on her bag.

'You see, I've always been unlucky. At first, Couchet didn't even pay the maintenance money regularly. And, for a sensitive woman, it's painful to see her second husband paying for the upkeep of a child who's not his.'

No, Maigret was not asleep, even though his eyes were half-closed and his pipe had gone out.

This was becoming more and more harrowing. The woman's eyes started brimming. Her lips began to tremble in a disconcerting manner.

'No one else knows what I've suffered. I put Roger through school. I wanted to give him a good education. He wasn't like his father. He was affectionate, caring . . . When he was seventeen, Martin found him a job in a bank, so he could learn the profession. But that's when he met Couchet, I don't know where.'

'And he got into the habit of asking his father for money?'

'Couchet had always refused to give me anything, mind you! For me, everything was too expensive! I made my own dresses and I wore the same hat for three years.'

'And he gave Roger everything he asked for?'

'He corrupted him! Roger left home to go and live on his own. He still comes to see me from time to time. But he also used to go and see his father.'

'How long have you lived at Place des Vosges?'

'About eight years. When we found the apartment, we didn't even know that Couchet was in serums. Martin wanted to move out. That was all I needed! If it was up to anyone to move, it should have been Couchet, shouldn't it? Couchet grown rich somehow or other. I'd see him rolling up in a chauffeur-driven car! He had a chauffeur, you know. I saw his wife.'

'At her house?'

'I watched her from the street, to see what she looked like. I'd rather not say anything. She's nothing special, in any case, despite her airs and graces and her astrakhan coat.'

Maigret drew his hand across his forehead. This was becoming obsessive. He'd been staring at the same face for fifteen minutes and right now he felt that he would never be able to get it out of his mind.

A thin face, drained of colour, with fine features, which seemed set in an expression of resigned suffering.

And that too reminded him of certain family portraits, even of his own family. As a child, he had had an aunt, plumper than Madame Martin, but who also complained all the time. When she visited his family, he knew that the moment she sat down she'd pull a handkerchief out of her bag.

'My poor Hermance!' she'd begin. 'What a life! You'll never guess what Pierre's done now.'

And she had that same mobile mask, those too-thin lips and eyes that sometimes registered a flicker of disarray.

Madame Martin suddenly lost her train of thought. She grew flustered.

'Now, you must understand my situation. Naturally, Couchet remarried. All the same, I was his wife, I shared his early life, in other words, the hardest years. Whereas she's just a doll.'

'Are you saying you have a claim on his estate?'

'Me!' she cried indignantly, 'I wouldn't touch his money with a barge pole! We're not rich. Martin lacks drive, he doesn't know how to put himself forward and he allows the grass to grow under his feet while less clever colleagues . . . but even if I had to be a cleaner to make a living, I wouldn't want — '

'Did you send your husband to tell Roger?'

She didn't blanch, because it wasn't possible. Her complexion remained uniformly ashen. But her gaze clouded.

'How do you know?'

And suddenly, indignant, 'We're not being followed, I hope? Tell me! That would be outrageous! And, if it is the case, I shall have no hesitation in taking this to the highest authority.'

'Calm down, madame . . . I didn't say any such thing. I ran into Monsieur Martin by chance this morning.'

But she was still mistrustful, staring at the

chief inspector with dislike.

'I'm going to end up wishing I hadn't come. One tries too hard to do the right thing! And, instead of being grateful — '

'I assure you I'm infinitely grateful to you for coming to see me.'

She still had the feeling that something was amiss. She felt terrified by this big man with broad shoulders and a hunched neck who was looking at her with innocent eyes as if his mind were completely vacant.

'Besides,' she said shrilly, 'it's better you hear it from me than from the concierge . . . You'd have found out one way or another — '

' . . . That you are the first Madame Couchet.'

'Have you seen Madame Couchet number two?'

Maigret struggled to repress a smile.

'Not yet.'

'Oh! She'll weep crocodile tears. Mind you, she'll be all right now, with the millions Couchet made.'

And suddenly she began to cry, her lower lip came up, transforming her face, softening its sharp angles.

'She didn't even know him when he was struggling, when he needed a wife to support and encourage him — '

From time to time, a muffled sob, barely audible, escaped from her slender throat encircled by a silk moiré ribbon.

She rose and glanced around to make sure she hadn't forgotten anything. She sniffed, 'But none of that counts.'

A bitter smile, beneath her tears.

'Well, anyhow, I've done my duty. I don't know what you think of me, but — '

'I assure you that — '

He would have been hard put to continue if she had not finished the sentence for him.

'I don't care. I've got a clear conscience! It's not everyone who can say as much.'

She was missing something but she didn't know what. She glanced round the room again and shook one hand as if surprised to find it empty.

Maigret had risen to his feet and saw her to the door.

'Thank you for coming to see me.'

'I did what I felt was my duty.'

She was in the corridor where inspectors were chatting and laughing. She swept past the group, head held high, without looking round.

And Maigret, his door closed, walked over to the window and flung it wide open, despite the cold. He felt weary, like after a tough criminal interrogation. In particular he felt that sort of vague unease one feels when forced to consider certain aspects of life one generally prefers to ignore.

It wasn't dramatic. It wasn't horrifying.

She hadn't said anything extraordinary. She hadn't given Maigret any new leads.

Even so, the conversation with her had left him with a faint feeling of disgust.

On a corner of the desk, the police gazette lay open, showing twenty or so photographs of wanted individuals. Most of them faces of thugs.

Faces that bore the scars of degeneracy.

*Ernst Strowitz, sentenced in absentia by the Caen tribunal for the murder of a farmer's wife on the Route de Bénouville . . .*

And the warning, in red:

*Dangerous. Still armed.*

A fellow who would not sell himself cheaply. Well! Maigret would have preferred that to all this syrupy greyness, to these family sagas, to this still inexplicable murder, which he found mind-boggling.

His head was full of images: he pictured the Martins out for their Sunday stroll. The putty-coloured overcoat and the black silk ribbon around the woman's neck.

He rang a bell. Jean appeared, and Maigret sent him to fetch the records of all those connected to the murder case that he had requested.

There wasn't much. Nine had been arrested once, only once, in Montmartre, in a raid, and had been released after proving that she did not make her living from prostitution.

As for the Couchet boy, he was being watched by the vice squad, which suspected him of drug trafficking. But they had never been able to pin anything on him.

A call to the vice squad. Céline, whose surname was Loiseau and who was born in Saint-Amand-Montrond, was well known to them. She had a record. They picked her up fairly frequently.

'She's not a bad girl!' said the brigadier. 'Most of the time she's content with one or two regular friends. It's only when she ends up back on the street that we find her.'

Jean had not left the room and was signalling to Maigret.

'That lady forgot her umbrella!'

'I know.'

'Oh!'

'Yes, I need it.'

And the inspector rose with a sigh, went over and shut the window, and stood with his back to the fire in his habitual thinking posture.

⋆ ⋆ ⋆

An hour later, he was able to make a mental summary of the notes he'd received from various departments and which were spread out on his desk.

First of all, the result of the autopsy confirming the pathologist's theory: the shot had been fired from around three metres away and death had been instantaneous. The dead man's stomach contained a small amount of alcohol, but no food.

The photographs from the Criminal Records Office, located under the eaves of the Palais de Justice, showed that no fingerprint matches had been found.

And lastly, the Crédit Lyonnais confirmed that at around three p.m., Couchet, who was a well-known customer, had dropped into the bank's head office and withdrawn 300,000 francs in new bills, as was customary on the penultimate day of each month.

It was pretty much established that on arriving at Place des Vosges, Couchet had placed the 300,000 in the safe, alongside the 60,000 already in there.

And since he still had work to do, he had not locked the safe again but was leaning against it.

The lights in the laboratory suggested that at some point he had left the office, either to inspect another part of the building or, more likely, to go to the toilet.

Had the money still been in the safe when he sat down at his desk again?

Probably not, for if it had been, the murderer would have had to move the body to open the heavy door and take the wads of cash.

So much for the technicalities. But was it a *thief and murderer* or a *murderer* and a *thief* operating separately?

Maigret spent ten minutes with the examining magistrate, apprising him of the progress to date. Then, since it was just after noon, he set off home, hunching his shoulders, a sign he was in a bad mood.

'Is it you who's investigating the Place des Vosges case?' asked his wife, who had read the newspaper.

'It is!'

And Maigret had a very particular way of sitting down and looking at Madame Maigret,

209

with a mixture of increased affection and a hint of anxiety.

He could still picture Madame Martin's thin face, black clothes and sorrowful eyes.

And those tears that had suddenly welled up, then disappeared, as if consumed by an inner fire, only to flow again a little later!

Madame Couchet who had furs . . . Madame Martin who didn't . . . Couchet who fed the Tour de France cyclists while his first wife had to wear the same hat for three years.

And what about the son . . . And the bottle of ether on the bedside table in Hôtel Pigalle?

And Céline, who only went on the streets periodically, when she didn't have a regular boyfriend?

And Nine?

'You don't look happy . . . You don't look well, you look as though you're coming down with a cold.'

It was true! Maigret could feel a tickle in his nostrils and his head was like cotton wool.

'What's that umbrella you've brought in? It's horrible!'

Madame Martin's umbrella! The Martins, putty-coloured overcoat and black silk dress, out for a Sunday stroll down the Champs-Élysées!

'It's nothing. I don't know what time I'll be back.'

★  ★  ★

There are impressions that cannot be explained: something felt wrong, something that emanated

210

from the façade itself.

Was it the flurry of activity in the shop that made beaded funeral wreaths? Of course, the residents must have clubbed together to buy a wreath.

Or the anxiety on the face of the ladies' hairdresser on the other side of the archway whose salon faced on to the street?

In any case, there was something unsavoury about the building that day. And, since it was four p.m. and beginning to grow dark, the feeble little lamp under the archway was already lit.

Opposite, the park keeper was locking the gates. In the Saint-Marcs' first-floor apartment, the manservant was drawing the curtains, slowly, meticulously.

When Maigret knocked at the door of the concierge's lodge, he found Madame Bourcier telling the whole story to a Dufayel credit collector in the store's navy blue livery who wore a little inkwell pendant on a chain around his neck.

'This is a respectable residence where nothing has ever happened . . . Sssh! . . . Here comes the inspector.'

She vaguely had something in common with Madame Martin, in that both women were ageless, and sexless. And both had suffered, or considered they had.

Except that the concierge seemed more resigned, displaying an almost animal acceptance of her fate.

'Jojo . . . Lili . . . Don't stand in the way . . . Good evening, Detective Chief Inspector

. . . I was expecting you this morning . . . What a business! . . . I thought it was the right thing to do to go round to all the residents to ask them to club together for a wreath. Do we know when the funeral will be? . . . Oh, by the way . . . Madame de Saint-Marc . . . you know! . . . Please don't say anything to her . . . Monsieur de Saint-Marc came by this morning . . . He doesn't want her upset, in her condition.'

In the dusky light of the courtyard, the two lamps, the one hanging in the archway and the one on the wall, threw long yellow lines.

'Madame Martin's apartment?' asked Maigret.

'Second floor, third door on the right, after the bend.'

Maigret recognized the window, where a light was on, but there was no shadow against the curtain.

A clatter of typewriters could be heard coming from the offices. A delivery man arrived.

'Doctor Rivière's Serums?'

'At the back of the courtyard. Right-hand door. Jojo! Leave your sister alone!'

Maigret started walking up the stairs, Madame Martin's umbrella under his arm. The building had been renovated up to the first floor, the walls repainted and the stairs varnished.

From the second floor, it was a different world — grubby walls and a rough floor. The apartment doors were painted an ugly brown and had either name cards tacked on to them or little spun aluminium plates.

A calling card at three francs a hundred: *Monsieur and Madame Edgar Martin*. To the

212

right, a three-colour braided bell-pull with a silk tassel. When Maigret yanked it, a reedy bell rang in the hollowness of the apartment. Then there were rapid footsteps. A voice asked, 'Who is it?'

'I've brought back your umbrella.'

The door opened. The entrance hall was reduced to one square metre with a coat stand from which the putty-coloured overcoat hung. Directly opposite, the open door of a room, part living room, part dining room, with a wireless set on a sideboard.

'Forgive me for the intrusion. This morning you left this umbrella in my office.'

'There you go! And I was convinced I'd left it on the bus. I was saying to Martin — '

Maigret did not smile. He was used to women who were in the habit of calling their husbands by their surnames.

Martin was there, in his striped trousers over which he'd slipped a chocolate-coloured, coarse-cloth smoking jacket.

'Do come in.'

'I wouldn't want to disturb you.'

'You never disturb people who have nothing to hide!'

The primordial characteristic of a home is probably its smell. Here, the smell was indistinct, a blend of caustic soda, cooking and musty old clothes.

A canary was hopping about in a cage, occasionally spraying a drop of water.

'Offer the detective chief inspector the armchair.'

*The* armchair! There was only one, a

high-backed Voltaire leather armchair so dark that it looked black.

And Madame Martin, very different from how she had been that morning, simpered, 'You'll have a drink, won't you ... Oh you must! Martin! Pour an aperitif.'

Martin was flustered. Perhaps there was nothing to drink? Perhaps they were nearly out?

'No thank you, madame. I never drink on an empty stomach.'

'But you have the time — '

It was sad. So sad that it almost made you want to give up on being a man, on living on this earth, even though the sun shines over it for several hours a day and there are real birds flying freely!

These people didn't seem very fond of light, for the three electric bulbs were carefully shrouded in heavy, coloured shades that let only the tiniest amount of light through.

'Caustic soda mainly,' thought Maigret.

That was the dominant *smell*! What's more, the surface of the solid oak table was polished as smooth as an ice rink.

Monsieur Martin wore the smile of a man entertaining.

'You must have a marvellous view over the Place des Vosges, which is the only square of its kind in Paris,' said Maigret, who was perfectly aware that the windows overlooked the court-yard.

'No! The apartments at the front, on the second floor, have very low ceilings, because of the architectural style ... All the buildings

214

around the square are classed as historical monuments, you know. We can't change anything, which is a great shame! We've been wanting to put in a bathroom for years and — '

Maigret had walked over to the window He casually tweaked the shadow-puppet blind. And stood stock still, so stunned that he forgot to make polite conversation.

Facing him were the Couchet firm's offices and laboratory.

From downstairs he had noticed that there were frosted-glass windows, but from up here, he saw that only the lower panes were frosted. The others were clear, transparent, washed two or three times a week by the cleaning women.

There was a clear view of the spot where Couchet had been killed, and of Monsieur Philippe signing the typed letters that his secretary was handing to him one at a time. He could see the lock on the safe.

And the communicating door to the laboratory stood ajar. Through the laboratory windows, a row of women in white overalls, sitting at a massive bench, could be seen packing glass tubes.

Each woman had a particular task. The first took the bare tubes from a basket and the ninth passed the neat packages with their patient information leaflets to an office worker, in other words, goods ready to be delivered to the pharmacists.

'Pour him a drink anyway,' said Madame Martin's voice behind Maigret.

And her husband busied himself opening a

cupboard with a clinking of glasses.

'Just a thimbleful of Vermouth, Detective Chief Inspector! ... No doubt Madame Couchet is able to offer you cocktails — '

And Madame Martin gave a peeved smile, as if her lips were barbs.

# 5

## The Madwoman

Glass in hand, watching Madame Martin closely, Maigret said, 'If only you'd been looking out of the window yesterday evening, my investigation would be over! Because from here it is impossible not to see everything that goes on in Couchet's office.'

His voice and manner contained no insinuations. He sipped his Vermouth and carried on chatting.

'I'd even say that this case would have been one of the most unusual instances of witnessing a criminal act. Someone who was present at a murder from a distance! What am I saying? With binoculars, you'd be able to see the lips of the speakers so clearly that you could work out what they were saying.'

Not knowing what to think, Madame Martin remained guarded, a vague smile frozen on her pale lips.

'But also, how upsetting for you! Standing at your window, minding your own business, and suddenly seeing someone threatening your ex-husband! Even worse, for the scenario must have been more complicated than that. I can picture Couchet all alone, absorbed in his accounts. He gets up and goes to the toilet. When he comes back, someone has ransacked

217

the safe but hasn't managed to get away. But there is one odd detail, which is that Couchet sat down again. True, perhaps he knew the thief? . . . He speaks to him . . . He chides him, asks him to hand back the money — '

'The only thing is, I'd have had to be at the window,' said Madame Martin.

'Perhaps other windows on this floor afford the same view? Who lives on your right?'

'Two girls and their mother . . . The ones who play records every night.'

Just then came a scream, which Maigret had heard before. He said nothing at first, then murmured, 'That's the madwoman, isn't it?'

'Sssh!' said Madame Martin tiptoeing over to the door.

She flung it open and in the dimly lit corridor the shape of a woman beating a hasty retreat could be seen.

'Old cat!' grumbled Madame Martin loudly enough to be heard by the receding figure.

Coming back into the room, furious, she explained, 'It's old Mathilde! A former cook. Did you see her? She looks like a fat toad! She lives in the room next door with her sister, who's mad. I don't know which one's the ugliest. The mad one hasn't left her room once in all the years we've had this apartment.'

'Why does she scream like that?'

'Why indeed! She screams when she's left alone in the dark. She's afraid, like a child. She screams . . . I've finally worked out what's going on. From morning till night, old Mathilde roams the corridors. You're bound to come

218

across her lurking behind a door. And when you catch her, she's not even embarrassed . . . She wanders off with her ugly, placid grin. You don't feel at home here any more, you have to talk in whispers if you want to discuss private matters. I just caught her at it, didn't I? Well, I bet she's already back.'

'It's not very pleasant,' agreed Maigret. 'But can't the landlord do anything about it?'

'He's done his best to throw them out, but unfortunately there are laws. To say nothing of the fact that it's both unhealthy and repugnant, those two old women in one tiny room! I bet they never wash.'

Maigret had grabbed his hat.

'Forgive me for having disturbed you. It's time for me to go.'

Now he had a clear picture of the apartment in his mind, from the doilies to the calendars on the walls.

'Be very quiet and you'll catch the old lady at it.'

That was not entirely the case. She wasn't in the corridor, but behind her half-open door, like a plump spider waiting to ambush her prey. She must have been disconcerted when the inspector greeted her politely as he walked past.

★　★　★

Aperitif time found Maigret sitting in the Select, not far from the American bar where all the talk was of horse-racing. When the waiter came over, he showed him the photo of Roger Couchet,

219

which he had 'borrowed' from the young man that morning.

'Do you know this young man?'

The waiter looked surprised.

'That's strange.'

'What's strange?'

'He left not even fifteen minutes ago. He was sitting at this table! I wouldn't have noticed him except that instead of telling me what he wanted to drink, he said, 'Same as yesterday!' But I didn't recall seeing him, so I said, 'Can you remind me what that was?' 'A gin-fizz, remember?', and that's the oddest part. Because I'm sure I didn't serve a single gin-fizz yesterday evening.

'He stayed for a few minutes and then he left . . . It's strange that you should come in just now and show me his photograph.'

It wasn't strange at all. Roger had been determined to establish that he had been at the Select the previous evening, as he had told Maigret. He had used quite a clever trick but his mistake had been to choose a drink that was out of the ordinary.

A few minutes later, Nine came in, looking downcast, and sat at the table closest to the bar. Then, spotting Maigret, she rose, dithered, and came over to him.

'Did you want to talk to me?' she asked.

'Not especially. Actually yes! I'd like to ask you a question. You come here almost every evening, don't you?'

'Raymond always asked me to meet him here.'

'Do you have a regular table?'

'Over there, where I sat when I came in.'

'Were you there yesterday?'

'Yes, why?'

'And do you remember seeing the original of this portrait?'

She looked at the photo of Roger and murmured, 'But that's my next-door neighbour!'

'Yes, he's Couchet's son.'

Troubled by this coincidence, her eyes opened wide as she wondered what it meant.

'He came over shortly after you left this morning. I'd just got back from the Moulin Bleu.'

'What did he want?'

'He asked me if I had an aspirin for Céline, who was ill.'

'And did they hire you at the theatre?'

'I have to go there this evening. One of the dancers is injured. If she's not better, I'll stand in for her and perhaps they'll give me a permanent job.'

She lowered her voice and went on, 'I have the hundred francs. Give me your hand.'

And that gesture revealed her entire character. She didn't want to give Maigret the money in public. She was afraid of embarrassing him! So she had the note folded into a tiny oblong in the palm of her hand. She passed it to him as if he were a gigolo.

'Thank you, you were so kind.'

She sounded despondent. She looked about her without taking the slightest interest in the pantomime of people coming and going. She gave a wan smile and said, 'The head waiter's looking at us. He's wondering why I'm with you. He must think I've already replaced Raymond . . . This must be awkward for you!'

'Would you like a drink?'

'No, thank you,' she said discreetly. 'If ever you need me . . . At the Moulin Bleu, my stage name is Élyane . . . Do you know where the stage door is, in Rue Fontaine?'

★   ★   ★

It wasn't too difficult. Maigret rang the bell of the apartment on Boulevard Haussmann a few minutes before dinner time. The moment he stepped inside there was an overpowering smell of chrysanthemums. The maid who opened the door walked on tiptoe.

She thought the inspector simply wanted to leave his card and wordlessly she showed him to the room where the body was laid out, draped in black. By the door were numerous calling cards on a Louis XVI tray.

The body was already in its casket, which was invisible under all the flowers.

In a corner, a tall, very distinguished young man in mourning nodded briefly at Maigret.

Opposite him kneeled a woman in her fifties, with coarse features, dressed like a country-woman in her Sunday best.

The inspector went up to the young man.

'May I see Madame Couchet?'

'I'll ask my sister if she can see you. You are Monsieur — ?'

'Maigret! The detective chief inspector in

charge of the investigation.'

The countrywoman stayed where she was. A few moments later, the young man returned and steered his guest through the apartment.

Apart from the all-pervasive scent of flowers, the rooms retained their usual look. It was a magnificent late nineteenth-century apartment, like most of the buildings on Boulevard Haussmann. Vast rooms. Slightly over-ornate ceilings and doors.

And classy period furniture. In the drawing room, a monumental crystal chandelier tinkled when people walked underneath it.

Madame Couchet sat flanked by three people, whom she introduced. First of all, the young man in mourning:

'My brother, Henry Dormoy, barrister.'

Then a gentleman of a certain age:

'Colonel Dormoy, my uncle.'

And lastly, a lady with magnificent silver hair:

'My mother.'

And all of them, in mourning, looked extremely distinguished. The table had not yet been cleared of the tea things and there was toast and cakes.

'Please sit down.'

'One question, if I may. The lady who is sitting with the body — '

'My husband's sister,' replied Madame Couchet. 'She arrived this morning from Saint-Amand.'

Maigret did not smile, but he understood. He clearly sensed that they were not overly keen to see the Couchet family turn up, dressed like

223

bumpkins or got up like petty bourgeois.

There were the relatives on the husband's side and the relatives on the Dormoy side.

The Dormoys were elegant, discreet. For a start, everyone was wearing black.

From the Couchets, for the moment there was only this countrywoman, whose black silk blouse was straining under the arms.

'May I have a few words with you in private, madame?'

She apologized to her family, who made to leave the drawing room.

'Please stay, we'll go into the yellow boudoir.'

She had been crying, there was no doubt. Then she had powdered her face and her puffy eyelids barely showed. There was a note of genuine weariness in her voice.

'You haven't received any unexpected visits today, have you?'

She looked up, vexed.

'How do you know? Yes, early this afternoon, my stepson came.'

'Had you met him before?'

'Very briefly. He used to go and see my husband at his office. But we ran into him at the theatre on one occasion and Raymond introduced us.'

'What was the purpose of his visit?'

Embarrassed, she looked away.

'He wanted to know if we'd found a will. He also asked me the name of my lawyer so he could contact him concerning the formalities.'

She sighed by way of an apology for all this unpleasantness.

'He's entitled to. I think that half the inheritance goes to him, and I don't intend to stand in his way.'

'May I ask a few personal questions? When you married Couchet, was he already wealthy?'

'Yes. Not as wealthy as he is today, but his business was beginning to flourish.'

'A love marriage?'

An enigmatic smile.

'You could say so. We met in Dinard. After three weeks, he asked me if I'd consent to be his wife. My parents made inquiries.'

'Were you happy?'

He looked her in the eyes and needed no reply. He murmured the answer himself, 'There was a certain age gap. Couchet had his business. In other words, there was not a great deal of intimacy. Is that so? You ran his household. You had your life and he had his — '

'I never criticized him!' she said. 'He was a man with a great appetite for life, who needed excitement. I didn't want to hold him back.'

'Weren't you jealous?'

'At first. Then I got used to it. I believe he loved me.'

She was quite attractive, but with no spark, no spirit.

Rather nondescript features. A soft body A sober elegance. She probably made a gracious hostess, serving her friends tea in the warm, comfortable drawing room.

'Did your husband often talk to you about his first wife?'

Then her pupils contracted. She tried to hide

225

her anger, but realized that Maigret was no fool.

'It's not for to me to — ' she began.

'My apologies. Given the circumstances of his death, I'm afraid I have to be direct.'

'You don't suspect — ?'

'I suspect nobody. I'm trying to piece together your husband's life, and the lives of those around him, his movements and actions during his last evening. Did you know that his ex-wife lived in the building where Couchet had his offices?'

'Yes! He told me.'

'In what terms did he talk about her?'

'He resented her . . . Then he was ashamed of his feelings and claimed that in reality she was a sad creature.'

'Why sad?'

'Because nothing could satisfy her . . . and also — '

'And also?'

'You can guess what I mean. She's very grasping. In short, she left Raymond because he didn't earn enough money. So when she found out that he was rich . . . after she'd ended up the wife of a petty bureaucrat!'

'She didn't try to — '

'No! I don't think she ever asked him for money. It's true that my husband wouldn't have told me if she had. All I know is that for him every time he bumped into her at Place des Vosges it was awkward. I think she deliberately waylaid him. She never spoke to him, but she gave him malicious looks.'

Maigret couldn't help smiling at the thought of those encounters, under the archway: Couchet getting out of the car, fresh and pink, and Madame Martin, starchy, with her black gloves, her umbrella and her handbag, her spiteful face . . .

'Is that all you know?'

'He was looking for new premises, but it's difficult to find laboratories in Paris.'

'I presume you are not aware of your husband having any enemies?'

'None! Everyone loved him. He was too kind. Kind to the point of making a fool of himself. He didn't just spend money, he threw it away. And when criticized, he'd reply that he'd spent enough years counting every *sou*, now he could afford to be generous.'

'Did he often see your family?'

'Very little! They have nothing in common, do they? And different tastes — '

Maigret found it hard to imagine Couchet in the drawing room with the young lawyer, the colonel and the stately mother.

All this made sense.

A strong, fiery, coarse young man who had started out with nothing and who had spent thirty years of his life struggling to make his fortune.

He had grown rich. In Dinard, at last he had access to a world that had hitherto been closed to him. A real young lady, a bourgeois family, tea and *petits fours*, tennis and outings to the country.

He had got married. To prove to himself that now, the world was his! To have a home like those he had only ever seen from the outside!

He had got married, too, because he was in awe of this nice, well-brought-up young lady.

And then it was the apartment on Boulevard Haussmann, with the most traditional trappings.

Except he needed outside stimulation, to see other people, talk to them without having to mind his 'P's and 'Q's ... go to brasseries, bars ...

And other women.

He loved his wife. He admired her. He respected her. He was in awe of her.

But precisely because he was in awe of her, he needed girls like Nine to relax with.

Madame Couchet had a question on the tip of her tongue. She was reluctant to ask it. Then she took the plunge, averting her gaze.

'I wanted to ask you if ... It's a delicate matter ... I'm sorry ... He had girlfriends, I know ... He only kept it quiet — and barely — out of consideration. I need to know whether, on that front, there'll be any problems, a scandal — '

She obviously imagined her husband's mistresses to be like prostitutes in a novel, or screen vamps!

'You have nothing to be afraid of!' smiled Maigret, who was thinking of little Nine with her distraught face and the handful of jewellery she had taken that same afternoon to the Crédit Municipal.

'There won't be any need to — ?'

'No! No allowance.'

She was astonished. Perhaps a little put out, because if these women were making no

228

demands, it must be because they were fond of her husband! And he of them.

'Have you decided on the date of the funeral?'

'My brother is dealing with it. It will take place on Thursday at Saint-Philippe-du-Roule.'

A clatter of plates came from the dining room next door. Was the table being laid for dinner?

'All that remains is for me to thank you and take my leave. I apologize again.'

And, walking down the Boulevard Haussmann, he caught himself muttering as he filled his pipe, 'Good old Couchet!'

The words escaped his lips as if Couchet had been an old friend. And the feeling was so strong that the thought that he had only seen him dead astounded him.

He felt as if he knew him literally inside out.

Perhaps because of the three women?

First, there'd been the confectioner's daughter, in the apartment in Nanterre, despairing at the thought that her husband would never have a proper job.

Then the young lady from Dinard, and Couchet's pride and satisfaction at becoming the nephew of a colonel.

Nine . . . Their dinners at the Select . . . Hôtel Pigalle . . .

And the son who came to sponge off him! And Madame Martin who contrived to run into him under the archway, hoping perhaps to plague him with remorse.

A strange ending! All alone, in the office where he came as seldom as possible. Leaning against the half-open safe, his hands on the table.

Nobody had noticed or heard anything. The concierge, crossing the courtyard, had seen him sitting in the same place as usual behind the frosted glass, but she was mainly concerned about Madame de Saint-Marc, who was giving birth.

The madwoman upstairs had screamed! In other words, old Mathilde, padding around in felt slippers, had been concealed behind a door on the landing.

Monsieur Martin, in his putty-coloured overcoat, had come downstairs to hunt for his glove by the dustbins.

One thing was certain: right now, someone had the stolen 360,000 francs in their possession!

And someone had committed a murder!

'All men are self-centred!' Madame Martin had said bitterly, with her pained expression.

Was she the one who had the 360 brand new thousand-franc notes handed over by the Crédit Lyonnais? Did she now have money, a lot of money, a whole wad of fat notes promising years of comfort with no worries about the future or about the pension she would receive on Martin's death?

Was it Roger, with his puny body, ravaged by ether, and that Céline he'd picked up to moulder away with him in the dampness of a hotel bed?

Was it Nine, or Madame Couchet?

In any case, there was one place from which the whole thing could have been witnessed: the Martins' apartment.

And there was a woman prowling around the

building, loitering in the corridors, listening at every keyhole.

'I'd better pay old Mathilde a visit!' thought Maigret.

But when he arrived at Place des Vosges the next morning, the concierge, who was sorting the post (a big pile for the Couchet laboratory and only a handful of letters for the other residents), intercepted him.

Are you on your way up to the Martins'? I'm not sure that's a good idea. Madame Martin was taken very ill last night. We had to call the doctor out urgently. Her husband is out of his mind.'

The laboratory staff were crossing the courtyard on their way to the offices and the lab. At a first-floor window, a manservant was shaking rugs.

A baby could be heard wailing and a nanny was crooning monotonously.

# 6

## A Raging Fever

'Sssh! . . . She's asleep . . . Come in anyway.'

Monsieur Martin stood aside, resigned. Resigned to showing his home in a state of disorder. Resigned to showing himself ungroomed, his moustache drooping, a greenish colour, which betrayed the fact that it was dyed.

He had sat up with his wife all night. He was worn out, listless.

He tiptoed over to close the door that communicated with the bedroom, through which Maigret glimpsed the foot of the bed and a bowl on the floor.

'The concierge told you?'

He whispered, glancing anxiously at the door. As he spoke, he turned off the gas ring on which he had been making coffee.

'Some coffee?'

'No thank you. I shan't disturb you for long. I wanted to inquire after Madame Martin.'

'You're too kind!' said Martin emphatically.

He really did not suspect any ulterior motive. He was so distraught that he must have lost his critical faculties, although it was not certain he had ever possessed any.

'It's terrible, these attacks she has! Would you excuse me for drinking my coffee in front of you?'

He grew flustered on noticing that his braces were flapping against his calves. He hastily adjusted his clothes and removed the bottles of medicine that were sitting on the table.

'Does Madame Martin often suffer these attacks?'

'No. And especially not as violent as this. She's very highly strung. When she was a girl, apparently she had nervous fits every week.'

'And still does?'

Martin gave him a hangdog look, barely daring to admit, 'I have to make allowances for her. One little disagreement and she's seething!'

With his putty-coloured overcoat, carefully waxed moustache and leather gloves, he had been ridiculous. A caricature of the pretentious petty official.

But now the dye had faded from his moustache, the look in his eyes was that of a defeated man. He hadn't had the time to shave, and was still wearing his nightshirt under an old jacket.

And he cut a pathetic figure. He was, astonishingly, at least fifty-five.

'Did something upset her last night?'

'No . . . No — '

He became agitated, looking about him, panic-stricken.

'No one came to see her? Her son, for example?'

'No! You came, then we had dinner. And then — '

'What?'

'Nothing. I don't know . . . It just came over

233

her . . . She's very sensitive. She's had so much unhappiness in her life!'

Did he really believe what he was saying? Maigret sensed that Martin was trying to convince himself.

'In short, you personally have no ideas about the murder?'

And Martin dropped the cup he was holding. Was he of a nervous disposition too?

'Why would I have any ideas? I swear . . . If I did, I . . . '

'You — '

'I don't know. It's a terrible business! Just when we're inundated at the office. I haven't even had the time to inform my boss this morning.'

He wiped his thin hand across his forehead then busied himself picking up the pieces of broken china. He spent ages looking for a cloth to clean the wooden floor.

'If only she'd listened to me, we wouldn't have stayed here.'

He was afraid, that was patent. He was beside himself with fear. But fear of what, fear of whom?

'You're a good man, aren't you, Monsieur Martin? And an honest man.'

'I have thirty-two years' service and — '

'So if you knew something that could help the police unmask the culprit, you would feel duty-bound to tell me.'

Were his teeth chattering?

'I would most definitely do so . . . but I don't know anything . . . and I too would like to know!

This is no life . . . '

'What do you think of your stepson?'

Martin stared at Maigret in amazement.

'Roger? He's . . . '

'He's depraved, I know!'

'But he's not a bad boy, I swear. It's all his father's fault. As my wife always says, you shouldn't give young people so much money. She's right! And as she says I don't think Couchet did it out of generosity or fatherly love, he had no interest in his son. He did it to get rid of him, to salve his conscience.'

'His conscience?'

Martin turned red, and became even more flummoxed.

'He treated Juliette badly, didn't he?' he said quietly.

'Juliette?'

'My wife, his first wife. What did he ever do for her? Nothing! He treated her like a skivvy. And she was the one who helped him through the hard times, and later — '

'He didn't give her anything, obviously. But she had remarried.'

Martin's face had turned beetroot. Maigret watched him with amazement, and pity. For he realized that the poor man was in no way to blame for this staggering story. He was merely repeating what he must have heard hundreds of times from his wife.

Couchet was rich! She was poor! And so . . .

But the civil servant was straining to listen.

'Did you not hear something?'

They kept quiet for a moment. A faint cry was

heard coming from the bedroom. Martin went over and opened the door.

'What are you telling him?' asked Madame Martin.

'But . . . I — '

'It's Inspector Maigret, isn't it? . . . What does he want now?'

Maigret couldn't see her. The voice was that of someone lying in bed, very weary but who still has all her wits about her.

'The detective chief inspector came to inquire after you.'

'Tell him to come in. Wait! Pass me a wet towel and the mirror. And the comb.'

'You'll get yourself all upset again.'

'Hold the mirror straight, will you! No! Put it down . . . You're hopeless . . . Take away that bowl. Honestly, men! As soon as their wife's not there, the place looks like a pigsty. You can show him in now.'

Like the dining room, the bedroom was drab and cheerless, furnished in poor taste with a profusion of old curtains, old fabrics and faded rugs. The minute he stepped inside, Maigret felt Madame Martin's eyes boring into him. Her gaze was calm and extraordinarily clear.

Her drawn face broke into an invalid's syrupy smile.

'The place is a terrible mess! Please don't take any notice,' she said. 'It's because I was taken ill.'

And she stared mournfully in front of her.

'But I'm feeling better. I must be back on my feet tomorrow, for the funeral. It is tomorrow, isn't it?'

'Yes, it's tomorrow! You're prone to these attacks — '

'I had them even as a child, but my sister — '

'The sister who — ?'

'I had two sisters. Now don't you go believing what's not . . . The youngest suffered fits too. She got married. Her husband turned out to be a good-for-nothing and one fine day, when she was having an attack, he had her put away She died a week later.'

'Don't get upset!' implored Martin, who didn't know where to put himself or where to look.

'Insane?' asked Maigret.

The woman's features hardened again and there was malice in her voice.

'In other words, her husband wanted to get rid of her! Not even six months later, he married someone else. Men are all the same . . . You devote yourself, you kill yourself for them — '

'I beg you!' sighed her husband.

'I don't mean you! Although you're no better than the others.'

And Maigret suddenly sensed a whiff of hatred in the air. It was fleeting, hazy, but he was convinced he was not mistaken.

'All the same, if it weren't for me — ' she went on.

Did her voice contain a threat? Her husband busied himself doing nothing. To keep up appearances, he counted out drops of a potion into a glass, one by one.

'The doctor said — '

'I don't give a fig for what the doctor said!'

'But you must . . . Here! Drink it slowly. It's not so bad.'

She looked at him, then she looked at Maigret, and finally she gave a resigned shrug and drank.

'You haven't really come to inquire after my health,' she stated suspiciously.

'I was on my way to the laboratory when the concierge told me — '

'Have you found any clues?'

'Not yet.'

She closed her eyes, to indicate fatigue. Martin looked at Maigret, who rose.

'Well, I wish you a speedy recovery. You're already much better.'

She let him leave. Maigret stopped Martin from seeing him out.

'Please, stay with your wife.'

Poor fellow! He seemed afraid to stay; it was as if he were clinging to Maigret because when there was another person there, things were not so dreadful.

'You'll see, it will turn out to be nothing serious.'

As he walked through the dining room, he heard a rustle in the corridor. And he caught up with old Mathilde just as she was about to go back into her room.

'Good morning.'

She looked at him fearfully, without replying, her hand poised on the door knob.

Maigret spoke quietly. He guessed that Madame Martin was listening; she was perfectly capable of getting out of bed to eavesdrop.

'As you probably know, I'm the detective chief

238

inspector in charge of the investigation.'

He already sensed that he would get nothing out of the woman with her placid, moonlike face.

'What do you want from me?'

'Only to ask you if you have anything to tell me. How long have you been living here?'

'Forty years!' she replied curtly.

'You know everyone.'

'I don't talk to anyone!'

'I thought perhaps that you might have seen or heard something. Sometimes a tiny clue helps set the police on the right track.'

Someone was moving around inside the room. But the old woman kept the door determinedly shut.

'You saw nothing?'

She did not reply.

'And you heard nothing?'

'You'd do better to tell the landlord to put the gas in.'

'The gas?'

'Everyone else here has gas. But because he's not allowed to put my rent up, he refuses to install it in my room. He wants to boot me out! He's doing everything he can to force me out, but he'll be leaving before me, feet first! And you can tell him that from me.'

The door opened a tiny crack, so tiny that it seemed impossible that the fat woman could squeeze through. Then she closed it behind her and only muffled sounds came from inside the room.

\* \* \*

'May I have your card?'

Maigret proffered his visiting card, and the butler in a striped waistcoat took it before disappearing inside the apartment, which was extraordinarily light, thanks to its five-metre-high windows. Such windows have become rare and are only found in the buildings on Place des Vosges and the Ile Saint-Louis.

The rooms were vast. From somewhere the hum of an electric vacuum cleaner could be heard. A nanny in a white uniform with a pretty blue headdress was going from one room to another. She shot the visitor an inquisitive glance.

A voice, close at hand.

'Show the detective chief inspector in.'

Monsieur de Saint-Marc was in his study, in his dressing gown, his silvery hair carefully smoothed. First he went over and closed a door, through which Maigret had the time to glimpse an antique bed, the face of a young woman on the pillow.

'Please take a seat. Naturally you want to speak to me about this terrible Couchet business.'

Despite his age, he gave an impression of health and vigour. And the atmosphere in the apartment was that of a happy home, where everything was full of light and joy.

'I was particularly saddened by this tragedy, which took place at a time of great emotion for me.'

'I am aware of that.'

There was a little glint of satisfaction in the

eyes of the former ambassador. He was proud of having a child at his age.

'May I ask you to keep your voice down, as I'd rather keep this business from Madame de Saint-Marc. In her condition, it would be unfortunate . . . But what was it you wanted to ask me? I barely knew this Couchet. I'd caught a glimpse of him crossing the courtyard a couple of times. He belonged to one of the clubs I go to occasionally, the Haussmann, but he must rarely have set foot in the place. I just noticed his name in the latest directory. I believe he was quite vulgar, wasn't he?'

'In other words, he was working-class. He had struggled to become successful.'

'My wife told me he had married a woman from a very good family, a former school friend of hers. That's one of the reasons why it's better not to tell her . . . so, you wanted to ask me . . . ?'

The vast windows afforded a view of the entire Place des Vosges bathed in soft sunshine. In the square, gardeners were watering the lawns and flower beds. Drays plodded heavily past.

'Just a simple question. I know that you were on edge while your wife was in labour, which is only natural, and that several times you came down and paced up and down the courtyard. Did you meet anyone? Did you not see someone heading towards the offices at the back?'

Monsieur de Saint-Marc thought for a moment, fiddling with a paper knife.

'Wait . . . No! I don't think so. Don't forget, I had other things on my mind. The concierge

241

would be in a better position to — '

'The concierge doesn't know anything — '

'And I . . . No! . . . Or rather . . . But it can't have anything to do with — '

'Tell me anyway.'

'At one point, I heard a noise by the dustbins. I was at a loose end, so I went over and I saw one of the residents from the second floor — '

'Madame Martin?'

'I believe that's her name. I confess, I don't know my neighbours very well. She was rummaging in one of the zinc bins . . . I remember her saying, '*One of our silver spoons must have fallen into the rubbish bin.*' I asked, '*Have you found it?*' And she said, quite excitedly, '*Yes! Yes!*''

'Then what did she do?' asked Maigret.

'She hurried back up to her apartment. She's a jittery little woman who always seems to be running . . . If I recall, we lost a valuable ring in the same manner . . . and the astonishing thing is that it was returned to the concierge by a rag-picker who'd found it when he was rummaging with his hook.'

'You couldn't tell me roughly what time this incident occurred?'

'That would be difficult . . . Wait . . . I didn't want any dinner . . . But at around eight-thirty, Albert, my butler, urged me to have something and, since I refused to come to the table, he brought me some anchovy tarts in the drawing room. That was before — '

'Before eight-thirty?'

'Yes. Let us say that the incident, as you call it,

242

took place just after eight o'clock, but I don't think it is of any significance whatsoever. What is your opinion about this business? There's a rumour going around, apparently, that the murder was committed by someone who lives here, but personally I refuse to believe it. When you think that anyone can just walk into the courtyard. By the way I'm going to write to the landlord to request that the main door be locked at dusk.'

Maigret had risen.

'I haven't yet formed an opinion,' he said.

The concierge brought up the post and, since the door had remained open, she suddenly caught sight of the inspector conversing with Monsieur de Saint-Marc.

Poor Madame Bourcier! She was all flustered! Her expression betrayed a world of anxieties.

Would Maigret be so bold as to suspect the Saint-Marcs? Or even simply to bother them with his questions?

'Thank you, monsieur . . . and please forgive my intrusion — '

'A cigar?'

Monsieur de Saint-Marc had the airs of a gentleman, with a tiny hint of condescending familiarity more suggestive of the politician than the diplomat.

'I am entirely at your service.'

The butler closed the door behind him. Maigret made his way slowly down the stairs and found himself in the courtyard where the delivery man from a department store was trying to find the concierge.

In the lodge, there was only a dog, a cat and the two children busy smearing milk soup all over their faces.

'Isn't your mother here?'

'She'll be back, m'sieur! She's taking the post up.'

In the ignominious corner of the courtyard, near the lodge, there were four zinc bins into which, at night, the residents came one by one to throw their household waste.

At six a.m., the concierge unlocked the main door and the municipal rubbish collectors emptied the bins into their cart.

At night, that corner was not lit up. The only light in the courtyard was on the other side, at the foot of the stairs.

What had Madame Martin come down to look for, more or less at the time when Couchet was killed?

Had she taken it into her head to look for her husband's glove?

'No!' grunted Maigret struck by a memory. Martin had only brought the rubbish down much later.

So what had she been up to? There couldn't have been a lost spoon! During the daytime, the residents are not allowed to throw anything into the dustbins.

So what were the pair of them looking for, one after the other?

Madame Martin had been rummaging in the bin itself.

Martin, on the other hand, had been looking in the area around the bins, striking matches.

And by the next morning, the glove had been found!

'Did you see the baby?' asked a voice behind Maigret.

It was the concierge, who was talking about the Saint-Marcs' child with more emotion than about her own.

'You didn't say anything to Madame, I hope? She mustn't be told — '

'I know! I know!'

'For the wreath . . . I mean the residents' wreath . . . I'm wondering whether we should have it delivered to the undertakers today or whether it's the custom only to send it to the funeral . . . The staff were very generous too, they've collected over three hundred francs.'

And, turning to the delivery man, 'What is it?'

'Saint-Marc!'

'Right-hand staircase. First floor facing. And knock gently!'

Then, to Maigret, 'You should see how many flowers she's received! So many they don't know where to put them all. Most of them have had to be taken up to the servants' rooms. Won't you come in? Jojo! Leave your sister alone!'

The inspector was still staring at the dustbins. What on earth could the Martins have been looking for in them?

'This morning, did you put the bins out as usual?'

'No! Since I've been widowed, it's impossible! Or I'd have to take someone on, because they're much too heavy for me . . . the bin men are very kind, I give them a glass of wine from time to

245

time and they come into the courtyard to collect them.'

'So the rag-pickers can't rummage through them!'

'Do you think so? They come into the courtyard too. Sometimes there are three or four of them, and they make an unholy mess.'

'Thank you for your help.'

And Maigret left, pondering, either forgetting or not considering it worth his while to visit the Couchet offices again as he had planned to do earlier in the day.

When he arrived at Quai des Orfèvres, he was told, 'Someone was asking for you on the telephone. A colonel.'

But he decided to pursue his hunch. Opening the door of the inspectors' office, he called out, 'Lucas! I want you to get on to this straight away. Question all the rag-pickers who operate around the Place des Vosges. If necessary, go as far as the Saint-Denis plant, where the rubbish is incinerated.'

'But — '

'We need to know if they noticed anything unusual in the dustbins of 61, Place des Vosges, the morning before yesterday.'

He slumped in his armchair and a word came back into his mind: colonel.

What colonel? He didn't know any colonels.

Oh yes he did! There was one colonel in this case! Madame Couchet's uncle! What on earth did he want?

'Hello! Élysée 1762? This is Detective Chief Inspector Maigret from police headquarters

246

. . . Excuse me? . . . Colonel Dormoy wants to speak to me. I'll hold the line, yes. Hello! Is that you, Colonel? . . . How? . . . A will? . . . I can't hear you very well. No, on the contrary, lower your voice! Hold the receiver a little further away. That's better. So? You have found a will that no one knew about? And not even stamped? Understood! I'll be with you in half an hour. No! There's no point my taking a taxi.'

And he lit his pipe, pushed back his armchair and crossed his legs.

# 7

## The Three Women

'The colonel is waiting for you in Monsieur's bedroom. Please follow me.'

The room where the body had been laid out was closed. There was someone moving around next door, which must have been Madame Couchet's bedroom. The maid opened a door and Maigret glimpsed the colonel standing by the table, his hand resting lightly on it, his chin high, dignified and calm as if he were posing for a sculptor.

'Please sit down!'

Maigret ignored his invitation to sit and simply unbuttoned his heavy overcoat, placed his bowler hat on a chair and filled his pipe.

'Did you find the will yourself?' he then asked, looking about him with curiosity

'Indeed I did, earlier today My niece doesn't know about it yet. I have to say that it is so shocking — '

A strange bedroom, typical of Couchet! True, the furniture was period, like the rest of the apartment. There were a few items of value, but mixed in with them were things that revealed the man's vulgar tastes.

In front of the window was a table that pretty much served as his desk. On it were Turkish cigarettes and also a whole set of cheap, cherry-wood pipes which Couchet must have seasoned lovingly.

A purple dressing gown! The gaudiest he could have found! Then, at the foot of the bed, slippers with holes in their soles.

The table had a drawer.

'Note that it wasn't locked!' said the colonel. 'I don't even know if there is a key. This morning, my niece needed cash to pay a supplier and I wanted to save her the trouble of writing a cheque. I searched this room, and this is what I came across.'

An envelope with the Grand-Hôtel crest. Pale blue note-paper with the same letterhead.

Then a few lines that appeared to have been written distractedly, like a rough draft.

*This is my last will and testament . . .*

And further down, these surprising words:

*Since I shall probably not get around to finding out about inheritance law, I instruct my lawyer, Maître Dampierre, to do his utmost to ensure that my fortune is shared as equally as possible between:*

*1 My wife Germaine, née Dormoy;*

*2 My first wife, now Madame Martin, residing at 61, Place des Vosges;*

*3 Nine Moinard, residing at Hôtel Pigalle, Rue Pigalle.*

'What do you make of that?'

Maigret was jubilant. This will endeared Couchet to him even further.

'Naturally,' continued the colonel, 'this will does not hold water. There are numerous reasons why it would be deemed null and void and, immediately after the funeral, wc intend to contest it. But the reason I felt it was useful and urgent to discuss it with you is that — '

Maigret was still smiling, as if he had witnessed a good prank. Even the Grand-Hôtel letterhead! Like many businessmen, Couchet probably held some of his meetings there. So, while waiting for someone, probably, in the lobby or the smoking room, he had picked up a blotter and scribbled those few lines.

He hadn't sealed the envelope! He'd stuffed the whole thing in his drawer, postponing the business of having a proper will drawn up.

That had been two weeks ago.

'You must have been struck by one outrageous detail,' the colonel was saying. 'Couchet simply doesn't mention his son! That alone is enough to render the will null and void and — '

'Do you know Roger?'

'Me? . . . No.'

And Maigret was still smiling.

'I was saying earlier that if I asked you to come here, it was because — '

'Do you know Nine Moinard?'

The poor man jumped as if someone had stepped on his toe.

'I don't need to know her. Her address alone, Rue Pigalle, gives me an idea of . . . Now what was I saying? . . . Oh yes! Did you notice the date on the will? It is recent! Couchet died two weeks after writing it. He was murdered! Now imagine that one of the two women concerned was aware of these provisions . . . I have every reason to believe that neither of them is rich.'

'Why two women?'

'What do you mean?'

'Three women! The will names three women! Couchet's three women, if you like!'

The colonel assumed that Maigret was joking.

'I was being serious,' he said. 'Don't forget that there is a dead man in the house. And that this affects the future of several people.'

Of course. All the same, Maigret felt like laughing. He himself couldn't have said why.

'Thank you for letting me know.'

The colonel was vexed. He could not understand this attitude on the part of a police inspector of Maigret's senior rank.

'I suppose — '

'Goodbye, Colonel. Kindly pay my respects to Madame Couchet.'

In the street, he couldn't help muttering, 'Good old Couchet!'

Coldly, just like that, in complete seriousness, he had put his three women in his will! Including his first wife, now Madame Martin, who was constantly appearing in front of him with her contemptuous gaze, like a living reproof! Including courageous little Nine, who did everything she could to entertain him.

On the other hand, he had forgotten that he had a son!

For a good few minutes, Maigret wondered whom to tell first. Madame Martin, who would probably leap out of her bed at the news of a fortune? Or Nine?

'But they haven't got their hands on the cash yet.'

This business could go on for years! The family would contest the will. Madame Martin, in any case, wouldn't allow them to push her around.

'Even so, the colonel has been honest. He could have burned the will and no one would ever have known.'

And a light-hearted Maigret crossed the Europe district on foot. A wan sun gave out a little warmth and there was joy in the air.

'Good old Couchet!'

He entered the lift of Hôtel Pigalle without announcing himself and a few moments later he was knocking at Nine's door. He heard footsteps inside the room. The door opened a fraction, just enough for a hand to poke through. The hand remained dangling in the air.

A woman's hand, already wrinkled. Since Maigret didn't respond, the hand grew impatient and the face of an elderly Englishwoman appeared. She launched into an unintelligible tirade.

Or rather, Maigret guessed that the English-woman was expecting her post, which explained the outstretched hand. What was clear was that Nine no longer occupied her room and that she probably didn't live in the hotel any more.

'Too expensive for her,' he thought.

And he paused uncertainly outside the neighbouring door. A valet decided him, asking him suspiciously, 'Can I help you?'

'Monsieur Couchet — '

'Is he not answering?'

'I haven't knocked yet.'

And Maigret was still smiling. He was in a buoyant mood. That morning, he suddenly felt as if he were playing a part in a farce. Life itself was a farce! Couchet's death was a farce, especially his will!

' . . . C'min!'

The bolt slid back. The first thing Maigret did was to march over and draw the curtains and open the window.

Céline had not even woken up. Roger rubbed his eyes and yawned, 'Oh! It's you.'

There was an improvement: the room didn't reek of ether. The clothes were in a heap on the floor.

' . . . What d'you want?'

Roger sat up in bed, picked up the glass of water from his bedside table and drained it in one go.

'The will has been found!' announced Maigret covering up a naked thigh belonging to Céline, who was lying curled up.

'So what?'

Roger showed no excitement. Barely a vague curiosity.

'So what? It's a strange will! It will certainly cause much ink to flow and earn the lawyers a lot of money. Can you imagine, your father has left his entire fortune to his three women!'

The young man struggled to understand.

'His three . . . ?'

'Yes! His current lawful wife. Then your mother! And lastly his girlfriend Nine, who was living in the room next door till yesterday! He has instructed the lawyer to ensure they each receive an equal share.'

Roger didn't bat an eyelid. He appeared to be thinking. But not to be thinking about something that concerned him personally.

'That's priceless!' he said at length in a serious tone that belied his words.

'That's exactly what I said to the colonel.'

'What colonel?'

'An uncle of Madame Couchet's. He's playing the head of the family.'

'I bet he's not happy!'

'Too right!'

The young man thrust his legs out of the bed and grabbed a pair of trousers draped over the back of a chair.

'You don't seem particularly bothered by this news.'

'Oh me, you know . . . '

He buttoned up his trousers, looked for a comb and closed the window, which was letting in the cold air.

'Don't you need money?'

Maigret was suddenly solemn. His gaze became probing, questioning.

'I don't know.'

'You don't know whether you need money?'

Roger darted Maigret a shifty look and Maigret felt ill at ease.

'I don't give a — !'

'It's not as if you are earning a good living.'

'I don't earn a bean!'

He yawned and looked mournfully at his reflection in the mirror. Maigret noticed that Céline had woken up. She didn't move. She must have overheard some of the conversation, for she was watching the two men with curiosity.

She too needed the glass of water! And the atmosphere in that untidy room, with its stale smell, those two listless beings, was the quintessence of a dispirited world.

'Do you have any savings?'

Roger was beginning to tire of this conversation. He looked around for his jacket, took out a slim wallet embossed with his initials and threw it to Maigret.

'Have a look!'

Two 100-franc notes, a few smaller ones, a driving licence and an old cloakroom ticket.

'What do you intend to do if you are deprived of your inheritance?'

'I don't want any inheritance!'

'You won't contest the will?'

'No!'

That was strange. Maigret, who had been staring at the carpet, looked up.

'Three hundred and sixty thousand francs are enough for you?'

Then the young man's attitude changed. He walked over to the inspector, stopped within inches of him, at the point where their shoulders were touching. And, his fists clenched, he snarled, 'Say that again!'

At that moment, there was something thuggish about him, a coarse air, the scent of the café brawl.

'I'm asking you if Couchet's 360,000 francs are — '

He just managed to grab Roger's arm in mid-air. Otherwise he would have received one of the biggest punches of his life!

'Calm down!'

But Roger was calm! He wasn't struggling! He was pale. He stared fixedly. He was waiting until the inspector was prepared to release him.

Was it to strike again? Meanwhile, Céline had jumped out of bed, despite being half-naked. Maigret could sense she was about to open the door to call for help.

Everything happened peacefully. Maigret only held on to Roger's wrist for a few seconds, and when he gave him back his freedom of movement, the young man did not move.

There was a long silence. It was as if each one of them was afraid to break it, the way, in a fight, each opponent is reluctant to deliver the first punch.

Finally it was Roger who spoke.

'You've got to be kidding!'

He picked up a mauve dressing gown from the floor and threw it over to his companion.

'Do you want to tell me what you plan to do, once you've spent your 200 francs?'

'What have I done until now?'

'There's just one little difference: your father's dead and you can no longer sponge off him.'

Roger shrugged as if to say that Maigret had

got the wrong end of the stick.

There was an indefinable atmosphere, not exactly of drama, but something else — a poignancy perhaps, a bohemian atmosphere but devoid of poetry. Perhaps it was the sight of the wallet and the two 100-franc notes? Or was it the anxious woman, who had just realized that tomorrow would not be like the previous days, that she'd have to find a new source of support?

But no! It was Roger himself who was frightening. Because his behaviour and actions were out of character, contradicting what Maigret knew of his past.

His calmness . . . and it wasn't an act! He was truly calm, calm like someone who —

'Give me your gun!' suddenly commanded the chief inspector.

The young man pulled it out of his trouser pocket and proffered it with the ghost of a smile.

'Promise me you'll — '

He stopped in mid-sentence when he saw the woman about to scream in terror. She couldn't grasp what was going on, but she knew it was something very bad.

Irony, in Roger's eyes.

Maigret almost ran out of the room. Having nothing further to say, no gesture to make, he beat a retreat, banging into the door frame on his way out and stifling a curse.

Back in the street, his cheery mood of that morning had dissipated. He no longer found life a joke. He looked up at the couple's window. It was closed. You couldn't see a thing.

He was uneasy, as one is when nothing makes sense any more.

Roger had given him two or three looks . . . He couldn't have explained it, but they were not the looks he was expecting. They were looks that were somehow at odds with the rest.

He retraced his steps, because he had forgotten to ask at the hotel for Nine's new address.

'Don't know!' said the porter. 'She paid for her room and left carrying her suitcase! Didn't need a taxi. She must have gone to the cheapest hotel around here.'

'Look, if . . . if anything were to happen here . . . Yes . . . something unexpected . . . would you kindly inform me personally at police headquarters? Detective Chief Inspector Maigret.'

He was annoyed at himself for having said that. What could happen? Even so he recalled the two 100-franc notes in Roger's wallet and Céline's look of fear.

A quarter of an hour later, he entered the Moulin Bleu via the stage door. The auditorium was empty, dark, the seats and the sides of the boxes covered in glossy green silk fabric.

On the stage, six women, shivering despite their coats, were repeatedly rehearsing the same step — 'a ridiculously easy step' — while a short, pudgy man bellowed a tune at the top of his lungs.

'One! . . . Two! . . . Tra la la la . . . No! . . . Tra la la la . . . Three! . . . Three, for heaven's sake!'

Nine was the second woman in the line. She recognized Maigret, who was standing by a column. The man had spotted him too, but he wasn't bothered.

'One! . . . Two! . . . Tra la la — '

It went on for fifteen minutes. It was colder in here than outside and Maigret's feet were frozen. At last the squat man wiped his forehead and cursed his dancers by way of a farewell.

'Come to see me?' he yelled at Maigret from a distance.

'No! . . . I've come to see — '

Nine walked over, embarrassed, wondering whether she should hold out her hand to the inspector.

'I have some important news for you — '

'Not here . . . We're not allowed to have visitors at the theatre . . . Except in the evenings, because they have to pay.'

They sat at a pedestal table in a little bar next door.

'They've found Couchet's will. He left his fortune to three women.'

She looked at him in amazement, without suspecting the truth.

'First of all, his first wife, even though she's remarried, then his second wife . . . And then you.'

She continued to stare at Maigret, who saw her pupils dilate and then mist over.

And finally she buried her face in her hands to cry.

# 8

## The Home Nurse

'He had heart disease. He knew it.'

Nine sipped her ruby-coloured aperitif.

'That's why he took things easy. He said he'd worked enough, that it was time for him to enjoy life.'

'Did he sometimes talk about death?'

'Often! But not . . . not that kind of death! He was thinking of his heart disease.'

They were in one of those little bars where all the customers are regulars. The owner watched Maigret covertly as if he were a bourgeois meeting his mistress. At the counter, the men were talking about the afternoon's racing.

'Was he sad?'

'It's hard to explain! Because he wasn't like other men. For example, when we were at the theatre, or somewhere else, he'd be enjoying himself. Then, for no reason, he'd say with a deep laugh, *'Life's a bitch, isn't it, Ninette!'*'

'Did he take care of his son?'

'No.'

'Did he talk about him?'

'Almost never! Only when he came to scrounge.'

'And what did he say?'

'He'd sigh, *'What a stupid idiot!'*'

Maigret had already intuited that, for one reason or another, Couchet had little affection

260

for his son. It even seemed as if he was disgusted by the young man. Disgusted to the point of not trying to come to his rescue!

For he had never lectured him. And he gave him money to get rid of him, or out of pity.

'Waiter! How much do I owe you?'

'Four francs sixty!'

Nine left the bar with him and they stood on the pavement of Rue Fontaine for a moment.

'Where are you living now?'

'Rue Lepic, the first hotel on the left. I haven't even looked at the name yet. It's fairly clean.'

'When you're rich you'll be able — '

She gave him a watery smile.

'You know very well I'll never be rich! I'm not the sort for all that.'

The strangest thing was that Maigret had that very impression. Nine didn't look like someone who would be rich one day. He couldn't have said why.

'I'll accompany you to Place Pigalle, where I'm going to get my tram.'

They walked slowly, Maigret huge, burly, and Nine petite next to his broad back.

'If you knew how lost I feel being on my own! Luckily there's the theatre, with two rehearsals a day until the show opens.'

She had to take two steps to each of Maigret's strides, and was almost running. At the corner of Rue Pigalle, she stopped abruptly, while the inspector frowned and muttered under his breath, 'The fool!'

But they couldn't see anything. Opposite Hôtel Pigalle, around forty people were gathered. A police officer stood in the doorway trying to move them on.

That was all, but there was that particular atmosphere, that silence that you only encounter in the street when a tragedy occurs.

'What's going on?' stammered Nine. 'In my hotel!'

'No! It's nothing! Go back to your room — '

'But . . . something — '

'Go!' he snapped.

And she obeyed, scared, while Maigret elbowed his way through the crowd. He charged like a ram. Women shouted abuse at him. The police sergeant recognized him and asked him to step inside the hotel.

The district detective chief inspector was already there, talking to the porter, who cried out, pointing at Maigret, 'It's him! I recognize him — '

The two inspectors shook hands. From the little lounge that opened off the lobby, sobs, groans and indistinct murmurs could be heard.

'How did he do it?' asked Maigret.

'The girl who lives with him states that he was standing by the window, very calm. She got dressed, and he watched her, whistling. He only paused to tell her she had lovely thighs, but that her calves were too thin. Then he started whistling again, and suddenly everything went quiet. She felt a terrible emptiness . . . He was no longer there! He couldn't have left via the door.'

'Got it! Did he injure anyone as he landed on the pavement?'

262

'No one. Killed outright. Spine broken in two places.'

'Here's the ambulance,' announced the sergeant coming over to them.

And the district detective chief inspector explained to Maigret, 'There's nothing more to be done. Do you know whether he has any family who need to be informed? When you arrived, the porter was just telling me that the young man had had a visitor this morning . . . a tall, well-built man. He was giving me a description of this man when you turned up. It was you! Should I write a report anyway, or will you deal with everything?'

'Write a report.'

'What about the family?'

'I'll deal with them.'

He opened the door to the lounge, saw a shape lying on the floor, completely covered with a blanket from one of the beds.

Céline, crumpled in an armchair, was now making a regular wailing noise, while a plump woman — the owner or the manager — was trying to comfort her.

'It's not as if he killed himself for you, is it? It's not your fault, you never refused him anything.'

Maigret did not lift up the blanket, did not even make Céline aware of his presence.

A few moments later, the body was carried out to the ambulance, which set off in the direction of the mortuary.

Then, gradually, the crowd in Rue Pigalle dispersed. The last stragglers didn't even know whether there had been a fire, a suicide or the arrest of a pickpocket.

★  ★  ★

*He was whistling . . . and suddenly everything went quiet.*

Slowly, slowly Maigret climbed the staircase of the Place des Vosges and, as he reached the second floor, he scowled.

Old Mathilde's door was ajar. She was probably lurking behind it, spying. But he shrugged and pulled the bell cord by the Martins' front door.

He had his pipe in his mouth. For a second he considered putting it in his pocket, then, once again, he shrugged.

The sound of bottles clinking. A vague murmur. Two male voices coming closer and at last the door opened.

'Very good, doctor . . . Yes, doctor . . . Thank you, doctor.'

A crushed Monsieur Martin, who had not yet had time to get dressed and whom Maigret found in the same sorry get-up as that morning.

'It's you?'

The doctor headed for the staircase while Monsieur Martin showed the inspector in, glancing furtively in the direction of the bedroom.

'Is she worse?'

'We don't know . . . The doctor won't say . . . He'll be back this evening.'

He picked up a prescription that was lying on

top of the wireless, and stared at it with vacant eyes.

'I don't even have anyone to send to the pharmacy!'

'What happened?'

'More or less the same as last night, but more violent. She began shivering, mumbling incoherently . . . I sent for the doctor and he tells me she has a temperature of nearly forty.'

'Is she delirious?'

'You can't understand anything she says, I tell you! We need ice and a rubber pouch to place on her forehead.'

'Do you want me to stay here while you go to the pharmacy?'

Monsieur Martin was about to say no, then he resigned himself.

He put on an overcoat and left, gesticulating, a tragic and grotesque figure, and then came back because he had forgotten to take any money.

Maigret had no ulterior motive for remaining in the apartment. He showed no interest in anything, didn't open a single drawer, didn't even glance at a pile of correspondence sitting on a table.

He could hear the patient's irregular breathing. From time to time she gave a long sigh, then babbled a jumble of syllables.

When Monsieur Martin came back, he found him in the same spot.

'Have you got everything you need?'

'Yes . . . This is terrible! . . . And I haven't even let my office know!'

Maigret helped him break up the ice and put it

in a red rubber pouch.

'And yet you didn't have any visitors this morning?'

'Nobody . . . '

'And you didn't receive any letters?'

'Nothing . . . Circulars.'

Madame Martin's forehead was perspiring and her greying hair was plastered to her temples. Her lips were pale, but her eyes remained extraordinarily alert.

Did they recognize Maigret, who was holding the ice-filled pouch on her forehead?

It was impossible to say. But she seemed to have quietened down a little. She lay still with the red pouch on her forehead, staring at the ceiling.

The inspector led Monsieur Martin into the dining room.

'I've got several pieces of news for you.'

'Oh!' he said with a shiver of anxiety.

'Couchet's will has been found. He has left a third of his fortune to your wife.'

'What?'

And the civil servant floundered, panic-stricken, overwhelmed by this news.

'You say he's left us . . . ?'

'A third of his fortune! It's likely that things won't be straightforward. His second wife will probably contest the will. Because she only receives a third, too. The last third goes to another person, Couchet's most recent mistress, a certain Nine — '

Why did Martin seem so crestfallen? Worse than crest-fallen, devastated! As if his arms and legs had been severed! He stared fixedly at the floor, unable to regain his composure.

'The second piece of news is not so good. It concerns your stepson — '

'Roger?'

'He committed suicide this morning, by jumping out of the window of his room in Rue Pigalle.'

Then he saw the petty official's hackles rise, as he shot him a look of anger, of rage, and shouted, 'What are you telling me? You're trying to drive me mad, aren't you? Admit that all this is a trick to get me to talk!'

'Not so loud! Your wife — '

'I don't care! You're lying! It isn't possible.'

He was unrecognizable. In one fell swoop his shyness, the good manners that were of such importance to him had all deserted him.

It was strange to see his face distraught, his lips quivering and his hands waving around in mid-air.

'I swear to you,' said Maigret, 'that both items of news are official.'

'But why would he have done that? I tell you, it's enough to drive a person insane! Actually, that's what's happening! My wife is going mad! You've seen her! And if this goes on, I'll end up going mad, too. We'll all go mad!'

His eyes were darting around wildly. He had lost all self-control.

'Her son jumping out of the window! And the will — '

His features were tense and suddenly he burst into tears — it was tragic, comical, horrible.

'Please! Do calm down — '

'An entire lifetime ... Thirty-two years ... Every day ... At nine o'clock ... Never a foot wrong ... All that for — '

'Please ... Remember your wife can hear you, and that she's very unwell — '

'What about me? Do you think I'm not unwell too? Do you think I could stand such a life for long?'

He didn't look the sort to cry and that made his tears all the more poignant.

'It's nothing to do with you, is it? He's only your stepson. He's not your responsibility.'

Martin looked at the chief inspector, suddenly calm, but not for long.

'He's not my responsibility — '

He flew off the handle.

'Even so, I'm the one who has to deal with all the trouble! You dare to come here telling these stories! On the stairs, the residents give me strange looks. And I bet they suspect me of killing that Couchet! Absolutely! And, anyway, how do I know you don't suspect me as well? What do you want with us? Huh! Huh! You don't answer! You wouldn't dare answer. People choose the weakest! A man who's unable to defend himself ... And my wife is sick ... And — '

As he gesticulated, he banged the wireless with his elbow. It wobbled and crashed on to the floor amid a tinkle of broken bulbs.

Then the petty official resurfaced.

'That wireless cost twelve hundred francs! ... I saved up for three years to buy it.'

A groan came from the bedroom next door.

He listened out, but didn't move.

'Does your wife need anything?'

It was Maigret who put his head inside the bedroom. Madame Martin was still in bed. The inspector met her gaze and would have been unable to say whether it was a look of acute intelligence or one clouded by fever.

She did not attempt to speak, but let him go.

In the dining room, Martin was resting both elbows on a dresser, holding his head in his hands and staring at the wallpaper, a few centimetres from his face.

'Why would he kill himself?'

'Suppose for example that it was he who — '

Silence. A crackling. A strong smell of burning. Martin hadn't noticed.

'Is there something on the stove?' asked Maigret.

He went into the kitchen, blue with steam. On the gas ring he found a milk pan whose contents had boiled over and which was about to explode. He turned off the gas, opened the window and caught a glimpse of the courtyard, Doctor Rivière's Serums laboratory, the director's car parked in front of the porch. And he could hear the clatter of typewriters in the offices.

If Maigret was lingering, it was not without a reason. He wanted to give Martin the time to calm down, even to decide on an attitude to adopt. He slowly filled his pipe and lit it with an igniter hanging above the gas stove.

When he came back into the dining room, the man had not budged, but he was calmer. He straightened up with a sigh, fumbled for a handkerchief and blew his nose loudly.

'All this is going to end badly, isn't it?' he began.

'There are already two dead!' replied Maigret. 'Two dead.'

An effort. An effort that must have been extremely harrowing, but Martin, who was about to get all agitated again, managed to remain composed.

'In that case, I think it would be best — '

'That it would be best . . . ?'

Maigret barely dared speak. He held his breath. He felt a pang in his chest, for he sensed he was close to the truth.

'Yes,' groaned Martin to himself. 'Too bad! It's essential . . . ess-en-tial — '

But then he walked automatically over to the door of the bedroom, and looked deep into the room.

Maigret was still waiting, motionless, not saying a word.

Martin said nothing. His wife remained silent. But something must have been happening.

The situation dragged on and on. The inspector was growing impatient.

'Well?'

Martin turned slowly towards him, with a different face.

'What?'

'You were saying that — '

Monsieur Martin tried to smile.

'That what?'

'That it was best, to avert any further tragedies — '

'That it was best to what?'

He wiped his hand across his forehead, like someone finding it difficult to remember.

'Please forgive me! I'm so distraught — '

'That you have forgotten what you wanted to say?'

'Yes . . . I don't remember . . . Look! . . . She's asleep.'

He pointed to Madame Martin, who had closed her eyes and whose face had turned purple, probably from the ice being applied to her forehead.

'What do you know?' asked Maigret in the tone he used for smart-aleck prisoners.

'Me?'

And from then on, all his answers were in that vein! What's known as acting dumb. Repeating a word in astonishment.

'You were on the point of telling me the truth — '

'The truth?'

'Come on! Don't try and pretend you're an idiot. You know who killed Couchet.'

'Me? . . . I know?'

If he had never been given a clout, he was within a whisker of receiving an almighty one from Maigret's hand!

Maigret, his jaws clenched, watched the unmoving woman who was asleep, or pretending to be, then the man whose eyelids were still puffy from the previous outburst, his features drawn, his moustache drooping.

'Will you take responsibility for what might happen?'

271

'What might happen?'

'You're wrong, Martin!'

'Wrong how?'

What was going on? For a minute, perhaps, the man who had been about to speak had stood between the two rooms, his eyes riveted on his wife's bed. Maigret had not heard a sound. Martin had not moved.

Now she was asleep, and he was feigning innocence!

'Forgive me ... I think there are moments when I don't know what I'm saying ... Admit that a person can go mad if — '

All the same, he remained sad, lugubrious even. He had the attitude of a condemned man. His gaze avoided Maigret's face, fluttered over familiar objects and finally settled on the wireless set, which he proceeded to pick up, crouched on the floor, his back to the inspector.

'What time will the doctor be coming?'

'I don't know. He said 'this evening'.'

Maigret left, slamming the door behind him. He found himself nose-to-nose with old Mathilde, who got such a fright that she stood transfixed, her mouth open.

'You haven't anything to tell me either, have you? ... Eh? ... Perhaps you're going to claim you don't know anything either?'

She tried to compose herself. She had both hands beneath her apron in the classic pose of an elderly housewife.

'Come and let's go back to your room.'

Her felt slippers glided over the floorboards. She paused, reluctant to push her half-open door.

'Go on, go inside.'

And Maigret followed her in, kicked the door shut, not even sparing a glance for the madwoman sitting by the window.

'Now, talk! Understood?'

And he sank with his full weight on to a chair.

# 9

## The Man with the Pension

'First of all, they spend their whole time arguing!'

Maigret didn't bat an eyelid. He was up to his ears in all this day-to-day unpleasantness, which was more repulsive than the murder itself.

The old woman before him had a malevolent expression of jubilation and menace. She was talking! She was going to talk some more! Out of hatred for the Martins, for the dead man, for all the residents of the building, out of hatred for the whole of humanity! And out of hatred for Maigret!

She remained standing, her hands clasped over her soft, fat belly, and it was as though she had been waiting for this moment all her life.

It was not a smile that hovered on her lips. It was bliss that melted her!

'*First of all*, they spend their whole time arguing.'

She had time. She distilled her words. She allowed herself the leisure of expressing her contempt for people who argue.

'Worse than ragamuffins! It's always been like that! I sometimes wonder how he's managed not to wring her neck yet.'

'Ah! You were expecting . . . ?'

'When you live in a place like this, you have to expect anything . . . '

She placed careful emphasis on her words. Was she more loathsome than ridiculous or more ridiculous than loathsome?

The room was large. There was an unmade bed with grey sheets that can never have been hung out to dry in the open air. A table, an old wardrobe, a stove.

The madwoman sat in an armchair staring in front of her with a gentle half-smile.

'Do you ever have visitors, may I ask?' said Maigret.

'Never!'

'And your sister never leaves this room?'

'Sometimes, she gets out on to the staircase.'

A depressing drabness. A smell of unsavoury poverty, of old age, of death even?

'Mind you, it's always the wife who goes for him!'

Maigret barely had the energy to question her. He vaguely looked at her. He was listening.

'Over money matters, of course! Not over women . . . Although once she suspected, when she did the accounts, that he had visited a house of ill-repute, and she gave him a hard time.'

'Does she hit him?'

Maigret spoke without irony. The idea was no more preposterous than any other. There were so many implausibilities that nothing would be surprising.

'I don't know if she hits him, but in any case she smashes plates . . . Then she cries, saying that she'll never have a happy marriage.'

'In other words, there are scenes almost every day?'

'Not big scenes! But carping. Two or three big scenes a week.'

'That must keep you busy!'

She wasn't sure she had understood and began to look slightly anxious.

'What does she complain about most often?'

''*When you can't afford to feed a wife, you don't marry!*

''*You don't deceive a woman telling her you'll be getting a rise when it's not true.*

''*You don't steal a wife from a man like Couchet, who's capable of earning millions.*

''*Civil servants are cowards. You should work for yourself, be prepared to take risks, be entrepreneurial, if you want to get anywhere.*''

Poor Martin, with his gloves, his putty-coloured overcoat and his waxed moustache! Maigret could imagine the hail of criticism she constantly rained on him.

But he had done his best! Couchet before him had been subjected to the same criticisms, and she must have said to him, 'Look at Monsieur Martin! Now there's a clever man! And he hopes to have a wife one day! She'll get a pension if anything happens to him! Whereas you — '

All this sounded like a sinister accusation. Madame Martin had been wrong, had been wronged, had wronged everyone!

There was a terrible mistake at the root of all this!

The confectioner's daughter from Meaux wanted money. That was an established fact. It was a necessity! She felt it. She was born to have money, and consequently, it was up to her husband to earn it!

But Couchet didn't earn enough. And she wouldn't even be entitled to a pension if he died.

So she had married Martin.

Except that it was Couchet who had become a millionaire, when it was too late! And there was no way of giving Martin wings, no way to convince him to leave the Registry Office and to sell serums too, or something that would bring in money

She was unhappy. She had always been unhappy. Life seemed determined to cheat her cruelly!

Old Mathilde's glaucous eyes stared at Maigret, making him think of jellyfish.

'Did her son ever visit her?'

'Sometimes.'

'Did she quarrel with him too?'

This was Mathilde's big moment! She took her time. After all, she had all the time in the world!

'She used to advise him: '*Your father's rich! He should he ashamed of himself, not getting you a better job! You don't even have a car . . . and do you know why? Because of that woman who married him for his money! Because that's the only reason she married him!*

''*And God knows what she's got in store for you later . . . Will you even get a share of the fortune that should be yours?*

''*That's why you should get money out of him now, put it away in a safe place. I'll look after it*

277

*for you if you like. Do you want me to look after it for you?'*

And Maigret, gazing at the filthy floor, thought hard, his forehead furrowed.

He concluded that among this hodgepodge of sentiments he could identify one overriding feeling which had perhaps led to all the others: anxiety! A morbid, pathological anxiety verging on madness.

Madame Martin always talked about what might happen: her husband's death, poverty if he didn't leave her a pension . . . She was afraid for her son!

It was a nightmare, an obsession.

'What did Roger reply?'

'Nothing! He never stayed long! He must have had better things to do elsewhere.'

'Did he come the day of the murder?'

'I don't know.'

And the madwoman in her corner, as old as Mathilde, still gazed at the inspector, smiling her blissful smile.

'Did the Martins have a conversation that was more interesting than usual?'

'I don't know.'

'Did Madame Martin go downstairs at around eight o'clock in the evening?'

'I don't remember! I can't be in the corridor all the time.'

Was it thoughtlessness, transcendent irony? In any case, she was holding something back. Maigret could tell. Not all the pus had come out.

'That evening, they had an argument.'

'Why?'

'I don't know.'

'Weren't you listening?'

She did not reply. Her expression signified: 'That's my business!'

'What else do you know?'

'I know why she's ill!'

And that was her trump card. Her hands trembled, still clasped over her stomach. This was the high point of her entire career.

'Why?'

The moment needed savouring.

'Because . . . Wait a minute, let me ask my sister if she needs anything . . . Fanny, are you thirsty? . . . Hungry? . . . Not too hot?'

The little cast-iron stove was red hot. The old woman floated around the room, gliding soundlessly across the floor in her felt slippers.

'Because?'

'Because he didn't bring home the money!'

She spelled out this sentence and then clammed up once and for all. It was over! She would not say another word. She had said enough.

'What money?'

A waste of time! She wouldn't answer any more questions.

'It's none of my business! That's what I heard! Make of it what you will . . . Now, I have to see to my sister.'

He left, leaving the two old women to heaven-knows-what routine.

He was all churned up. His stomach heaved, as in seasickness. *He didn't bring home the money . . .*

Was there not an explanation? Martin decided to rob the first husband, perhaps to stop her from criticizing his mediocrity. She watched him out of the window. He left the office with the 360 notes . . .

Except that, when he came back, he no longer had them! Had he hidden them somewhere safe? Had he been robbed in turn? Or had he become scared and got rid of the money by throwing it into the Seine?

Was mediocre Monsieur Martin in his putty-coloured overcoat a killer?

Earlier on, he had wanted to talk. His weariness was that of a guilty man who no longer has the strength to keep quiet, who prefers immediate prison to the anguish of waiting.

But why was his wife the one who was ill?

And above all, why was it Roger who had killed himself?

Was all this perhaps a figment of Maigret's imagination? Why not suspect Nine, or Madame Couchet, or even the colonel?

Making his way slowly down the stairs, the inspector met Monsieur de Saint-Marc, who turned around.

'Oh! It's you.'

He extended a condescending hand.

'Any news? Do you think you'll get to the bottom of it all?'

Then came the scream of the madwoman upstairs, who must have been abandoned by her sister, gone to stand guard behind some door.

★ ★ ★

A lovely funeral. A big turnout. Distinguished people. Especially Madame Couchet's family and their neighbours on Boulevard Haussmann.

Only Couchet's sister in the front row looked out of place, even though she had gone to impossible lengths to be elegant. She was crying. Above all, she had a noisy way of blowing her nose that prompted the dead man's mother-in-law to glare at her every time.

Immediately behind the family sat the laboratory staff.

And, with the employees, old Mathilde, very dignified, sure of herself, sure of her right to be there.

The black dress she wore must have served for just that purpose: attending funerals! Her eyes met Maigret's, and she deigned to give him a slight nod.

The singing, accompanied by the organ, burst forth, the cantor's bass, the deacon's falsetto: *Et ne nos inducas in tentationem . . .*

The scraping of chairs. The catafalque was high, and yet it was invisible beneath all the flowers and wreaths.

### The residents of 61, Place des Vosges

Mathilde must have given her share. Had the Martins added their names to the list of contributors too?

Madame Martin was not there. She was still in bed.

*Libera nos, domine . . .*

The absolution. The end. The master of

281

ceremonies slowly leading the procession. Maigret, in a corner, by a confessional box, came across Nine, whose little nose was all red. She hadn't bothered to give it a dab of powder.

'It's terrible, isn't it?' she said.

'What's terrible?'

'Everything! I don't know! That music . . . and that smell of chrysanthemums.'

She bit her lower lip to stifle a sob.

'You know . . . I've thought a lot about . . . Well, I sometimes think he suspected something.'

'Are you going to the cemetery?'

'What do you think? People might see me, mightn't they? Perhaps it's better if I don't go . . . Even though I'd so like to know where they put him.'

'You can always ask the keeper.'

'True.'

They were whispering. The footsteps of the last of the guests died away on the other side of the door. Cars started up.

'You were saying that he suspected something?'

'Perhaps not that he would die in that manner . . . but he knew he didn't have long. He had quite a serious heart disease.'

Maigret could sense that she had been fretting, that for hours and hours on end a single question had been on her mind.

'Something he said came back to me.'

'Was he afraid?'

'No! On the contrary. When anyone happened to mention cemeteries, he would laugh and say,

'The only place where you'll find peace and quiet . . . A nice little corner in Père-Lachaise.''

'Did he joke a lot?'

'Especially when he wasn't happy . . . Does that make sense? He didn't like to show he was worried. At those times, he tried somehow to snap out of it, to find something to laugh about.'

'When he spoke of his first wife, for example?'

'He never talked to me about her.'

'What about his second wife?'

'No! He didn't talk about anyone in particular . . . He would talk about people in general . . . He found they were strange creatures. If a waiter cheated him, he would look at him more affectionately than the others. 'A *rascal!*' he would say. And he'd say it in an amused tone, pleased even!'

It was cold. A real November day. Maigret and Nine had no business in this district of Saint-Philippe-du-Roule.

'Is everything all right at the Moulin Bleu?'

'It's fine!'

'I'll come by and say hello one evening.'

Maigret shook her hand, and jumped on to the platform of an omnibus.

He needed to be alone, to think, or rather to let his mind wander. He pictured the procession arriving soon at the cemetery . . . Madame Couchet, the colonel, the brother, the people who must be gossiping about the strange will . . .

What had the Martins been up to, rummaging around the bins?

For that was the crux of the story. Martin had poked around the dustbins claiming he was looking for a glove, which he hadn't found but had been wearing the next morning. Madame Martin had also rifled through the rubbish, talking of a silver spoon thrown out accidentally.

' . . . *because he didn't bring home the money,*' old Mathilde had said.

In fact, things must have been lively at that hour in Place des Vosges! The madwoman, who must be on her own, wouldn't she be screaming as usual?

The omnibus was full, and drove past bus stops without stopping. A man, pressed up against Maigret, was saying to his neighbour, 'Did you read about that business with the thousand-franc notes?'

'No! What was that?'

'I wish I could have been there . . . At the Bougival weir . . . Two mornings ago . . . Thousand-franc notes floating on the tide . . . It was a sailor who spotted them first and who managed to fish out a few . . . but the lock-keeper saw what was going on and called the police and an officer kept an eye out for anyone trying going after the loot.'

'No kidding? I don't suppose that stopped them putting a bit aside.'

'The paper says they found around thirty notes, but that there must have been a lot more, because they fished out a couple down river in Mantes too . . . Huh! Cash swimming down the Seine! It's better than gudgeon.'

Maigret stood a head taller than everyone else. He remained impassive, his face composed.

. . . *because he didn't bring home the money.*

So was that it? Meek Monsieur Martin, overcome by fear or remorse at the thought of his crime? Martin who admitted he went for a walk that evening on the Ile Saint-Louis to relieve his neuralgia!

Maigret couldn't help smiling a little as he pictured Madame Martin, who had seen it all from her window and was waiting.

Her husband came home, weary, defeated. She watched his every action and movement. She was eager to see the notes, perhaps to count them.

He got undressed and prepared for bed.

Didn't she pick up his clothes to search his pockets?

She started to feel anxious. She looked at Martin with his droopy moustache.

'The . . . the . . . money?'

'What money?'

'Who did you give it to? Answer me! Don't try and lie.'

And Maigret, alighting from the omnibus at Pont-Neuf, from where he could see the windows of his office, caught himself saying in a low voice, 'I bet once he was in bed, Martin began to cry!'

285

# 10

## Identity Cards

It began at Jeumont. The time was eleven p.m. A few third-class passengers walked towards the customs shed while the customs officers began inspecting the second- and first-class carriages.

Meticulous people had got their suitcases down in advance and spread the contents out on the seats. This included a man with anxious eyes in second class, in a compartment where the only other passengers were an elderly Belgian couple.

His luggage was a model of neatness and forethought. His shirts were wrapped in newspaper to prevent them getting dirty. There were twelve pairs of detachable cuffs, winter drawers and summer drawers, an alarm clock, shoes and a pair of worn-out slippers.

A woman's hand had clearly done the packing. There was no wasted space. Nothing would get creased. A customs officer poked around carelessly, observing the man in the putty-coloured overcoat, who looked just the type to have such suitcases.

'All right!'

A chalk cross on the cases.

'Anything to declare, the rest of you?'

'Excuse me,' asked the man, 'where exactly does Belgium begin?'

'You see the first hedge over there? No! You can't see anything! But look ... Count the lamps ... the third on the left ... Well, that's the border.'

A voice in the corridor, repeating at the door of each compartment, 'Have your passports ready, your identity cards!'

And the man in the putty-coloured overcoat struggled to put his suitcases back in the overhead net.

'Passport?'

He turned around and saw a young man wearing a grey peaked cap.

'French? Your identity card, then.'

It took a few moments. His fingers rummaged in his wallet.

'Here you are, monsieur!'

'Good! Martin, Edgar Émile ... That's correct! ... Follow me — '

'Where to?'

'You can bring your luggage.'

'But ... the train — '

The two Belgians now stared at him, aghast, although they were amused to have shared a compartment with a fugitive. Monsieur Martin, his eyes wide, clambered up on to the seat to retrieve his suitcases.

'I swear ... What the — ?'

'Hurry up ... The train's about to leave.'

And the young man in the grey cap rolled the heaviest suitcase on to the platform. It was dark. In the glow of the lamplight, people were hurrying back from the buffet. The whistle was blown. A woman was arguing with the customs officers who refused to allow her back on to the train.

'We'll see about that in the morning — '

And Monsieur Martin followed the young man, struggling to carry his suitcases. He had never thought a station platform could be so long. It went on and on, endless, deserted, with mysterious doors leading off it.

Finally, they went through the last one.

'Come in!'

It was dark. Nothing but a lamp with a green shade, hanging so low above the table that it only shed light on a few papers. And yet something was moving at the far end of the room.

'Good evening, Monsieur Martin,' said a cordial voice.

And a burly form stepped out of the shadows: Detective Chief Inspector Maigret, encased in his heavy overcoat with a velvet collar, his hands in his pockets.

'Don't bother taking off your coat. We're getting the train back to Paris, which is due to arrive on platform three.'

This time it was definite! Martin was crying, silently his hands paralysed by his neatly packed suitcases.

⋆   ⋆   ⋆

The inspector who had been placed on sentry duty at 61, Place des Vosges had telephoned Maigret a few hours earlier, 'Our man is running off. He's just taken a taxi to the Gare du Nord.'

288

'Let him get away. Carry on watching the wife.'

And Maigret had caught the same train as Martin. He had travelled in the neighbouring compartment with two sergeants who had told lewd stories for the entire duration of the journey.

From time to time, the chief inspector peeped through the spy hole between the two compartments and glimpsed a gloomy Martin.

Jeumont . . . Identity card! . . . Border police.

Now, they were both on their way back to Paris, in a reserved compartment. Martin was not handcuffed. His suitcases were in the net above his head, and one of them, precariously balanced, threatened to fall on him.

They had reached Maubeuge and Maigret still hadn't asked a single question.

It was unbelievable! He was ensconced in his corner, his pipe between his teeth. He puffed away continually, watching his companion with his laughing little eyes.

Ten times, twenty times, Martin opened his mouth without saying anything. Ten times, twenty times, the chief inspector took absolutely no notice.

And eventually it happened: an indescribable voice, which Madame Martin herself would probably not have recognized.

'It's me — '

And Maigret still didn't say a word. His pupils seemed to say, 'Really?'

'I . . . I was hoping to make it across the border — '

There is a way of smoking that is aggravating for the person watching the smoker: with each puff, his lips part sensuously, making a little 'puk' sound. And the smoke isn't puffed out in front, but escapes slowly and forms a cloud around his face.

Maigret smoked like this and his head nodded from right to left and left to right to the rhythm of the train.

Martin leaned forward, his hands hurting inside his gloves, his eyes feverish.

'Do you think it'll be long? . . . It won't, will it? Because I confess . . . I confess everything — '

How did he manage to hold back his sobs? His nerves must have been utterly frayed. And his eyes, from time to time, were beseeching Maigret: 'Please help me! . . . You can see that I have no strength left.'

But the chief inspector did not budge. He was as calm, with the same curious, detached gaze as if he were in front of an exotic animal's cage at the zoological gardens.

'Couchet caught me . . . So — '

And Maigret sighed. A sigh that meant nothing, or rather that could be interpreted in a hundred different ways.

Saint-Quentin! Footsteps in the corridor. A portly passenger tried to open the door of the compartment, realized it was locked, stood there for a moment looking in, his nose pressed to the pane, and then finally resigned himself to looking for another seat.

'Because I confess everything, you see? There's no point denying — '

Exactly as if he had spoken to a deaf man, or to a man who did not understand a wretched word of French. Maigret filled his pipe, meticulously tapping it with his index finger.

'Do you have any matches?'

'No . . . I don't smoke, as you know very well. My wife doesn't like the smell of tobacco. I want it to be done quickly do you understand? I'll say so to the lawyer that I'll have to choose. No complications! I confess everything. I read in the paper that some of the money's been found. I don't know why I did that. I could feel it in my pocket and I had the impression that everyone in the street was looking at me. At first I thought of hiding it somewhere, but to do what with it?

'I walked along the embankment. There were barges. I was afraid of being seen by a bargeman. So I crossed the Pont-Marie and was able to get rid of the bundle on the Ile Saint-Louis.'

The compartment was boiling hot; condensation ran down the windows, pipe smoke curled around the lamp.

'I should have confessed everything to you the first time I saw you. I didn't have the courage. I hoped that — '

Martin fell silent and stared curiously at his companion, who had half-opened his mouth and closed his eyes. His breathing was regular like the purring of a fat, satiated cat.

Maigret was asleep!

Martin glanced over at the door, which only needed a push. And, as if to avoid the temptation, he huddled in a corner, clenching his buttocks, his twitching hands resting on his scrawny knees.

★ ★ ★

Gare du Nord. A grey morning. And the herd of commuters, still drowsy, streaming out.

The train had stopped a long way from the concourse. The suitcases were heavy. Martin didn't want to stop. He was out of breath and his arms hurt.

They had to wait a long time for a taxi.

'Are you taking me to prison?'

They had spent five hours on trains and Maigret hadn't uttered ten sentences. If that! Words that had nothing to do either with the murder or with the 360,000 francs. He had talked about his pipe, or the heat, or the arrival time.

'Sixty-one, Place des Vosges!' he instructed the driver.

Martin implored him, 'Do you think it's necessary to — ?'

And to himself, 'What must they be thinking at the office! There wasn't time to let them know — '

The concierge was in her lodge, sorting out the post: a huge pile of letters for Doctor Rivière's Serums. A tiny pile for the rest of the residents.

'Monsieur Martin! Monsieur Martin! Someone came from the Registry Office to see if you were ill . . . Apparently you've got the key to — '

Maigret dragged his companion away. And

Martin had to lug his heavy suitcases up the stairs. There were milk cans and fresh bread outside the apartment doors.

Old Mathilde's door moved.

'Give me the key.'

'But — '

'Open it yourself.'

A profound silence. The click of the lock. Then they saw the tidy dining room, every object in its rightful place.

Martin hesitated for a long time before saying out loud, 'It's me! . . . And the detective chief inspector — '

Someone moved in the bed in the adjacent bedroom. Martin closed the door behind them and groaned, 'We shouldn't have . . . She's not in any way to blame, is she? And in her condition — '

He didn't dare enter the bedroom. To maintain his composure, he picked up his suitcases and placed them on two chairs.

'Shall I make some coffee?'

Maigret knocked on the bedroom door.

'May I come in?'

No reply. He pushed open the door and received the full force of Madame Martin's stare. She was in bed, motionless, curling pins in her hair.

'I'm sorry to disturb you . . . I've brought home your husband, who made the mistake of panicking.'

Martin was behind him. He could sense him, but he couldn't see him.

Footsteps could be heard in the courtyard,

and voices, chiefly women's voices: the office and laboratory staff arriving. It was one minute to nine.

A muffled cry from the madwoman next door. Medication on the bedside table.

'Are you feeling worse?'

He knew very well that she wouldn't answer, that despite everything, she would maintain the same staunch reserve.

She seemed afraid of saying a word, a single one. As if one word could unleash disaster!

She had grown thinner and her complexion had become duller. But her eyes, on the other hand, those strange grey pupils, had a fiery, wilful life of their own.

Martin entered, his legs weak. His entire demeanour was apologetic, as if asking for forgiveness.

The icy grey eyes swivelled slowly to look at him, so piercingly that he looked away, stammering, It was at Jeumont station . . . One more minute and I'd have been in Belgium.'

Words, sentences, noise were needed, to fill the void that could be sensed around each individual. A void that was tangible, to the point that voices echoed as in a tunnel or a cave.

But no one spoke. They struggled to articulate a few syllables, with anxious glances, then silence fell in the implacable manner of a fog.

And yet something was happening. Something slow, insidious: a hand slid beneath the blanket and in an imperceptible movement inched its way up to the pillow.

Madame Martin's thin, clammy hand. Maigret, while looking elsewhere, followed its progress, waiting for the moment when that hand would finally reach its goal.

'Isn't the doctor supposed to be coming this morning?'

'I don't know . . . Is anyone looking after me? I'm lying here like an animal left to die.'

But her eyes became brighter because her hand finally touched the object she was seeking.

A barely audible rustle of paper.

Maigret took a step forward and seized Madame Martin's wrist. She seemed to have no strength, almost no life. Even so, from one moment to the next, she displayed an unimaginable vigour.

She refused to let go of whatever she was holding. Sitting up in bed, she fought back furiously. She raised her hand to her mouth. With her teeth she tore the sheet of white paper she was clutching.

'Let me go! Let me go or I'll scream! . . . And you? Are you just going to stand there?'

'Detective Chief Inspector . . . I beg you,' groaned Martin.

He was listening out. He was afraid the residents would come running. He didn't dare step in.

'Beast! Filthy beast! Hitting a woman!'

No, Maigret wasn't hitting her. He simply held her wrist in his grip, squeezing a little hard perhaps, to stop the woman from destroying the document.

'Aren't you ashamed! A dying woman — '

A woman who displayed an energy the like of which Maigret had rarely encountered in his career in the police! His bowler hat fell on to the bed. She suddenly bit the inspector's wrist.

But she could not keep her nerves so tensed for long, and he managed to prise her fingers open; she gave a howl of pain.

Now she was crying, crying without tears, crying out of vexation, out of rage, perhaps also to strike a pose?

'And you just stood there and let him — '

Maigret's back was too broad for the narrow bedroom. He seemed to fill the entire space, blocking out the light.

He went over to the fireplace, smoothed out the sheet of paper with bits missing, and ran his eyes over a typed text on letterhead paper.

Laval and Piollet
of the Paris bar
Counsels in chambers
Solicitors

On the right, in red: *Re Couchet vs. Martin. Advice of 18 November.*

Two pages of dense, single-spaced typing. Maigret only read fragments, in a quiet voice, while typewriters could be heard clattering in the offices of Doctor Rivière's Serums.

*In view of the law of . . .*

*Given that Roger Couchet's death occurred subsequent to that of his father . . .*

*. . . that no will can deprive a legitimate son of his rightful share . . .*

*. . . that the second marriage of the testator to Madame Dormoy was under the joint estate system . . .*

*. . . that Roger Couchet's natural heir is his mother . . .*

*. . . have the honour of confirming that you are entitled to claim half of Raymond Couchet's estate, including both movable and immovable assets . . . which, according to the specific information we have received and subject to adjustment for errors or omissions, we value at around five million, the establishment known as 'Doctor Rivière's Serums' itself being estimated at three million . . .*

*. . . We remain at your service to take any steps necessary to nullify the will and . . .*

Confirm that of the sums recovered we will retain a commission of ten per cent (10%) for costs . . .

Madame Martin had stopped crying. She was lying down again and her frosty gaze was once more directed at the ceiling.

Martin stood in the doorway more disconcerted than ever, not knowing what to do with his hands, his eyes, his entire body.

'There's a postscript!' muttered Maigret to himself.

The postscript was preceded by the words: *Strictly confidential.*

*It is our belief that Madame Couchet, née Dormoy, is also minded to contest the will.*

*Furthermore, we have made enquiries about the third beneficiary, Nine Moinard. She is a woman of dubious reputation, who has not yet taken any steps to claim her due.*

*Given that she is currently without any resources, it seems to us that the most expeditious solution would be to offer her a sum of money as compensation.*

*We would suggest the sum of twenty thousand francs, which is likely to delight a person in Mile Moinard's situation.*

*We await your decision on this matter.*

Maigret had allowed his pipe to go out. He slowly folded the document and slipped it into his wallet.

Around him, all was absolute silence. Martin seemed to be holding his breath. His wife, on the bed, staring fixedly already looked like a corpse.

'Two million, five hundred thousand francs,' murmured the chief inspector. 'Minus the twenty thousand francs to be given to Nine to ensure she would be accommodating . . . It's

298

true that Madame Couchet will probably contribute half — '

He was certain that a triumphant smile, faint but eloquent, hovered on the woman's lips.

'That's a hefty sum! . . . I say Martin — '

Martin gave a start, tried to put himself on the defensive.

'What do you expect to receive? . . . I'm not talking about money . . . I'm talking about your sentence . . . Theft . . . Murder . . . Perhaps they'll establish that there was premeditation . . . In your opinion? . . . No acquittal, naturally, since it wasn't a crime of passion . . . Oh! If only your wife had resumed relations with her former husband . . . but that is not the case . . . A question of money, purely of money . . . Ten years? . . . Twenty years? . . . Do you want to know what I think? . . . Mind you, it's never possible to guess at the decisions of jurors . . . Although there have been precedents . . . Well, we can say that in general, while they tend to be lenient when it comes to crimes of passion, they are extremely harsh in cases involving personal gain . . . '

It was as if he were talking for the sake of talking, playing for time.

'That's understandable! They are petty bourgeois, traders . . . They believe they have nothing to fear from mistresses they don't have or who they trust . . . but they have a lot to fear from thieves . . . Twenty years? . . . Well, no! . . . I reckon it'll be the guillotine — '

Martin didn't budge. He was now even more ashen-faced than his wife. He had to hold on to

299

the door frame for support.

'Except that Madame Martin will be rich
. . . She's at the age when a person knows how to
enjoy life and wealth — '

He walked over to the window.

'Unless this window . . . This is the stumbling
block . . . It is bound to be pointed out that
everything could be seen from here . . . Everything, you hear! And that is serious! . . . Because
that would make her an accessory . . . And in
fact, the criminal code states that accessories to a
murder are prohibited from being beneficiaries
of the victim's will. It's not only the murderer,
but the accomplices too . . . You see now how
important this window is — '

It was no longer silence that was surrounding
him, it was something more absolute, more
worrying, almost unreal: a total absence of any
life.

And suddenly, a question, 'Tell me, Martin!
What did you do with the gun?'

A rustle in the corridor: old Mathilde, of
course, with her moon face and her soft belly
under her gingham apron.

The concierge's shrill voice in the courtyard.

'Madame Martin! . . . It's the Dufayel man!'

Maigret sat in a wing chair that wobbled but
didn't break straight away.

# 11

## The Drawing on the Wall

'Answer me! The gun — '

He followed Martin's gaze and noticed that Madame Martin, who was still staring at the ceiling, was moving her fingers against the wall.

Poor Martin was making desperate efforts to understand what she meant. He grew impatient. He could see that Maigret was waiting.

'I — '

What could that square or trapeze that she was outlining with her thin finger mean?

'Well?'

At that moment, Maigret truly pitied him. This must be terrible for him. Martin was gasping with impatience.

'I threw it in the Seine.'

The die was cast! As the chief inspector pulled the gun out of his pocket and placed it on the table, Madame Martin sat up in bed, fuming.

'I did eventually find it in the dustbin,' said Maigret.

And then the feverish woman hissed, 'There! Do you understand now? Are you happy? You missed your chance, once again, as you always have done! Anyone would think you did it on purpose, for fear of going to prison . . . but you'll go to prison anyway! Because you were the thief! The 360 notes that monsieur threw into the Seine — '

She was terrifying. It was clear that she had bottled everything up inside her for too long. The release was violent. And she was so carried away that sometimes several words reached her lips at the same time and tumbled over each other.

Martin bowed his head. His part was over. As his wife said, he had failed miserably.

' . . . Monsieur takes it into his head to steal, but he leaves his glove on the table — '

All Madame Martin's resentment was going to burst out, messily, chaotically.

Behind him Maigret heard the voice of the man with the putty-coloured overcoat.

'For months she'd been pointing at the office to me through the window, Couchet, who was always going to the toilet . . . and she rebuked me for making her so miserable, for being incapable of feeding a wife . . . I went down there — '

'Did you tell her that you were going?'

'No! But she knew. She was at the window.'

'And from a distance you saw the glove that your husband had left behind, Madame Martin?'

'As if he were leaving a calling card! Anyone would think he did it on purpose to annoy me — '

'You picked up your gun and you went there . . . Couchet returned while you were in the office . . . He thought it was you who had stolen — '

'He wanted to have me arrested! That's what he wanted to do! As if it weren't thanks to me

302

that he'd become rich! . . . Who'd looked after him, in the early days, when he barely earned enough to eat bread without any butter? . . . All men are the same! . . . He even reprimanded me for living in the building where he had his offices. He accused me of sharing the money he gave my son.'

'And you shot him?'

'He had already picked up the telephone to call the police!'

'You headed for the dustbins. Saying you were looking for a silver spoon, you hid the gun in the rubbish. Who did you bump into then?'

She spat, 'That stupid old man from the first floor.'

'Nobody else? I thought your son came by. He was out of money.'

'So what?'

'He hadn't come to see you, but his father, isn't that right? Only you couldn't allow him to go into the office, where he would have discovered the body You were both in the courtyard. What did you say to Roger?'

'I told him to go away. You can't understand a mother's heart.'

'And he left. Your husband came home. Neither of you mentioned anything . . . Is that right? . . . Martin was thinking of the notes he'd ended up throwing into the Seine, because deep down he's a poor devil of a good man.'

'Poor devil of a good man!' echoed Madame Martin with an unexpected fury. 'Ha! Ha! And what about me? I've always been unhappy — '

'Martin doesn't know who has killed . . . He

goes to bed. A day goes by without you saying anything . . . But the following night you get up to search the clothes he's taken off . . . You look for the money in vain . . . He watches you . . . You question him . . . And it's the outburst of anger that old Mathilde overheard behind the door . . . You've killed for nothing! That idiot Martin has thrown the money away! He has thrown a fortune in the Seine, for lack of guts! It makes you ill . . . You go down with a fever . . . And Martin, who is unaware that you are the killer, goes and tells Roger the news. And Roger realizes the truth. He saw you in the courtyard . . . You stopped him from going into the office. He knows you. He thinks I suspect him. He imagines that he'll be arrested, accused . . . and he can't defend himself without accusing his mother . . . Perhaps he's not a very nice boy . . . But there are probably good reasons why he ended up living as he did. He's full of loathing . . . loathing for the women he sleeps with, loathing for the drugs, for Montmartre where he hangs around, and, above all, for this family tragedy in which he alone is aware of all the motives. He jumps out of the window!'

Martin was leaning against the wall, his face buried in his folded arms. But his wife gazed fixedly at the inspector, as if she were just waiting for the right time to interrupt his account, and attack him back.

Then Maigret produced the lawyers' written advice.

'During my last visit, Martin was so panic-stricken that he was about to confess his theft . . . but you were there . . . He could see you through the doorway . . . You frantically signalled to him and he held his tongue. Is that not what finally opened his eyes? He questioned you. Yes, you had killed! You screamed in his face! You killed because of him, to make up for his mistake, because of that glove left on the desk! And, because you have killed, you won't even inherit, despite the will! Oh! If only Martin were a man! Let him go abroad. People will believe he's guilty. The police will go away and you'll go and join him with the millions. Poor old Martin!'

And Maigret almost crushed the man with a formidable clap on the shoulder. He spoke in a muted voice. He let the words fall without insisting.

'To have done all that for the money! Couchet's death, Roger throwing himself out of the window, and then to realize at the last minute that you won't get it! You'd rather pack Martin's bags yourself. Neatly arranged suitcases. Months' worth of underwear — '

'Stop!' begged Martin.

The madwoman screamed. Maigret flung open the door and old Mathilde almost tumbled into the room!

She fled, terrified at the inspector's tone of voice, and for the first time she shut her door properly and turned the key in the lock.

Maigret glanced around the room one last time. Martin didn't dare move. His thin wife sitting up in bed, her shoulder blades prominent beneath her nightshirt, followed the police officer with her eyes.

She was so serious, so calm all of a sudden, that Maigret wondered, anxiously, what she had up her sleeve.

He remembered certain looks, during the earlier scene, certain movements of her lips. And he intuited, at exactly the same time as Martin, what was happening.

There were unable to stop her. The whole thing happened independently of them, like a nightmare.

Madame Martin was very, very thin. And her features became even more tormented. What was she staring at, in places where there was nothing but the usual bedroom objects?

What was she watching attentively moving around the room?

Her forehead furrowed. Her temples throbbed. Martin cried, 'I'm scared!'

Nothing had changed in the apartment. A lorry drove into the courtyard and they could hear the concierge's shrill voice.

It was as though Madame Martin was making a huge effort, all alone, to scale an impossible mountain. Twice her hand made a movement as if to swat something away from her face. Finally, she swallowed her saliva and smiled like someone who has reached their goal, 'All the same, you'll all come and ask me for money. I'm going to tell my lawyer not to give you any.'

Martin was twitching from head to toe. He realized that this was no passing delirium caused by her fever.

She had lost her mind, permanently!

'You can't blame her. She's never been like everyone else, has she?' he moaned.

He was awaiting the inspector's confirmation. 'Poor Martin — '

Martin was crying! He seized his wife's hand and was rubbing his face against it. She pushed him away. She had a superior, contemptuous smile.

'No more than five francs at a time. I've suffered enough, I have, of — '

'I'm going to call Sainte-Anne's' said Maigret.

'Do you think? Does she . . . does she need to be locked up?'

Force of habit? Martin was panic-stricken at the idea of leaving his home, that atmosphere of resentment and daily quarrels, that sordid life, that wife who, one last time, was trying to think but who, disconsolate and defeated, lay back with a great sigh, stammering, 'Bring me the key — '

A few moments later, Maigret crossed the teeming street like a stranger. He had a throbbing headache, something that occurred rarely, and he went into a pharmacy to buy a pill.

He couldn't see anything around him. The sounds of the city blended with others, with voices in particular, which continued to resonate in his head.

One image in particular haunted him: Madame Martin getting up, picking her husband's clothes up from the floor and looking for the money. And Martin watching her from the bed.

The woman's questioning gaze!

'*I threw it into the Seine.*'

It was at that moment that something had snapped. Or rather there had always been something not right in her brain! It was already so when she lived in the confectioner's at Meaux.

Only it wasn't noticeable. She was an almost-pretty girl. No one worried about her too-thin lips.

And Couchet had married her!

'*What would become of me if something happened to you?*'

Maigret had to wait to cross the Boulevard Beaumarchais. For no reason, Nine came into his mind.

'She'll get nothing, not a *sou*,' he murmured. 'The family will have the will revoked. And it is Madame Couchet, née Dormoy — '

The colonel must have begun the formalities. It was natural. Madame Couchet would get everything. All those millions — '

She was a distinguished woman, who would maintain her station.

Maigret slowly climbed the stairs and pushed open the door of the apartment in Boulevard Richard-Lenoir.

'Guess what happened?'

Madame Maigret was setting four places on the white tablecloth. Maigret noticed a small jug of plum brandy on the sideboard.

'Your sister!'

It wasn't difficult to guess, because each time she came from Alsace, she brought fruit brandy and a smoked ham.

'She's gone to buy some things with André.'

The husband. A good fellow who managed a brickworks.

'You look tired. I hope you're not going out again today at least?'

Maigret did not go out. At nine p.m., he was playing Pope Joan with his sister and brother-in-law. The dining room was fragrant with the smell of plum brandy.

And Madame Maigret kept giggling because she'd never understood cards and she made every silly mistake imaginable.

'Are you sure you haven't got a nine?'

'No, I've got one — '

'So why don't you put it down?'

For Maigret, all that had the soothing effect of a hot bath. His headache was gone.

He no longer thought about Madame Martin, who had been taken by ambulance to Sainte-Anne's, while her husband sobbed alone in the empty stairwell.

We do hope that you have enjoyed reading this large print book.

Did you know that all of our titles are available for purchase?

We publish a wide range of high quality large print books including:
**Romances, Mysteries, Classics**
**General Fiction**
**Non Fiction and Westerns**

Special interest titles available in large print are:
**The Little Oxford Dictionary**
**Music Book**
**Song Book**
**Hymn Book**
**Service Book**

Also available from us courtesy of Oxford University Press:
**Young Readers' Dictionary**
**(large print edition)**
**Young Readers' Thesaurus**
**(large print edition)**

For further information or a free brochure, please contact us at:
**Ulverscroft Large Print Books Ltd.,**
**The Green, Bradgate Road, Anstey,**
**Leicester, LE7 7FU, England.**
**Tel: (00 44) 0116 236 4325**
**Fax: (00 44) 0116 234 0205**